OLD BOOKSTORE MYSTERIES

Volumes 1-3

Isabella Bassett

Copyright © 2021 Isabella Bassett

All rights reserved. The moral right of the author has been asserted.

Old Bookstore Mysteries: Volumes 1-3
(Out Of Print, Murderous Misprint, Suspicious Small Print)

Kindle Edition
Published July 1, 2021
ASIN: B08W57VZW5

This is a work of fiction. Names, characters, places, and incidents either are the product of the author's imagination or are used fictitiously. Any similarity to real persons, living or dead, is coincidental and not intended by the author.

No part of this book may be reproduced, or stored in a retrieval system, or transmitted in any form or by any means, electronic, mechanical, photocopying, recording, or otherwise, without express written permission of the publisher.

CONTENTS

Title Page
Copyright
Books by Isabella Bassett   1
Book 1: Out Of Print   2
1 On the way back from Italian class   4
2 An old bookstore   12
3 The unwelcome customer   24
4 A death in the newspaper   31
5 A trip to Isola Caresio   38
6 A garden party   49
7 A Bishop's curse   58
8 A visit from the island   65
9 A book on the counter   77
10 A chase through cobblestone alleys   88
11 A secret revealed   93
12 A night of bonfires   102
13 To save a treasure   113

14 In a meadow	118
Out Of Print Author's Notes	125
Book 2: Murderous Misprint	127
1 Scaredy-cat	129
2 The sorcerer's house	139
3 Death of a witch	152
4 A book out of place	159
5 Last-minute customer	173
6 Witchwort	178
7 The witching hour	186
8 The coven	200
9 The thief's story	208
10 Old friends	220
11 Who is lying	227
12 Not so scenic drive	234
13 Under a cherry tree	239
Murderous Misprint Author's Notes	246
Book 3: Suspicious Small Print	248
1 A treasure map	250
2 A party at the castle	258
3 Zweihander, a sword for two hands	269
4 Voices among the shadows	275
5 A visit from the past	286
6 Sticky fingers in the treasure trove	293

7 Longswords and other forms of exercise	304
8 Man is not mightier than the sword	313
9 Lady Justice	322
10 The Executioner	333
11 Of two maps	343
12 A secret passage	348
13 A dead end	351
14 The Executioner's daughter	360
15 Coffee and cake	368
About The Author	374

Books by Isabella Bassett

The Old Bookstore Two-Hour Cozy Mysteries Series

Out Of Print
Murderous Misprint
Suspicious Small Print
Reckless Reprint
Incriminating Imprint
Scandalous Snowprint: A Christmas Whodunnit

Book 1: Out Of Print

The Old Bookstore Two-Hour Cozy Mysteries Book 1

By Isabella Bassett

Copyright © 2021 Isabella Bassett
All rights reserved. The moral right of the author has been asserted.

Out Of Print
(Old Bookstore Two-Hour Cozy Mysteries Book 1)
Kindle Edition
Published March 15, 2021

ASIN: B08W57VZW5

This is a work of fiction. Names, characters, places, and incidents either are the product of the author's imagination or are used fictitiously. Any similarity to real persons, living or dead, is coincidental and not intended by the author.

No part of this book may be reproduced, or stored in a retrieval system, or transmitted in any form or by any means, electronic, mechanical, photocopying, recording, or otherwise, without express written permission of the publisher.

1 On the way back from Italian class

Spring is so different here, Anne thought as she walked back from Italian class–'for adults and recent newcomers'. Anne liked lingering, exploring the old streets of the small town, looking for clues to its history in the details she noticed. She wondered if other people noticed them as well.

Deep peals of church bells echoed off the stone walls surrounding her. Anne checked her watch, *seven o'clock*, and hurried along the cobblestone path. She looked up at the bell tower of Chiesa dei Santi Pietro e Paolo soaring above a cluster of brightly painted houses. Built in the Middle Ages from the same gray Ticino granite Anne saw used everywhere–cobbles, garden walls, houses–the tower was visible from anywhere in town and marked the center of the pedestrians-only Old Town.

She wound her way through the narrow alley, the stone walls radiating heat stored from earlier in the day. The smell of blossoms hung in the still evening air. Now and then, glimpses of bright pink azaleas hinted at luscious gardens beyond the high walls, while the crown of a palm tree suggested other exotic plants–banana trees, agave, cacti–growing hidden from view. It was only the beginning of April, but spring was in full swing in Ascona.

In Boston, snow is probably just starting to melt, Anne thought.

A couple of European-tour vacations, years ago, during which she had visited the big Swiss cities in the north, had given Anne the impression that Switzerland was like New England–lots of snow with plenty of good skiing and hiking.

But this was Southern Switzerland.

Anne had moved to Switzerland last year with her husband, giving up her career so he could advance his. The pictures of Ascona online–a Mediterranean-looking town with exotic gardens, palm trees, and candy-colored houses nestled in the folds of the Alps–had enchanted them. The town had the old-world charm and history Anne craved and was just a 30-minute drive to Ben's new job. She didn't have to think twice about the move to Europe. She saw it as a chance to leave the mundane behind and follow her dreams, much like in the escape-to-the-country memoirs–*A Year in Provence* or *Under the Tuscan Sun*–she had enjoyed reading.

But eight months on, Anne had to admit that she hadn't achieved much.

The stone-walled alleyway ended abruptly

and opened to a street flanked by elegant old buildings, in faded pinks and yellows, accented with green window shutters. Designer clothes and accessories filled the storefronts dominating the ground floors. Strolling past, Anne liked to imagine what these buildings were before they became boutiques, jewelers, or wine sellers. Two round lemon trees in square galvanized pots stood guard at the entrance–closed for the day–of a small shop that sold locally-made cheese, olive oil, and wine. Wicker chairs, stacked three-high, lined the walls of a cafe. *Why does everything close so early here*, Anne wondered in disbelief.

Anne followed the shopping street as it turned and merged into the lakeside promenade that ran along the shore of Lago Maggiore. Italianate villas in vivid hues, now converted into expensive lake-view hotels, lined one side of the promenade, and plane trees, with their characteristic knobby branches, lined the other. The whole ensemble gave the pedestrian avenue an allure of a by-gone era of privilege and glamor.

Ascona was a place where the rich, mostly from the north, came for vacation, to bask in its Mediterranean warmth without having to leave the reliable efficiency of Switzerland. Tourists flocked to the shopping streets, packed with glossy boutiques, or to crowded cafes on the promenade where they could people-watch presided over by neatly dressed waiters.

Anne turned to look at the smooth expanse of the lake. Its surface danced with dappled gold, and white sailboats glided along the horizon. The Brissago Islands were visible in the distance. She had visited the botanical park on the larger island last summer, and had enjoyed sending photos from the gardens back home to her friends, and having them doubt that the luxuriant collection of exotic subtropical plants could be Switzerland.

Visible across the lake was Italy. Ascona's long history was intimately entwined with that of its southern neighbor. The town's coat of arms still displayed the papal keys, a testament to an earlier alliance and dependence. To Anne, Ascona looked and felt much like Italian towns she had visited: nineteenth century palazzos dotted the shores of the lake, ancient stone houses crowded the narrow cobbled alleys leading away from the shore, and restaurants served, almost exclusively, Italian staples like pizza, pasta, polenta, and Tiramisu.

And everyone spoke Italian.

Anne sighed. As her brother–who vacationed every summer in Tuscany–never failed to mention, Italian was such an easy language to pick up. But she was having a hard time learning it. And her lack of Italian was preventing her from making local friends or looking for a part-time job.

She knew she was one of the lucky few who got to quit her job and go on a permanent European vacation. And she had to admit, she had it good: she didn't need to work; she could travel on a whim to Italy or France for a weekend getaway; and she didn't have to shovel snow for what had felt like six months out of the year back home.

So what is my problem? Anne shook her head as she walked.

Well, if she were being honest, the problem was that while her husband's career was advancing, she had started to regret all she had left behind. It's true that back in Boston she had been unhappy with her job as a pharmaceutical lab technician. Her career was stagnating, and a bit boring. But now she realized that at 37, which was very close to 40, she would have a hard time switching careers, or even rebuilding her old career in a language she hardly spoke.

Anne had recently learned that there was a term for people like her–people who gave up their jobs to follow their significant other to Switzerland–a 'trailing spouse'. Anne felt that nothing summed up her current predicament with a more succinct brutality.

Though none of this is Ben's fault, Anne thought. She felt guilty having these negative feelings, while surrounded by so much beauty. And the conflicting emotions were driving her crazy.

But this evening her thoughts were more pleasantly occupied. This evening she had a plan. And she couldn't wait to share it with Ben.

She rounded a corner and came to a pastel two-storey house. The pink stucco covered the thick rough stones that formed the house's walls and hid its age. The color made it blend with its more modern neighbors, but the building's small size and slate-tiled roof hinted at its age–perhaps late medieval–to the careful observer. An art gallery occupied the first floor, and her own apartment was on the second.

Closing the heavy wooden street-level door, Anne ran up the stairs to the apartment. Soft light greeted her as she entered. On the inside, the apartment revealed more of its ancient provenance. When they had moved in, she had instantly loved the apartment's whitewashed stone walls, the exposed dark wood beams, and open plan layout. The generous windows knocked out into the thick stone walls bathed the apartment in bright light all day. And a tiny balcony that overlooked the lake–if she leaned forward and looked to the left–completed the magic.

Ben, reading on his phone at the kitchen table, looked up. The last rays of the golden hour made his hair even blonder, and Anne marveled at how boyish he still looked at 40.

"Hi," said Anne. And without waiting for a

reply, because she was excited to share this piece of information with her husband, she continued, "You know that old bookstore I like?"

Ben nodded in response.

"Well, on the way to Italian class I saw a sign in the window that they are looking for an assistant," she said, waiting to see how he would react.

"Okay," he said, encouraging her to give him more details. "But you don't speak Italian," he added.

The store in question was one Anne loved walking past. It was just the type of store that piqued her interest. She loved to stop and look through its windows after hours.

Although situated on the Old Town shopping street, the bookstore was little noticed by visitors to Ascona. Its windows displayed neither flashy art, as the art galleries, nor expensive accessories, as the boutiques, so the eyes of tourists slid past its windows to the sparkling displays of the jewelry store further down the street.

But the bookstore's windows were exactly what drew Anne's attention to it. Two gothic windows stood on each side of the store's entrance, each outlined in a dark wood frame that curved to a sharp point at the top. To Anne, those gothic windows hinted at so much mystery inside.

"Yes, but the ad is for an English-speaking assistant," Anne replied.

"They'll still require you to speak Italian, I would think," her husband said. "And why do you want to work in a bookstore, anyway? You've never worked in a bookstore."

"I know, but I've always wanted to," Anne said. "I still regret not accepting a job at the library during college. I remember I had already lined up another after-class job. But if I had taken that library job instead, who knows how my life would have turned out. I might have studied library science and become a librarian," she said, with a laugh. "You know I love books. And I can imagine that working with books is a very rewarding way to spend time."

"And what type of work?" her husband asked.

"It didn't mention that," Anne said, trying to remember the note on the store's door. "It just said apply within." In her excitement, Anne hadn't considered what the job might actually be. "Anyway. I'm going to go tomorrow morning and apply. At least it will give me a reason to go inside the bookstore." And with that, Anne twirled happily around and went to get a book to read for the evening.

2 An old bookstore

The aroma of Anne's cappuccino enveloped her, and her thoughts drifted to her fully automated Swiss coffee machine and how much joy she got from hearing the crunch of grinding beans and the hiss of frothing milk.

Anne knew good coffee. Thanks to her husband, a rising star in the coffee industry, with a nose for quality beans and the know-how for innovative roasting techniques, Anne always had access to the best roasts. She hadn't realized, until her husband applied for a job here, that Switzerland was one of the largest exporters of roasted coffee in the world, and that its citizens were some of the biggest consumers of coffee in the world.

Anne sat on her balcony–the one that almost overlooked the lake–sipping coffee. The fresh morning air carried a pleasant breeze from the lake. It was still early, but Anne could feel that the strong sun rays would make the day hot by lunchtime. She still had half an hour before she could go to the bookstore at 9 o'clock and apply for the English-speaking assistant's position.

Since last night, for a reason even Anne couldn't put her finger on, she had become fixated on getting the bookstore job. Maybe it was a left-over wish of working in the library from her college days, or maybe it was because she loved reading, or maybe it was because she wanted to feel useful, but she woke up this morning determined to get that job.

Almost everyone here spoke at least some English, in addition to Italian, and German, and sometimes even French, which made Anne feel quite inferior on the language front. But she had confidence in her transferable skills–organizational, research, and analytical–which she had developed during a Master's Degree in Biology, and a career in pharmaceutical research. All of which she had made sure to mention in the CV– the Swiss version of a resume–she had typed up last night.

And she loved books.

I hope that would be enough, she thought.

Because, not only had she never worked in a bookstore before, as her husband had pointed out, she had never worked in retail at all. Her college jobs had revolved around lab work.

Anne turned away from the lakeside promenade, with its bright sunshine and constant flow of tourists, and walked towards the tunnel-like alleyways that wound their way between houses. She needed to be alone and gather her thoughts.

Her pulse quickened as she got closer to the bookstore. *Stop acting like a teenager*, she laughed at herself. She was not some young girl going to her first job interview. She was an almost-middle-aged woman with a solid career behind her.

And yet, being in a new country where she didn't speak the language and where she had to rely on her husband for a lot of things–he spoke excellent Italian thanks to his Italian grandmother–made her feel infantile. But she knew her current state was only temporary, and applying for that bookstore job was a step in the right direction.

As she rounded the corner, she came out of the shaded alleyway and into full view of the pedestrian shopping street, bathed in sharp morning light. Anne had no problem locating the bookstore amid the storefronts.

Her eyes locked on the gothic broodiness of its grey stone facade, which stood in stark contrast to the brightly painted stores on the street. A hipster girl on her phone breezed by Anne. English conversation "– he said I wasn't the right fit –" caught Anne's attention. She shook off the thought that had slipped into her mind. It would be too much of a conscience if the girl had just been rejected for the bookstore assistant's job.

Right?

Anne wondered what would make someone right for the job. She hoped the bookstore job would be meted out based on personality rather than experience.

Even if she didn't get the job, Anne looked forward to having an opportunity, an excuse, really, to go into the bookstore. Though she had walked past it so many times in the last months, she had never dared go inside.

The bookstore was an antiquarian of Italian books. Books that Anne assumed were way out of her Italian-language league. So she had never ventured in.

If I lose my nerve to apply for the job, she thought, *I could ask for an Agatha Christie novel in Italian*. And with that comforting plan, she opened the store door.

The door in question was glass-paneled with a dark wood frame–with a pointed arch in the middle–that matched the windows. With a sinking feeling, Anne noticed the job notice from yesterday was gone. *Oh, no! How can the position be filled already*, she thought.

Her mind started spinning, and she was unsure of what to do. But as her hand was already on the door, she pushed it open. Gentle bells chimed above Anne's head. *Just like a normal bookstore*, she thought, *nothing to be intimidated about.*

Anne stood at the top of a short flight of stone steps leading down into the store. As her eyes adjusted to the gloomy interior, her breath caught. From the outside, Anne had found the store immensely interesting, with its gothic facade and stoic disregard for any sort of flourish that might attract tourists. Peeking inside, after hours, she had seen that the store was a converted apothecary, with the characteristic antique glass fronted cabinets still lining the walls.

The combination of old books and apothecary reminded Anne of alchemy, and she wondered what other surprising things the store might be hiding. Maybe part of the reason she had never gone in before was that she didn't want to spoil the fantasy she had constructed in her mind.

But even if Anne had found the store interesting from the outside, she was not prepared for the details displayed on the inside. Past the stone steps lay a floor covered in tiny tiles, arranged in a colorful geometric pattern. Dark wood counters framed the store on three sides. Behind them, nested in smooth stone walls, were the apothecary cabinets, which Anne had seen from the outside. Tall glass doors enclosed thick antique books with faded cloth bindings on the lower shelves, while the upper shelves were crammed with an array of white ceramic jars in different sizes with ornately painted labels. Each cabinet was framed with a twisting design of leaves, vines, and flowers carved into the dark wood. And above the cabinets, elegant stone ribs extended from the walls, traveled up in a curve, and met at the center of the store to form a soaring vaulted ceiling.

In the hushed interior, each of Anne's steps reverberated as she walked down into the store. It felt like walking into a cathedral.

As Anne descended the last step onto the tiled floor, a bang echoed through the store. She gave a start. Her heart pounded at the unexpected sound, and it took her a moment to realize that it wasn't her. The loud crash had come from a black cat as it jumped up on the counter and knocked over a tall stack of books.

The cat stood on the counter, sitting next to the tipped pile of books, examining Anne with an intense stare. Sitting behind the counter, a man with frameless glasses and greying hair smiled up at her.

"Ciao," Anne said.

"Salve," answered the man, using the more formal greeting reserved for strangers. *I should have used the same*, Anne thought.

She hesitated, but decided there was nothing to be shy about.

"I'm here to apply for the English-speaking assistant position," Anne said, uncertain if she should speak in Italian instead. "Is it still available?"

"Yes, just," said the man from behind the counter. *What does that mean*, Anne wondered.

"I'm Marco. Welcome to my store." Marco didn't move or get up and kept his hands on top of the counter. "So you are interested in the assistant position?" he asked. Anne noticed his English was excellent, though accented with an Italian annunciation.

"Yes, I brought my CV," she said as she stepped closer and handed the printed pages to him.

"I'm not interested in that," Marco dismissed them gently with his hand. "We'll just have a chat about the project, you'll tell me a bit about yourself, and we'll see how we get along."

He removed his hands from the counter and dropped them by his side. As he did, he started gliding backward. The movement surprised Anne, but she realized he was in a wheelchair. Marco spun the wheelchair to the side and started making his way around the counter. The black cat leapt off the counter into his lap.

He extended a hand towards Anne, "Nice to meet you," and invited her further into the store. "Okay, let's jump right into it," he said. "This is an antiquarian, and we buy and sell old books, and we sometimes also buy old maps, and documents, and archives from when people die –"

"From estate sales," Anne suggested.

"That's right," he said. He eased the cat off his lap and revealed a small brown leather book.

He wheeled toward the counter and opened the book. Anne followed him. He continued, "The project I'm hiring for involves this diary, and its companions. It belonged to a woman, Cecilia Holbourn, who established an art colony in the area in the 1900s. On the Isola Caresio," he pointed toward the lake. "Do you know it?"

Anne shook her head "No, not really. I've been to the botanical gardens on Brissago Islands, but know little about other islands."

"Ah, well, it's right behind the Brissago Islands, but difficult to see from here," he answered as he leaned over the pages of the diary. Anne looked at him more closely. Marco wore a thick cardigan despite the warm weather. And his haircut was like an army buzz cut, different from the longer hair–Anne had observed–men here preferred.

"The art colony has been on the island since the 1900s,", he said, bringing her attention back to the diary, "and in its heyday was quite popular with artists, philosophers, writers, and other luminaries. While it started off as a bohemian enclave, it turned into a strict vegetarian and nudist colony by the 1930s, with strong anarchist and bolshevik views", he continued as he leafed through the pages of the diary, "and then disintegrated into drugs and hedonism in the 1960s. By the 1980s, the current owner, a descendent of the art colony's founder, decided"–he closed the diary with a snap–"to close it down." He turned to look at Anne, "There were too many accidents involving wild parties, drugs, and alcohol. And there was probably some pressure from the town as well for the art colony to clean up its act or to close. When the art colony closed, the family decided to dispose of some of the archives. And since I collect documents of local history, I bought them."

The history of the island intrigued Anne, and she made a mental note to look up the island online when she got home.

"But now the art colony is being revived," Marco continued. "I think they are planning to turn it into a convention center and run it for profit. They have people on the island now to start restoration of the house. And I hear they also have some artists visiting already."

Maco turned towards the pile of books the cat had knocked over.

"Where we come in," he said, putting a hand on top of the pile, "is that the woman in charge of this venture wanted to buy the diaries back and display them at the house as a sort of museum, to recall the history of the art colony and its beginnings."

Anne's stomach had made a little jump at the "we", and she wondered if it was significant. *Was that 'we' as in Marco and other employees of the store, or 'we' as in Marco and me*, she thought.

"I sold the diaries back to them, of course," Marco continued, "but we agreed I can keep them for a while to digitize them. I think these are interesting little documents of local history, and I want to keep copies of them. So the position I'm interested in filling is to digitize the diaries and index any references to well-known people from the time of the diaries." Marco turned with a smile towards Anne and looked her straight in the eyes, "How is your Italian and Swiss history?"

The question threw her off. *Well, they are non-existent*, she thought. She caught a hint of mischief in his eyes and relaxed a bit. Seeing this as an opportunity to speak, Anne plunged right into the list of qualities and qualifications she had prepared for the interview.

"I don't know much about local history, but I'm willing to learn. I'm a quick learner. I love books and reading. And I think I would be perfect for this project. I'm organized, and I used to work as a researcher, so I'm good with summarizing data and finding patterns, and working on my own. I'm self-directed and self-motivated," she paused a little to go over her mental list and see if she missed anything.

She knew she probably looked like an eager student trying to please a teacher. *Ugh, what is it about this job that is getting me so worked up?* Anne thought. *Pull yourself together,* she told herself.

"Good, good. That's good," he said. "Do you

live in the area?"

"Yes, I live just a few streets away. Above the *Bellina Gallery*, near the promenade." Anne hoped living in town would give her some brownie points.

"Good," the man said again. "I'll see you tomorrow and we can complete the paperwork."

"So is that it?" she asked, unsure if the interview was done.

"That's it," he said. "Come at 9." The black cat jumped back in his lap as he pulled away from Anne, and swerved to go back behind the counter.

Anne left the store a bit confused. She seemed to have got the job. But she was not sure why. Marco hadn't asked many questions. She guessed he was going off personality, just like she had hoped. *And the project itself is not that complicated*, she thought. *I can handle it.*

Before joining the flow of tourists towards the promenade, she turned to look at the store. Funny, she had never noticed the name before. Mostly she didn't look at store names, because she couldn't translate them for herself. On a sign above the store she read "*Fuori Stampa*". *'Fuori'- outside and 'stampa'-printing*, she overtaxed her Italian knowledge. She couldn't make sense of it. She'd have to ask her husband.

As she walked home along the sun-dappled promenade, weaving among tourists, she got more and more excited about the job. It sounded like work that she would find interesting. It ticked so many of her ideal-job boxes–it involved books, and research, and analysis, and distilling information...

A happy jolt did a somersault in her stomach. She almost bounced as she turned the corner toward home.

3 The unwelcome customer

The bells over the front door chimed. *A customer*, thought Anne. Sitting in her office, a small room to the side of the bookstore's storage area, she scanned a page from the diaries.

In her first three days at the store, Anne had not had to serve a customer, yet. Because of her non-existent conversational Italian, Marco had taken care of that. Not that there were many customers. 'Out of Print', as Anne now knew the store was called, truly lived up to its name. Almost all the bookstore's business came through email enquiries from academics and researchers about old books and historical documents.

The slow pace of life in the store suited Anne. She discovered that Marco was the only other employee and that he was as quiet as she was. And, having never liked small talk at the office, she considered it a plus.

Anne was used to working on her own, from her lab days. She didn't mind spending long stretches of the day alone, digitizing the diaries. The rhythm of her work was relaxing and almost meditative, as she pressed each page to the scanner and waited for the digital copy to appear on her screen.

"Scusi!" A man's voice bellowed.

Anne jumped. She had forgotten about the customer. *I guess Marco didn't hear the customer come in,* Anne thought. She put down the diary and went to see if she could help.

The silhouette of a tall man with a hat stood out against the store windows. He was pacing across from one side counter to the other, flicking a pair of gloves in his hands.

"Buongiorno," Anne said as she stepped behind the counter.

The man turned, and she saw him more clearly. He wore a straw Panama hat arranged to one side for artistic flourish, a navy blue linen sport coat, and a long white scarf wrapped once around his neck. *Silk, probably*, Anne thought, *given the entire ensemble.* It reminded her of a caricature of an artist from a *Poirot* episode.

The man started speaking in rapid Italian.

Anne froze. She had no idea what he was saying. She knew any normal customer would expect a bookstore assistant to speak Italian, so she forced herself to interrupt him before he got any further.

"I'm sorry, I don't speak Italian," she said. The man stopped with an incredulous expression on his face. Anne thought she saw him roll his eyes under the brim of his hat.

"Are the diaries ready?" he switched to a measured, accented English, twirling the pair of light leather gloves in his hand to underlie his impatience at having to repeat himself.

Anne's confusion must have appeared on her face because the man continued with an irritated sigh. "The diaries of the grandmother from the art colony," he waved his gloves in the direction of the lake. While he was the same height as Anne, he still managed to hold his head in such a way as to be talking down to her.

"I'm sorry, but I don't know who you are. I can't give that information away." Anne felt protective of the diaries and the man was making her bristle.

"I've come from the Caresio island," he said, slowly, the way one would speak to a child. "I'm from the art colony. I'm the painter Paolo Duratti." He delivered all this with a hint of boredom, as if Anne should have known all this information.

Well, at least the artist part explains the outfit, Anne thought.

"The diaries are not finished yet. I haven't finished scanning all of them. It was my understanding that there was no rush on the project," Anne said.

"Well, when are you going to be done?" he demanded. A twirl of his gloves emphasized his question.

"There are still quite a lot of pages to be scanned and indexed," Anne explained. She waited to see what he would say, because she wasn't exactly sure what the man wanted with the diaries, and what he hoped to accomplish with his visit.

"Can I see them? I'm looking for some information," he said, switching to a more pleasant tone.

"I'm not sure I can let you see them," Anne said. She wasn't sure if she was supposed to show them. *I wish Marco were here*, she thought.

"Elaine, the director from the art colony, knows I'm here," the man pressed on. "You could say I'm here at her bidding. I'm just looking for some information and I can't wait. Who knows how long it would take you to finish with the diaries." He paused for a moment. "Here. I'll stand right here and you can watch me leaf through them, right here. Is that good for you?"

Where is Marco, Anne thought, a little irritated this time. Anne excused herself and went to the back to look for him.

The chapel-like feel of the front of the store belied the modern efficiency of the storage area in the back. Tall metal racks filled the space. Books, rolled up maps, and flat rectangular boxes filled with old documents and archives lined the shelves, stacked only as high as Marco's reach. Marco's office was to the side of the stacks. He wasn't in it.

Beyond the stacks was an area that looked disused. Metal stairs led to a second-floor gallery–also lined with book stacks–but that area was always dark, and Anne had not had a reason to explore it. A fireproof door beneath the gallery's balcony led to what Marco had explained was a climate controlled area for the oldest items in the store's inventory. Marco used a door to the side of the metal staircase to enter and exit the store.

She called out his name and looked for him among the stacks. But Marco was nowhere to be found. *He must have gone out for a bit*, Anne thought.

Anne didn't want to be away from the front too long, because she wouldn't put it past the pushy artist to go behind the counter and start looking for the diaries himself.

She walked back to the front. Maggie, the store's black cat, was pacing in front of the closed office door to Anne's office. *That's strange*, Anne thought. *I left it open.* She pressed on the handle, but the door did not open. She pushed her weight against it, thinking it was stuck, but it would not move. Worried that the artist had gone into her office, taken the diaries, and somehow locked the door, Anne ran to the front of the store.

But she found the artist still there, and more agitated than before.

"Well, can I see the diaries?" he shot out.

"I'm sorry," Anne said, and mentally kicked herself for apologizing. "I cannot find the store owner, and the door to the office with the diaries is locked."

"*Dio!*" He exclaimed, clearly not believing her. He let out a few curse words in Italian. Said, what sounded like, "I guess I have to wait for some incompetent girl to finish," under his breath, but loud enough for Anne to hear, and left the store with a huff. Anne could see him walking across the store windows, in the direction of the lake, his ridiculous white scarf flapping behind him.

"What happened?" Marco asked behind Anne.

She spun around, a hand on her chest. "Oh, you scared me," she said. "I didn't expect you."

Anne told Marco about the man. "I decided not to show him the diaries, mainly because he was rude, but also because I wasn't sure he had the right to see them," she said.

"You're probably right. He'll get to see them soon enough, if the art colony director lets him," Marco said. He shrugged, as if to dismiss the whole incident.

"And it was so strange," Anne continued, "but my door was stuck. I didn't lock it, but I couldn't budge it open."

Marco turned around and wheeled down the corridor towards her office door. He pressed the handle and with a slight push the door swung open in a smooth arc.

"How can that be? It was so stuck!" Anne said. Was Marco playing a trick on her? Had he locked the door and unlocked it again before coming to the front for some reason? *So strange*, Anne thought.

"The store is old," Marco called out over his shoulder as he rolled away towards his office.

4 A death in the newspaper

The calm waters of the lake sparkled gently in the morning sunlight. Along the promenade, as she made her way to the store, coffee in hand, Anne observed tourists and locals taking their place at the lake-side cafes for a day of leisure. Heavy-around-the-middle men in bright polo shirts hid behind large newspapers. Their young wives hid behind oversized sunglasses and sipped tiny coffees. Single ladies of retirement age, with coiffures hair-sprayed against the lake breeze, strode up and down the promenade behind small dogs.

Anne looked ahead. From far away, the bookstore reminded her of an unhappy old man among all the other cheerful stores. *A grumpy man who randomly locks doors*, she thought. She turned her eyes towards the lake, yesterday's unpleasant visit fresh in her mind. The art colony island was not visible from here, hidden behind Brissago Islands.

Why was the artist so insistent on seeing the diaries? What is inside them that he can't wait? Anne wondered.

After Paolo Duratti's visit, she had looked more closely through the text to see if some event jumped out at her. The diaries were interesting, but she couldn't find any information that would make an artist so desperate to see them. They contained nothing more than short snippets of Cicilia's daily life: her garden; her children; visitors to the art colony; descriptions of parties. Anne found those glimpses of life in the 1900s enchanting. The daily entries tugged on her imagination and transported her back in time. She imagined daily life on the island as pleasant, unhurried, and always drenched in sunshine. Ladies in long white frocks, lace parasols, hats held on with big pale blue bows, sitting in swaying meadows for impromptu afternoon picnics. Like a Monet painting. While the diaries were entertaining, they revealed nothing earth-shattering, as far as Anne could tell.

Anne passed a newsstand. A picture above the fold of the local newspaper caught her attention. It was the artist who had visited the store yesterday. She looked at the headline, but couldn't translate it. Hoping Marco would translate it for her, she bought a copy. She could also use the app on her phone, the one that translated text from pictures. *What did people do before translation apps*, Anne wondered. *They learned the language quicker*, she answered herself. She suspected that the ease of translating text with her phone was hindering her progress with Italian.

She tried to make out the words in the headline, but couldn't piece them together. Whatever it was, it was something important.

When Anne got to the store, Marco was already behind the counter. She flagged up the newspaper as she walked down the steps from the door.

"Look what I saw on my way here," Anne said, "but I can't make out all of it. It's something to do with the artist that came in yesterday." She spread the newspaper on the counter.

Marco glanced at it. "I've seen it," he said. Anne noticed a folded copy of the same newspaper by his elbow. After passing his eyes once more over the article, he continued, "There was a boating accident at the art colony last night and the artist, Paolo Duratti, drowned. It seems like the artists staying at the art colony had a party that involved a lot of wine and champagne." Marco shook his head.

"That's awful." Anne said. Her husband had mentioned last summer, when Anne wanted to take up paddleboarding on the lake, that people underestimated the tranquil waters of Lago Maggiore and its depth, and many drown in accidents on the lake every year.

Anne leaned over the newspaper, "Does the article say anything else?" There was a photo of the artists, but also a photo of the art colony villa. Even from the grainy print of the black-

and-white photo, Anne could see that it was an exquisite example of a Belle Epoque villa. Graceful white columns and elegant tall windows decorated the facade. She had seen other villas like it around the lake, and on lake Como in Italy, but most of those were now museums. *I can't believe there are still families who can afford to own an entire island and support the upkeep of such villas*, Anne thought.

"Not much," answered Marco. "Just a little about the history of the Isola Caresio and the art colony," he said. "It is a strange little place," he continued after some thought. "The art colony had always been accompanied by an outsized number of accidents. I guess that can be attributed to the fast and reckless lifestyle of the rich and idle. Lots of parties and lots of drinking. That doesn't mix well with proximity to a lake, and boating under the influence is never a good idea." Marco said, sounding reproachful.

"What is this word?" Anne pointed to one word in the title, printed big. "*La maledizione*", she read in her halting Italian.

"The curse. 'The curse has returned'," Marco translated.

"What curse?" Anne asked, her curiosity piqued.

Marco shook his head, "The history of the island goes way back, to before the art colony and its beautiful villa. Its beginnings are much darker."

Anne hoped he would continue without being prompted.

"The legend of the curse is well known around here. I'm surprised you haven't heard of it?" Marco said.

Too caught up in the promise of an interesting story to speak, Anne just shook her head.

Marco obliged. "Back in the 1400s, the lands all around here passed back and forth between Milanese princes and the fledgling Swiss federation. It was a constant battle between Italian princes and their grand families, which included bishops or even popes, and the republic of Swiss cantons. Isola Caresio was the Bishop of Milan's last stronghold in the area. There was a bitter battle on the island which led to his defeat; he had lost a lot of land in the process. The Bishop ordered his retreating army to burn everything to the ground, and cursed the island, any new building on it, and any people who tried to set foot on it. The only thing left was an old church and its tower. Left as a reminder of the curse. For a long time, it was the only building on the island.

"The island passed back and forth between Italian princes and the Swiss federation a few more times and finally settled into the possession of a family from the Italian nobility, descendents of the Bishop of Milan, but on the territory of Switzerland. In the late 1880s, the family built a villa as a summer retreat, which later became the art colony. The church is still there," Marco pointed to the photo of the villa. Anne looked closer and saw a dark tower, similar to the one in Ascona, among the tall trees behind the house. It seemed so out of place. "The local people here have blamed the curse for the accidents over the years at the art colony," he added.

Anne's brow creased, "But if the island belongs to the descendants of Italian princes, why are the diaries written in English?"

"Oh, like most aristocratic families, they were quite international in their bloodline, marrying suitably aristocratic partners from all over Europe. By the time the villa was built, and the diaries were written, the family, through marriages, had become quintessentially English."

The bells above the door announced a visitor and broke the spell of the island's story. Anne wanted to learn more, but she knew she had to get on with her work and walked to her office to start her day of digitizing.

She looked at the stack on her desk with a renewed interest. The curse added a new lens through which to read the diaries. Anne didn't believe in curses and thought they were just self-fulfilling prophecies of words taken too literally. She agreed with Marco that the accidents were probably due to the fast and reckless lifestyle of the rich. After all, how many rich and famous people die each year skiing, or flying their own planes, or doing some other extreme sport or activity. *It has probably been like that for centuries. Only the vehicles and modes of thrill-seeking have changed. Not human nature*, Anne thought.

5 A trip to Isola Caresio

"Done!" Anne stretched her back and rolled her shoulders. She had finished scanning all the diaries.

Scanning hadn't taken long. And even with the time she spent reading–and looking for clues as to why an artist would be so desperate to get his hands on what were essentially the diaries of an early 20th century housewife–Anne still had progressed through them with efficiency.

She gathered the leather-bound notebooks and carried them to the front of the store where Marco was hunched over a book.

"That's the last one," she announced. "I'll continue indexing them, but these can go to the island," she placed the stack on the counter. "Is there mail delivery to the island?" Anne asked.

Ever since her encounter with the artist, his inexplicable interest in the diaries, and his subsequent accident and death, Anne was curious about the art colony and its current residents. She wondered if anyone from the island would stop by the store to pick up the diaries.

"I'll phone them and see what they want to arrange," Marco said, rolling towards the phone on the wall. Anne remembered being surprised that the store still had a working landline.

While Marco was on the phone, Anne stepped out to get fresh air. After spending so much time in the windowless office, she welcomed the warm rays of the sun on her face. *Need to go for a long walk on the weekend*, she told herself.

She looked towards the lake, and her glance skimmed over the water in the direction of the island. Anne wondered what life was like on the art colony island now. She wanted to see the island up close. She knew it was private and therefore inaccessible to visitors without an invitation, but she decided that maybe her husband could rent a boat and they could sail by it one day.

Anne stepped back in. Marco greeted her with the news that they were invited to deliver the diaries to the island themselves. "Do you want to go for a boat ride?" Marco asked. "We can go during lunch."

Ascona, like the rest of Southern Switzerland, and the whole of Italy, resolutely hung on to the tradition of a long lunch break. Anne loved that people went home for an hour, or an hour and a half, and had lunch with family.

"How will we get there?" Anne asked.

"We'll take my boat." Marco answered. Anne didn't want to say it out loud, but she wondered how a person in a wheelchair could go on a boat, and operate a boat. Her hesitance must have shown because a mischievous smile spread across Marco's face and he added, "I have a specially designed boat. You'll see. I have it docked at the Old Port."

Anne had walked by the Old Port many times on her excursions through Ascona. 'Port' was a rather grand name for the rectangular pool of water enclosed by a low stone wall with boats moored inside. One wall had a narrow opening towards the lake so that boats could pass in and out. Unlike the more modern docks of Ascona–set in a prime location along the center of the promenade–from which tourist boats ferried visitors to other picturesque towns along the lake, and to Italy, the Old Port was tucked out of the way to the side of the promenade.

Anne locked the front door, and they left the store through the back. A paved lane behind the building sloped gently to the lake. Marco pointed out a modern white boat as his. Anne placed the box of diaries she was carrying into the boat and then got into the swaying vessel herself. Under Marco's instructions, she found the button to lower a platform on the back of the boat so that it was flush with the dock, and Marco wheeled on. Anne noticed he operated the boat with the practiced movements of an experienced boatman.

Marco guided the boat through the narrow opening in the stone wall at a low speed and picked up speed when they got to open water. Little splashes and bumps measured out the boat's progress across the lake in a rhythmic succession. A clear blue horizon opened up ahead of them. The breeze off the lake cooled down the sun's strong rays on Anne's face. She tried to tame the hair swirling wildly around her head, while she held the side of the boat for balance.

They rounded the two Brissago Islands–the larger, botanical gardens one, with its manicured exotic flora, and a smaller companion island, which, unlike the botanical park, was left to grow wild and untamed. Finally, the art colony island came into view. Anne's heart sped up. She looked forward to seeing the real thing after having spent so much time reading about it.

As they neared the island, a bell tower, much like the one in Ascona, rose out of the background of the island. The dark tower hunched menacingly over the pretty exuberance of a white villa. The contrast was striking. It reminded Anne of a pretty maiden trapped in the clutches of an ogre. A shiver ran down her spine. She had completely forgotten about the curse.

Anne had looked up the island's history online. Standing before her were the last remains of the vast fortune of the Trincini–now Fitzroy–family, that over the centuries fate and world events had whisked away.

Marco slowed down the boat. He aligned it

parallel with the middle of three docks jutting out from the island. The boat came to a stop with a light bump against the wooden planks.

Anne looked up, trying to focus on the details of the white palazzo. It was more beautiful and delicate than Anne had envisioned. The rectangular shape reminded her of a gilded jewelry box. A carved stone balustrade framed the flat roof, classic columns decorated the facade, and wrought-iron balconies adorned each of its many tall windows.

A tall woman, in sensible khakis and a white shirt with rolled-up sleeves, was waiting on the dock.

"Welcome," she said, with a wide smile showing off her perfect teeth.

"Hello," Marco answered. Marco turned towards Anne, "Anne, this is Elaine Mayer, the director of the art colony. She's the one who initiated the purchase of the diaries." Turning to Elaine, he said, "Anne has been working on digitizing and indexing the diaries."

"A pleasure to meet you," said Elaine. She walked to the boat and offered to take the box of diaries. "Marco, would the two of you like to come ashore and visit the island? We are having a little impromptu lunch outside with some drinks," she tipped her head towards the house, cradling the cardboard box against her body. "You can reach the top of the hill using that ramp on the side that the construction workers are using," she indicated a smooth dirt path sloping in a curve up from the right side of the docks. She spoke English with a predominantly British accent, but her speech was also laced with a pan-European accent Anne had become accustomed to in Switzerland, but which was hard to place.

A jolt of excitement passed through Anne, but she waited to see what Marco would say.

Marco shook his head, "No, thank you for the invitation, but I have to go back to the store and I was planning on having lunch with my wife." Disappointment washed over Anne–to have come so close to the island and not see it. "But maybe Anne would like to stay," Marco said, turning to Anne.

"I'd love to," Anne said, a little too loudly. She tried moderating her excitement. "It's such a beautiful place. And after reading through the diaries, I would love to see the island, and the house, in person." A thought crossed her mind– she couldn't ask Marco to come back and get her. "Only, how will I get back to Ascona?" she asked.

"We'll think of something," said Elaine, and paused for a moment. "We have the grocer's boat coming later in the afternoon. I'm sure he can take you back to the mainland."

Anne clambered off the boat and waved to Marco as he drove off. She reached in the back pocket of her jeans for an elastic, combed her fingers through her messy hair, and put her hair in a ponytail. Anne noticed the red and white police tape around the dock to the left. "My condolences," she said to Elaine.

"It's a terrible tragedy," Elaine said, following Anne's glance. "We all had quite a bit to drink that night. Paolo must have gone down to the dock for some reason and tried to go to the shore," Elaine pointed with her head to Ascona. "Goodness knows why, in the middle of the night. The police said he must have slipped or lost his balance trying to get on the boat, and hit his head, and then drowned," she was quiet for a moment. "No one heard anything, of course, or we would have tried to help. All the bedrooms we are currently using face the other way, and these shrubs," she swept her head, "hide much of the dock from view from the house. Poor Paolo." Elaine shook her head and continued walking ahead.

At the end of the dock they turned left and took white stone steps up the hill towards the house. Luscious greenery lined their way. Heavy purple clusters of wisteria blossoms hung over the path, the strong trunks twisting and crawling up the hill. The steps were worn in places and cracks in the stone had given way to weeds and grass. But Anne could see through their age and appreciated their elegance. She imagined the generations of joyful people–excited by the prospect of a summer spent on the lake–that had walked up these stairs from the dock to the house.

A stillness enveloped the island. The warm air was filled with the buzz of insects. Somewhere far away on the lake a motorboat purred. The leaves overhead rustled in the gentle breeze. A bumblebee flew low and slow from flower to flower on a purple bush.

"What a great idea to reopen the art colony," Anne said. "I can see how relaxing and inspiring this place must be to artists and even writers. Will the place be open to writers?" she turned to Elaine.

"At the moment it's only open to some artists, friends of the current owner, Barbara Fitzroy," Elaine answered. "But after the necessary repairs to the building have been completed, and a full business plan is drawn up, to make the art colony financially self-sufficient, we will open it up to the public," she said. "We're aiming to have it ready by next summer."

"Looks like an enchanting place to work," said Anne.

"Yes, I'm very lucky to have secured this position," said Elaine. They had reached the top of the steps, "Come, let me show you the house," she led the way towards the white building.

White gravel crunched under Anne's feet; a broad gravel path encircled the house. "This place must have been overgrown like a jungle when you first got here," Anne said, observing the wild mix of trees and bushes on every side of the house.

Elaine looked around, as if taking stock of the greenery surrounding them. "Oh, it wasn't so bad. We haven't actually done much to the gardens since we arrived. We've been focusing on getting the house back to working order," she said. "Even after the last art colony closed in the 80s, there has always been someone living on the island and taking care of it. You probably noticed the bell tower?" Elaine indicated the stone tower beyond the trees. "There has always been a priest at the church on the island. Ever since the church was built in the Middle Ages. I think the bell tower dates from the 1100s. There were other buildings on the island, but those were destroyed during battles. One day we'll get archaeologists to come excavate. Settlement here probably dates back to Roman time," Elaine said, and continued toward the house.

Three pairs of French doors lined the side of the house. The middle doors were open and they walked through them into a wide hall. The hall stretched the whole length of the house, with a sweeping white staircase in the center. Outside the weather was getting hot in the sharp midday sun, but inside the house was cool, even chilly.

Anne glanced around, taking in as much detail as she could. "It's absolutely breathtaking," she said. It reminded her of the grand Italian palazzos she had visited on lake Como in Italy. But those were museums; she couldn't believe someone actually owned this.

Her gaze fell on a group of paintings hanging on a wall to the side. "May I?" Anne asked, indicating the paintings, and walked over to take a closer look while Elaine went to put away the diaries.

"Being an art colony, the whole place used to be covered with paintings from various periods and various visitors," Elaine said walking back towards Anne. "We've left most of them in storage for now, but took out a few painted by the family."

Anne examined each painting. There were two very nice portraits, a group of landscapes, and a few decidedly modern paintings. One small painting in particular caught her attention. It showed a young girl in a white dress, in a field of tall wildflowers. Anne knew enough about art to appreciate the artist's confident brushstrokes and handling of light. It reminded her of an impressionist painting. *1911,* she read the date on the painting, *too late for impressionism. And no signature,* she observed.

"All of these were painted here at the art colony," Elaine said.

"That's a really nice one," Anne pointed to the

one with the girl.

"Yes, that's a really nice one. It's painted by Cecilia–Cece for short–whose diaries you've been working on. She's Barbara's great-grandmother. And the girl in the painting is Lily, Cece's daughter, Barbara's grandmother," Elaine explained. "Pitty, judging by this, she could have been a great artist, but didn't produce much beyond this painting. Her husband, John Holbourn, was somewhat well known at the time, but is now mostly forgotten," Elaine said, examining the painting. "This here," she said, pointing to one of the portraits, "is actually a portrait of Cece done at about the same time. She was in her mid-twenties here, from what Barbara said."

Anne looked over to the portrait with a renewed interest. She was excited to put a face to the diaries. Looking back at her was an attractive young woman with chestnut hair swept up in a voluminous pompadour, and a high white lace neck. The artist had captured a merriment in her clear blue eyes.

"Anyway, we'll have to go through all the pictures in storage and see what we have," Elaine said, looking at the paintings. "Let's join the others in the garden," she said after a few moments, and started walking towards the back of the house. Anne noticed the rectangular silhouettes of the absent paintings all along the walls of the hall.

6 A garden party

They walked through another set of open doors into a courtyard on the side of the house. Surrounded by a low balustrade wall, and lined with the same white gravel, the courtyard formed a terrace overlooking the lake. *This place just keeps getting better*, Anne marveled at the enchanted life of those who had lived here.

"This courtyard gets too hot in the middle of the day," Elaine said. "We've set up camp in a wilder bit of the island, with more shade." They walked out of the courtyard and up a path along the edge of a small forest. Anne appreciated the cool shade of the trees, as the sun really was warm by now. The path led them past a high stone wall.

"What's this?" Anne asked, indicating the wall.

"Oh, it's a walled garden," answered Elaine. "Quite charming. Complete with a thick wood door that locks and everything. It's like a secret garden, like in the kids' book," she smiled. "They really did not spare any expense when they were building this villa," Elaine said, echoing Anne's thoughts.

"We do yoga in here in the evenings sometimes," Elaine patted the large gray stones. "We leave our cell phones in the house and light a few candles. It's a magical experience," she said. "Sometimes we do naked yoga," her clear laughter bounced off the stone. "You should join us one evening. It's quite decadent," Elaine said, and smiled at Anne. Anne felt her cheeks burning, just smiled back, and continued walking.

Anne heard conversation punctuated with laughter in the distance. They walked into a clearing on the back of the walled garden. Among the tall grass, wildflowers bloomed in yellow, purple, and white. It reminded Anne of the painting inside the house. The breeze carried a delicate smell of warm grass.

A group of people lounged on lawn chairs, some in the sun, and some under the dappled shade provided by young spring leaves. A small table was laid with various plates, opened bottles of wine, and even a bottle of champagne. *Like a Renoir painting, just more upscale*, thought Anne.

"Everyone," Elaine said, her voice raised, "this is Anne from the bookstore. She came to deliver Cece's diaries." Elaine led Anne towards the others. "I've invited her to stay and join our little party for lunch." They stopped in front of the group. "Let me see," she said, looking round. "This is Nick. A terribly good painter. Don't let him convince you to paint you naked. Scandalous," Elaine said with a flirty note in her voice. *She's clearly hoping to be invited to do just that*, Anne thought.

Nick tipped back a straw hat, smiled in Anne's direction, and lowered the hat back over his eyes. He lay comfortably in his lawn chair in full sun, a pale blue linen shirt with the sleeves rolled up, khakis rolled up at the ankle, and suede loafers worn without socks. *In the habit of Italians*, Anne noticed. The whole ensemble radiated nonchalant elegance. Anne could appreciate why Elaine might hope to be painted by Nick.

"If I didn't know better," a bell-like voice rang out, "I would think Daniel is the one painting a nude woman in his room." Anne turned to the voice and saw a woman sitting in a contorted pose in one of the lounge chairs–a pose more suited for a glamor shot. The woman wore a short dress with spaghetti straps that showed off her slim legs. Smooth black hair, flipped to one side, cascaded down her tanned shoulders. "He's been so mysterious lately," the woman continued, "always locking himself up to paint. What are you working on so secretly, Daniel?" she turned to the man sitting next to her.

"Then we have Daniel and Poppy," Elaine's gaze traveled to the two people sitting under the shade of an old tree. "Daniel is also an artist, but more interested in painting what is selling than a true artist should be," Elaine said, laughing. "Although he is rather marvelous at painting like the old masters."

Daniel smiled a broad, good-natured smile, and pushed his hand through his dark wavy hair. "Elaine, you'll give our guest the wrong impression about me," he said in a voice thick like honey. *He would make a great voice actor*, Anne thought.

His voice certainly had an effect on the woman sitting next to him, who looked at him with the longing of someone who hoped to be noticed. "But I do think art is like any other profession. I'm good at what I do, I socialize with the right people, and I make good money selling my paintings to them," Daniel said, without a trace of defense in his voice.

"It helps to have an art dealer for a girlfriend," Nick spoke up from under his hat. He sat up in his chair, pushed back his hat, and turned to Daniel. "Where is dear Julia, anyway? I thought she would be here."

Daniel shrugged. "She got an urgent call to fly to Hong Kong for a valuation," he said. The woman sitting next to him readjusted in her chaise lounge, and Anne thought the sparkle in her smile dimmed a little at the mention of this Julia.

"And that's Poppy," Elaine said, pointing to the sulking woman next to Daniel.

"Penelope," the woman corrected her, and sighed, annoyed. Anne wasn't sure if that was due to being called Poppy or due to Daniel's girlfriend being mentioned.

"Penelope," Elaine stressed the name, "is a psychology professor and a successful author of controversial biographies of psychology luminaries. Her book on Freud caused quite a stir, and now she has her sights set on Carl Jung," Elaine added. There was a note in her voice which was either admiration or jealousy, Anne couldn't decide.

"And last–"

"As always," interjected a thin woman with delicate features. Dressed all in black despite the strong sun, she was sitting a bit off to the side of everyone else.

"–but not least," Elaine continued, irritated by the interruption, "is Maud, an installation artist. She creates light scapes and large scale outdoor installations in remote and inaccessible places." Elaine explained. "Terribly clever," she added, but in a tone that didn't sound like a compliment to Anne.

"Nice to meet you," Maud said.

Anne thought the introductions were strained. Clearly these people shared a lot of history together, but she felt uneasy in their company, as if she'd walked into the middle of a family argument.

"Nice to meet you all." Anne said to the group.

Elaine and Anne unfolded two lounge chairs and joined the semi-circle on the meadow. Still curious how this group of people, who didn't seem to like each other much, got to be here, Anne leaned forward in her chaise lounge and spoke to no one in particular, "How do you all know each other?"

"All our families know each other," Elaine said. "And we all run in the same social circles in London and New York. My parents are friends of Barbara's and we holidayed together in the Caribbean when I was a kid. Poppy, Maud and I were in a Swiss boarding school together, and then visited each other during school holidays. Nick went to university with Barbara's son, James. And Daniel is Barbara's family, of course," Elaine rattled off the tangled web of relationships. Anne gave up trying to keep up.

During Elaine's explanation, Daniel had walked to the table. He now walked back with two champagne glasses and gave one to Elaine. He handed the other one to Anne and sat on the edge of her lounge chair. This surprised Anne, and she scooted back. But Daniel appeared unphased. He examined Anne's face for a moment, as if assessing her. "Tell me, how did you end up working in a bookstore in Ascona?" he asked, with a smile. *Is he flirting with me*, Anne thought.

"There can't be anyone interested in books

here," Poppy said, interrupting. "It's all Russian oligarchs and their painted wives buying up property and art around here. Not books."

"And we know all about the Russian wives," Elaine laughed, and Poppy joined in the private joke.

"We used to work together in a medical spa in the north of Switzerland. Terribly exclusive and expensive," Poppy said, indicating herself and Elaine.

"So expensive that it priced itself out of business," Daniel said, smiling at Anne.

"Yes, I always thought that there would be an endless supply of fools to pay the price of a small car for a treatment at the spa," interjected Maude. "I guess even oligarchs have their limits."

"Yes, anyhow," Elaine cleared her throat. "Would you like something to eat?" she said, turning to Anne.

"Yes, please," said Anne, thankful for an opportunity to escape Daniel. She walked up to the table with Elaine. Helping herself to salad, Anne turned to Elaine, "Is this the meadow where the painting with the young girl I saw inside was painted?"

"Yes, it actually is. Well spotted," Elaine said. "And little has changed since then, except for the trees getting a little taller," she turned and looked around.

"What a shame, though," Nick spoke up. "If

Cecilia had continued painting, she could have been world famous."

"What do you mean?" Anne asked.

"He means that Cecilia had the talent to rival any male painter at the time, judging by her painting in the hall, but had to choose between having babies and having a career," Maud said, joining the conversation. "Even though she was the one with the money and the house, she had to bow to her husband's wishes and become a housewife," Maude continued, raising her voice. "Typical," she added. "That's why I've chosen to stay single."

"Yes, that's why," said Elaine under her breath, but not quietly enough. Maud threw her a withering look. Turning to Anne, Elain said, "Paolo thought the painting might be worth something, even if it was from a virtually unknown artist. He suggested getting it valued."

"Poor Paolo," said Nick, shaking his head. "Never could resist the bottle."

"What a fool for trying to go boating at that hour in that state," Elaine added.

"Oh, enough of this doom and gloom," Poppy said, getting up from her chair. "I'm sorry he's dead. Death is horrible. Bad luck and all, but he wasn't a nice person. He gave me the creeps."

"Poppy!" Elaine exclaimed. "What a beastly thing to say of a dead person!"

Poppy didn't pay her any attention. "Time to

work off that lunch. Let's dance, shall we," she walked toward the table and fumbled with her phone. A dance song came on from a speaker on the table, set among the plates.

Poppy sauntered towards Daniel. Her toned body moved gracefully to the beat of the music. She may have only been wearing a simple dress, but it fit her like couture, Anne noticed. Poppy pulled on Daniel's hand to join her.

Maud groaned, put her sunglasses on, and turned her face to the sun. Elaine walked over to Nick and started talking to him in a low tone.

Anne hoped Daniel would join Poppy so she could get her chair back.

7 A Bishop's curse

Daniel had relented and was now dancing with Poppy. Anne had taken the opportunity to sit back down and soak up the sun, while the others had gone on talking. The warm sun, the gentle breeze from the lake, and the buzzing insects lulled Anne into a state between relaxing and dozing off.

A crash through the bushes startled Anne. She opened her eyes and saw a dark figure coming out of the forest into the clearing of the meadow.

"*In nomine Domini*!" the dark figure yelled. "Enough! What are you all still doing here? Get out! Get off this island! It is not yours. It belongs to the church!" The man kept coming forward, slowly, as if stalking some invisible prey. Anne saw he wore the long black cassock and white collar of a priest. "You heathens! How many times do I need to warn you? The Bishop has spoken. No human shall set foot on this island." Now standing in the middle, surrounded by the lounge chairs, he delivered his speech with hands outstretched to the sky, "Be gone!" Then, turning towards the table, "And turn off that awful music!" he said, somewhat out of character.

He reminded Anne of the fire and brimstone Scottish preachers she had encountered in books, but this one with a British accent.

No one seemed disturbed by the whole incident.

"Get off of it, James," Nick said. "Oh, sorry, *Padre Giacomo*," he enunciated his name, and laughed, shaking his head, as if in disbelief.

Is this some sort of practical joke, Anne though.

"Yes, *Padre Giacomo*," said Poppy, stressing his name as well. "We are guests of Barbara. You have no authority here. Go hide in your dark tower," Poppy said, with venom in her voice. "You are pathetic," she stalked towards him like a lioness interrupted from enjoying her fresh kill. "Bugger off," she said, pointing towards the church tower.

As if coming out of a trance, James–Padre Giacomo–just stood there for a moment. He searched the faces of those around him. His clear blue eyes settled on Anne–the odd one out. Color crept up his neck and pale face. A gust of wind loosened a lock of blond hair and it fell over his forehead. He was younger than Anne first had thought. Finally, he looked away from Anne, pushed the hair back into place, and straightened his back.

He started backing out of the clearing and said, "Remember the curse. Paolo's death was not an accident. More deaths will follow." His voice was rising, "This island is cursed. No one shall set foot here but a man of God. Remember the words of the Bishop!" He was now at the edge of the forest and meadow, and his voice had risen to its previous crescendo, "*Igitur qui desiderat pacem, praeparet bellum!*" And as the forest engulfed his dark shape, he yelled, "*Igne natura renovatur integra.*"

Silence descended over the group. Everyone just looked at the spot where the forest had swallowed him. After a moment Elaine turned to Anne, "Sorry you had to witness that."

"Who was that?" Anne breathed her question.

"That was James, Barbara's son," Elaine said. "Padre Giacomo, as he is now known. He is the priest at St. Ignatius," Elaine pointed to the bell tower, "the church here on the island. Hard to believe that a few years ago we were all hanging out at the same parties," she said.

"And what was he saying at the end? Was that the curse? Was that Italian?" Anne asked.

"Latin," said Daniel, turning towards Anne. "Roughly translated he said, '*Whoever desires peace, let him prepare for war,*' and '*Through fire, nature is reborn whole*'. That last one is his favorite. He's got it into his head that the only way to break the curse is through fire. Nothing to worry about, though. It's not his first outburst. Just schoolboy Latin," Daniel smiled as if to dismiss the whole affair. "He's always threatening to burn this island down, drive all of us sinners away, and rebuild it in the name of God."

Daniel pushed a hand through his hair. "I must apologize for my cousin. He has always had a flair for the dramatic. And he has not gotten over the fact that my aunt wants to revive this art colony. A few years ago, James had a mental breakdown, broken heart or something, and joined the Catholic Church. He went to Italy to atone for his sins. The Bishop of Milan, who cursed this place, was a distant relative of his. And mine," Daniel explained.

"Very distant!" Poppy interrupted, with an indignant tone in her voice. "The *bloody* curse is from the *bloody* 1400s," she raised her voice. "He is only using it as an excuse to drive us off the island," she said, with a matter-of-fact certainty.

No one bothered to explain the curse. Just like Anne, everyone seemed to be familiar with it. Anne didn't want to ask any questions about it and how the Bishop was exactly related to the family, but the exchange had disturbed her.

"You don't think he is capable of doing more than just using words?" Anne asked. "You heard him, talking about Paolo's death, threatening war?"

"No," Daniel said, shaking his head. "James is a

sweet, gentle soul. It's all an act. He wants to keep the island all to himself and the church."

"Wouldn't he be inheriting the whole place anyway?"Anne asked, caught up in the family drama.

"Not if my aunt has anything to do with it. That's why she is reviving this art colony," he swept his hand, showing off the island. "If the art colony proves to be viable, she will transfer the island to a trust, thus removing it, the house, and the church from the line of inheritance, and James."

"That's awful," Anne said. She thought of her own loving parents and reminded herself to call them.

"There are a lot of family issues running really deep," Daniel said. "But suffice to say that my aunt doesn't approve of James' choice of vocation. She takes it as a personal affront. And it probably is, given her lack of mothering, and constant pursuit of artistic expression. And she couldn't live down the indignity that James picked the Catholic Church."

A boat horn cut through the quiet gloom that had settled over the recently merry group.

"That's the grocer's boat." Elaine jumped up from her chair. "Anne, I'll walk you to the dock."

Anne waved goodbye and walked down to the lake with Elaine.

At the dock, a man, in an Italian grandfathers'

cap, was unloading boxes of wine bottles and flat crates full of produce and bread off a boat. Anne stood beside Elaine while she spoke to the man in Italian. From the animated pointing towards herself and Ascona, Anne gathered they were negotiating her trip back to the mainland. Anne smiled at the man, hoping that would seal the deal.

While waiting for the last boxes to come off the boat, Anne got the distinct feeling that she was being watched. She turned around and looked up at the house. She searched the windows. Her attention was suddenly caught by a movement in the bushes near the construction. But she couldn't see anyone. *Must have been a bird*, Anne shook off the uneasy feeling.

The unloading complete, Anne thanked Elaine for her hospitality, and got in the boat.

She turned to the island as they motored away. *Who knows if I'll ever be back on this island*, Anne thought. *What a sad place.* Her thoughts drifted back to the incident with the priest, and to Paolo's fatal accident, and a chill passed through her body, despite the warm sun on her back. *Could this place really be cursed*? The priest's words sounded like threats to her. Why did he say Paolo's death was not an accident? Did he know something? Anne was concerned that all those people on the island who knew James from before his mental breakdown couldn't see him clearly now. To her, he looked deranged, sounded delusional, and she worried that he was dangerous. James had everything to lose if the art colony went ahead and was successful. Was he sabotaging the art colony? Did he kill Paolo?

As Anne sank deeper and deeper into dark thoughts, the boat sailed towards Ascona. Rounding the Brissago Islands, the colorful Old Town came into view, now bathed in warm afternoon light. Anne decided to share all that had happened with Marco, and her unease dissipated.

8 A visit from the island

This morning Anne couldn't wait to get to the bookstore. She wanted to share with Marco all she had heard and seen on the island yesterday.

It would be interesting to see what he thinks of all of this, Anne thought. There were so many threads she wanted to follow up on: the curse, the son who ran away and joined the church, the mother willing to deprive her son of inheritance in the name of art, and the group of silver-spoon artists. There was also the contempt everyone had shown toward James, and each other. It struck her as such a nihilistic attitude. *Probably brought on by a want for nothing and a life of privilege*, she thought.

And then there was Cecilia's story. Cecilia's choice to give up her painting–something she was obviously good at–to be a mother captivated Anne. She herself had had to give up her career to follow Ben to Switzerland, so she felt she could relate.

Anne had spent the previous evening researching the island's history online. As expected, almost all the articles were in Italian, and she had to use her translator app to make any sense of them. But she didn't get much more information beyond what she already knew–the current owner was Barbara there was a curse on the island; the island was known for its predisposition to accidents, which one camp of observers attributed to the curse and another to the loose lifestyle of the art colony. The only new piece of information she gained from her search was the fact that a lot of early and late 20th century luminaries visited the art colony. At the beginning of the century, it was artists; influential psychologists, such as Carl Jung; writers, such as Herman Hesse; and avant-garde thinkers, philosophers, even anarchists, such as Bukin. By the late 20th century, before the art colony closed down, the visitors had become mostly well-known musicians and their hangers-on.

Anne had more success looking up the island's current guests in the British press. As she pieced together snippets from articles, a picture of luxury and exuberance formed. They were children of Barons (Nick) or minor German princes (Maud), and moved in a rarefied social circle of pan-Europeans, made up of classmates from elite boarding schools and Oxbridge. Their friends worked in finance and art, ensuring none of the island's current residents was a penniless struggling artist. *None of them probably needs to work, but their art provides them with a legitimate way to make money without actually having to get a job,* thought Anne.

Intrigued by the evocation of the curse yesterday by James, Anne wanted to see if today she could find a reference to it in Cecilia's diaries. *Was the curse discussed in Cecilia's days? Did the island's residents leave in fear of it, or did they not spare it a second thought?* she wondered.

Anne adjusted the height of her swivel chair and opened a scanned file. Just then, the bells above the store door chimed. Since she was closest to the front and hadn't started work yet, Anne decided to see who it was. *Whoever it is*, she thought, t*he encounter can't be worse than with Paolo the other day*.

As she left the office, Maggie slipped in. "Guard my laptop," Anne said to the cat with a smile, "but don't sit on it." Anne had discovered that Maggie had a preference for placing herself, with all her heft, on top of the laptop keyboard. Probably because of the warmth it radiated, Anne suspected.

She walked to the front of the store, and the sight of Poppy surprised her.

"Ah, just the person I am looking for," Poppy said. "I wonder if you could help me with a bit of research. I'm working on a rather tantalizing biography of Carl Jung, and I hoped you could tell me if you've come across any references to him in the diaries."

"Yes, I've actually seen a few," Anne said. "It's hard to tell sometimes, though. Cecilia often referred to friends and guests by their first name only, and it's only through cross-references we can infer who was staying at the art colony at any given time."

"How terribly exciting!" Poppy said, a smile lighting up her face.

"But why don't you ask Elaine to show you the diaries?" Anne asked.

"What, those vultures?" Poppy laughed as if Anne's suggestion was ridiculous. "You know, I am the only one in that group that makes her living with actual work," she put her hands on her slim hips, as if getting ready for a challenge. "The rest of them are successful artists only because they have the friends and connections to whom to sell their artwork. I wouldn't trust any of them. And I absolutely refuse to let any of them into my research process. Even dear Elaine."

"I wonder why you trust me," Anne commented.

"Oh, I can tell you are a darling. Plus, who are you going to blab to about my work? It's not like you could leak details to the press. But I wouldn't put it past any of them," Poppy said, pointing in the general direction of the island with a wave of her manicured hand, as she sauntered towards Anne. She placed her hands on the counter and leaned in. "So, here is what I've got," she said in a hushed voice. "I've got a hold of some of Jung's diaries, and he mentions he stayed at the art colony in the summer of 1912. *And*," she emphasized, "he also mentions that Sargent stopped by for a few days on his way to Italy and Sicily. Rather exciting, don't you think, to have two greats staying here at the same time?"

"Are you referring to John Sargent, the painter?" Anne asked, surprised.

"Yes," Poppy said. "A cross-reference, anything in Cece's diaries referring to the meeting of the two 20th century greats and their time together on the island, would be a boon," she pressed on with her agenda. "I have to think exactly what angle to take, how to spin it to the book's advantage, you see, and make the most out of it, but I shall worry about that later."

"I haven't seen anything in the diaries about Sargent. But I haven't been looking for it. I'll have a second look." Anne said. As much as she disliked Poppy's cavalier attitude, the possibility that Sargent had stayed at the island excited Anne. Anne loved Sargent's art and had admired his paintings many times at Boston's Museum of Fine Art. If Cecilia's diaries indeed contained a reference to Sargent's stay, and if that information was new to scholars, Anne knew it would be a significant historical discovery.

"Great. You are marvelous. Give me a ring if you find anything. Here is my mobile," Poppy said, helping herself to a pen and paper from the counter and writing her phone number. Mission accomplished, Poppy turned to leave.

A recollection from the island flashed across Anne's mind as Poppy was about to open the door. "Is there anyone else on the island besides all of you and James?" Anne asked, calling out to her.

Poppy turned sharply. "No, of course not. Why do you ask?"

"I felt like someone was watching me as I was leaving yesterday."

"Well," Poppy said, and paused to think, "there are the workmen fixing the house. Maybe one of them came back in the afternoon to continue work. But that's highly unlikely. They come to the island only in the morning and are rather lazy. Toodles!" And with that, she twirled around and left the store.

Anne stayed at the counter for a few moments. She was excited by the prospect of reading through the diaries again and looking for references to both Carl Jung and John Sargent. She had made notes on Carl Jung and now she just needed to look in the same places for references to Sargent.

As she walked back to her office, she saw Maggie laying on top of the laptop.

"Of course!" Anne exclaimed playfully and pushed the cat away so she could resume work.

As she settled down and was about to look at her notes, she noticed that Maggie must have flipped through the pages on the screen while laying on top of the keyboard.

The diary page displayed now was April 12, 1911. As she glanced at the passage, a quick shiver passed through Anne and her arms broke out in tiny goosebumps. She usually had that reaction when she read a real-life unexplained mystery or a ghost story. In the diary, Cecilia referred to an oppressive feeling she sometimes got from the stone medieval church and its tower. And how she wished the church weren't there, casting its long cursed shadow through the centuries on the pretty villa, and the nascent art colony.

"Oh, wow!" Anne said, excited by an actual reference to the curse. So the specter of the curse was alive and well during Cecilia's time. Anne hadn't noticed it before. "Smart cat," she turned to pet the cat. Maggie had been trying to make her way back to the laptop keyboard the whole time Anne was reading, and now, encouraged by Anne's praise, saw an opportunity to push through and positioned herself again on top of the keyboard. She completed the maneuver with a purr.

"No, no, no!" Anne exclaimed, "I wasn't done with that passage."

Anne was about to scold the cat, but the diary

page on the screen grabbed her attention, and she halted. The date was now July 7, 1911. Maggie had again, inadvertently, turned the pages. Instead of scooping the cat off, Anne stroked the cat's soft fur and read.

The entry was a description of a picnic on the island on a shimmering sunny day. The entire party visiting the art colony was gathered on the meadow, lounging around in the afternoon's stillness and Lilly, Cecilia's young daughter, was playing in the tall grass among the flowers. 'I was painting next to dear John while he worked one of his lovely pictures', Cecilia wrote.

Anne stopped reading. *That must be the same meadow,* she said to herself. The description fit. And how many meadows would there be on the island?

Had she seen this passage before Poppy's visit, Anne would have assumed that 'dear John' was Cecilia's husband. He was named John, and he was a painter. But after what Poppy had discovered, that John Sargent had visited the island, the 'John' in the diary entry could also be a reference to John Sargent.

No, that can't be. It can't be that easy, Anne shook her head in disbelief. Plus, the dates didn't fit. This description was a year earlier than the date Poppy was interested in.

But who's to say Sargent visited the island only once, Anne thought.

Question after question popped up in Anne's mind. How could she confirm that this diary entry was indeed a reference to John Sargent and not simply to Cecilia's husband? Did Sargent keep diaries that would mention his stay at the island in 1911? Would there be electronic copies of them somewhere? A museum, perhaps? Were there records of his visit to Switzerland? Was that a well-known fact?

And if it is Sargent, would I be able to find a record of the picture he was painting in the meadow online, Anne wondered.

Anne decided she needed to look more into this. She would do research on John Sargent and any Swiss connections at home this evening. With any luck, she might even discover a reference to his stay at the art colony island.

◆ ◆ ◆

Anne had her laptop open on the coffee table. A sandwich sat on a plate in her lap, uneaten. With her husband gone on a business trip to South America, visiting an organic coffee plantation, Anne didn't feel like cooking dinner for one. She had become so absorbed in her research, she just now remembered about her sandwich.

Taking a bite out of it, she went over all she had discovered so far. She had spent the evening researching John Sargent online. It surprised her to find plenty of references to the artist's time in Switzerland. In the later part of his career, starting around 1900, Sargent spent the summers traveling in Switzerland and Italy with his sisters and family friends. These trips produced a collection of watercolors, and a few oil paintings, noted for their vivid colors and the expressive energy of their brushstrokes. Painted outdoors and free from the formal constraints of his commissioned portraits, art critics agreed that the paintings Sargent created during these summers were decidedly Impressionistic in style.

Anne scrolled through pages of effervescent paintings of Mediterranean gardens, Venetian canals, and ladies in white dresses–Sargent's sisters and nieces–reposing in verdant fields. But none of the references mentioned the area of Ascona specifically. Of course, there was the reference Poppy had found in Carl Jung's diary. So that confirmed John Sargent had stayed at the art colony at least once. But what was Sargent's connection to Cecilia and her family?

"If John Sargent were a family friend of Cecilia's then she could easily refer to him as 'dear John' without feeling the need to clarify, right?" Anne said, reasoning out loud.

But Anne had little success the rest of the evening finding any other information or any information linking John Sargent to Cecilia's family.

Anne felt a crick in her neck and decided to

stop for the night. She planned to spend a bit more time looking through the diaries tomorrow morning and then phone Poppy with what she had found.

She walked into the kitchen for a glass of water. She turned on the tap to let the water run cold. Their landlord had told them that the water came from springs high up in the nearby Alps, so the quality was better than any bottled water.

In the distance, Anne heard sirens. She looked out of her kitchen window, but she didn't have a clear view of anything except the neighboring houses. *You don't hear sirens in Ascona very often*, she thought. The area where Anne lived was a pedestrian zone, so it couldn't be a traffic accident. *Maybe someone got taken ill,* she decided.

Then Anne remembered that Ascona's annual Bonfire Night–Notte dei Falò–was tomorrow. She wondered if someone had started festivities early and the fire got out of control.

Bonfire Night was a traditional Swiss celebration held at the beginning of April to banish winter. Originating in Zurich, and called 'Sechseläuten' in the German-speaking part of the country, the town of Ascona had imported the festival a few years ago as a way to attract tourists in the slow days of spring. A large bonfire was set up on the lakefront promenade, in front of the town hall, and an effigy of a snowman–a Böög–was burned exactly at 6 o'clock in the evening, sending away the last vestiges of winter. Families brought sausages with them to roast on the fire. Others re-enacted the festivities at home with small bonfires in their backyards.

Anne was looking forward to the festival; this would be her first year. But if she wanted to go to the celebration, she would have to go alone. Her husband was away for another five days. She would ask Marco tomorrow if he planned on going with his wife.

9 A book on the counter

Preparations were underway for Bonfire Night, so Anne avoided the promenade this morning. She didn't want to spoil the surprise of seeing the whole setup for the first time this evening. She pictured the tall pyre lit up against the lake with the setting sun behind it.

The store was still closed when she got there. Waiting for Marco to arrive, Anne went over what she had to tell Poppy. It wasn't much–there was a reference in the diary to a 'John' painting at the art colony in 1911, but that was not the year Poppy was interested in. Plus, it could simply be a reference to Cecilia's husband. While Sargent had visited Switzerland for several summers in the 1900s, there was no specific mention of 'Sargent' in Cecilia's diaries. And Anne's attempts to establish a connection between Cecilia and John Sargent in her online search last night had failed.

"Sorry I'm late," a woman said, out of breath, behind Anne.

Anne turned around and saw Marco's wife. Anne had met Alex–short for Alexandra–several times before. In the mornings, she came to the store with Marco to unlock the front door, before heading over to a yoga studio she ran in the modern part of town; she also came at lunch and in the evenings to lock up and go home with Marco.

Alex's light blond–almost white–hair and golden tanned skin made her appear glowing. Years spent surfing, growing up in Australia, had given her the physique a 30-year-old would envy. Now in her late fifties, Alex maintained her agility with daily yoga. She radiated the serenity of someone at peace with herself. *I need to start yoga*, Anne thought.

"Marco will be in after lunch," Alex said. "He went to a book auction this morning. Here you go," she unlocked the door for Anne, "I have to run to the studio. See you later. Cheers."

Anne watched her rush up the street. The fluid movements of her long limbs, and her flowing dress sweeping the cobblestones, gave the impression that Alex was floating. She seemed somehow otherworldly to Anne.

Anne walked into the store and turned on the lights. At the end of each day, Marco made sure all books were put away, and the counters were always clean in the morning. So the open book on the counter–its white pages shining against the dark wood–stood out immediately. Anne went to put the book away, but when she looked down on the page, her arms broke out in goosebumps. A painting of a woman in a long evening dress, with an Edwardian pompadour and laughing eyes, filled the right-hand page. Anne grabbed the book and flipped to the cover–a Sotheby's auction catalog of paintings from about ten years ago. Anne turned back to the opened page and looked at the image and its description beneath:

'John Singer Sargent (1852-1925). Miss Cecilia Lester, a friend of the artist, painted as a coming out portrait, in the artist's London studio. Private collection. Oil on canvas. Painted 1904.'

"*This is too much of a coincidence!*" Anne said to herself. She looked around to see if anyone else was in the store, but she was alone.

Just then, Anne caught the creep of a black shadow across the floor out of the corner of her eye, and jumped back. But it was only Maggie coming to the front of the store. As if sensing Anne's unease, the cat leaped up on the counter and walked on silent paws towards her. Maggie butted her head against Anne's arm and purred. Anne's heartbeat slowed down. She scooped the cat in her arms and stroked it.

"Are you doing all this?" Anne addressed Maggie. Then shook off the thought. *What are you thinking, cats can't do that,* she told herself.

"But how are all these clues revealing themselves?" Anne breathed her question to the air around her. *First the diaries, now the catalog.* Each showed her the exact information she was searching for. She would need to tell Marco when he came in. She added that to the laundry list of things she wanted to discuss with him–the priest's outburst on the island, Poppy's visit yesterday, her online research. But somehow she hadn't found the right moment to talk to him.

Anne's mind wandered to the other odd times at the store: the time her office door wouldn't open when Paolo asked about the diaries; the diary entries Maggie inadvertently helped her find yesterday; and now a catalog of an old Sotheby's auction with a painting related exactly to the information she had been looking for last night.

A thought crystallized in Anne's mind–Maggie had been there each time she made a discovery. Anne looked down at the cat and suddenly wished Marco would get here already. The cat looked up at her with calm green eyes and continued to purr. *No, Maggie's appearance is just a coincidence*, Anne told herself. *She is always at the store, that's all.* Anne looked around the front of the store as if expecting something strange to happen. But the glass-fronted cabinets looked back in silence.

Having regained some of her composure, Anne's attention turned back to Cecilia, Sargent, and the catalog in front of her. No wonder she hadn't been able to find this painting in her search online yesterday. She had searched for Cecilia by her married name, not her maiden one. Plus, this work had been in a private collection before the sale, and probably went to another private collection, so its existence might not be well known.

Anne placed Maggie down on the counter and decided to call Poppy. She went to her office in search of the piece of paper with the phone number. This new discovery, of a painting of Cecilia by Sargent, excited Anne. Coupled with the note Poppy had discovered, it meant that John Sargent and Cecilia knew each other well. The John mentioned in Cecilia's diary–the one painting in the meadow–really could be John Sargent.

Poppy didn't answer her phone. Anne left her a message. She decided to continue looking through the diaries, and if Poppy didn't phone back, she would try her later.

❖ ❖ ❖

It was past lunchtime when Anne noticed Poppy hadn't called back and Marco hadn't returned. Anne dialed Poppy, but since she didn't pick up again, Anne phoned Elaine to see if she could locate Poppy for her. *And where is Marco*, Anne wondered, waiting for Elaine to pick up.

"Hello," Elaine's voice came on.

"Hi Elaine, it's Anne, from the bookstore in Ascona," Anne began. "Is Poppy around? She came into the store yesterday, and I have some information she was looking for."

"Um…" Elaine stumbled, "haven't you heard? There was an accident here yesterday evening," Elaine paused, "Poppy is dead!" she breathed out.

"What?" Anne knew she had heard correctly, but her brain couldn't process the information. For the second time this morning, a chill ran down the entire length of Anne's body. She needed to sit down. Seeing no chair, Anne slid down the wall to the floor and rested her head against the cool surface of the wall behind her for support.

"Look," Elaine sighed. Startled, Anne realized Elaine was still on the phone. "I have to go back to the police. They are still here," Elain said.

"No, wait!" Anne said, before Elaine could end the call. "Can you tell me what happened?"

Elaine sighed again, "A stone from the house fell on top of Poppy. It looks like an accident. It happened in the area undergoing restoration work. Goodness knows what she was doing there," she paused. "Look, I really need to go." Elaine hung up.

Anne remained on the floor. She couldn't believe that there had been a second accident on the island. Either it really was cursed, or something else entirely was going on.

A killer. The thought popped into Anne's mind and she shuddered. But she decided to follow its thread. Both Paolo and Poppy had come into the store asking about the diaries and then ended up dead. Was it all related to the diary? But why? Was it the priest, James? Poppy had been really rude to him that day on the island. And now she is dead! But why would he kill these people? Was he trying to get them off the island, so the art colony would close and he would have the island back to himself and his church? Was he just crazy and was fulfilling the prophecy of his ancestor, the Bishop of Milan? But if that were the case, why were the police not seeing it?

Anne wasn't sure how long she sat there, but she didn't stir until she heard Marco come in at the back. He wheeled into the front. The surprised look on his face showed he did not expect to see Anne sitting on the floor.

"Are you ill?"

Anne shook her head.

"What's going on?" Marco looked around, searching for the source of Anne's unusual behavior. But since there was no one else in the store, he returned his gaze to Anne, brow deeply furrowed.

Anne got up and placed Maggie back on the counter. She hadn't even noticed when the cat had jumped into her lap.

"I just phoned the island," Anne said. "Yesterday one of the women from the art colony stopped by the store, and now she's dead."

Marco nodded. "Yes," he said with a somber

tone and picked up the newspaper that lay folded in his lap, "it's in the newspaper."

He rolled forward to the counter and lay the newspaper flat so that Anne could have a look at it. Anne was reminded of the previous time they were bent over the newspaper reading about an accident on the island. This was an unwelcome déjà vu.

"What does it say?" Anne asked.

"Much of what it said the last time: the curse, the string of accidents over the decades at the island, the fast and reckless lifestyle of the art colony's residents," Marco listed the key points.

Anne hadn't really seen any fast and reckless lifestyle the day she visited the island, but there was no denying that all the current residents were used to an easy lifestyle. If that led to accidents, Anne didn't understand how. She could picture activities popular among the rich, such as skiing or paragliding, that could lead to fatal accidents, but simply relaxing at an artists' retreat should not be so deadly.

"The police have concluded that it was another accident. This Penelope," Marco glanced down at the newspaper to make sure he got the name right, "was found in a construction area where they were carrying out masonry work and restoring some of the stone decorations. One of them fell on her," Marco summarized.

Anne couldn't believe it was an accident. Not

this second time. What would Poppy be doing at the construction? She must have been lured there.

As if reading her thoughts, Marco continued, "It seems she was doing research for a book on Carl Jung, who had stayed at the colony at the beginning of the 1900s. She was looking to locate the bedroom where he had stayed. It was in the part of the house being renovated."

"Well, I guess that explains it," Anne said. But she was still unconvinced. "It's just so strange that so many accidents are happening on the island."

"Stranger things have happened," Marco replied. "I'm sure the police have done their job properly and have reached their conclusion based on the evidence." He paused. "There is one interesting piece of information, though," he tapped the newspaper. "It seems Penelope and the director of the art colony, Elaine, had worked together at a medical spa retreat–very exclusive–in northern Switzerland, but they both left under a cloud of some rumors of embezzlement, and the spa ended up going bankrupt soon after."

Interesting, Anne thought. She knew Poppy and Elaine had worked together before, but this new piece of information about embezzlement was surprising. How did that fit in the puzzle? A curse, accidents, the diaries. *And now embezzlement?*

All these different threads frustrated Anne. She wanted to run her theories by Marco. But was there even a theory to run by him? It was just a lot of unconnected pieces of interesting information. Anne felt lightheaded. Maybe it was the talk about Poppy. She needed to step out for some fresh air.

"Marco, do you mind, I want to just go get a cup of coffee. It's all a bit too much for me," she said.

"No problem, take you time, see how they are getting along with the bonfire," he said, swerving his chair around, towards the back of the store.

That's right, the bonfire, Anne thought.

"Marco," she called after him, "are you and Alex going to the bonfire tonight?"

"No, it's Friday. I have my therapy sessions Friday evenings, remember?"

Anne had forgotten. Marco and his wife did physical therapy on Fridays, and Alex was strict about them, and, since she was his therapist, she didn't let him miss a session.

"Actually, before you go," Marco turned around and wheeled back towards her, "I wanted to ask you if you could close up tonight. Alex and I wanted to get a head start, in case the streets get too crowded with tourists. It's hard maneuvering as it is. With crowds–it's impossible."

"Yes, no problem."

"Here, take my keys, just in case we leave before you're back," Marco said, handing her a bunch of keys. "You'll figure out which is which, if you need to," he said, with a smile.

"I'll be back in a few minutes, before you leave," Anne said, and headed for the front door.

10 A chase through cobblestone alleys

The brightness of the day outside startled Anne. After hearing about Poppy's death, the store had felt dark and oppressive. But out here, life went on as usual.

Tourists strolled down the street, stopping to look in at store windows. Others lingered by the gelato stand, eating ice cream from small paper cups with bright plastic spoons. But the general flow of people streamed towards the promenade, with its outdoor cafes and chairs lined to face the mirror-like expanse of the lake, and the majestic Alps, peaks still covered with snow, beyond its shores. It was hard to believe that anything bad could happen here. And yet, there had been two accidents.

Anne crossed the street, sidestepping a family, to get a cup of coffee at Luigi's. Carrying the hot drink, she headed down to the promenade to clear her mind. She gave up on her earlier resolve not to see the bonfire until this evening and walked toward the rising pyre.

Town workers had strung white and red tape

all around the bonfire. A yellow portable crane nimbly twisted back and forth, lifting tall logs into position. A crowd had gathered around the perimeter, watching the progress of the logs. Anne joined them, sipping her paper-cup cappuccino. Luigi–purveyor of expensive coffee to the rich and idle, as Marco called him–made the best cappuccino in Ascona. *The bonfire really is going to be a fantastic sight to see this evening*, she thought.

She stood there, watching, engrossed in the process.

Sargent, Anne's mind jumped to the catalog this morning, *I forgot to tell Marco about John Sargent! And the painting in the catalog, and the references to John in the diaries!* Anne remembered she had wanted to talk to Marco. She made up her mind to tell him all she had discovered. Even if she hadn't formed a clear idea about what it all meant, she wanted to see what he thought. She was sure there was a connection among all these facts, even if she couldn't see it. *Perhaps he will*, Anne thought.

About to head back to the store, Anne got the distinct feeling that she was being watched. She spun around quickly and locked eyes with a woman a few people behind her. The woman seemed startled by Anne. They stood there looking at each other for a few moments.

Deciding it was just a coincidence, Anne

broke eye contact, and began to weave her way through the people behind her. At the same time, the woman turned and started walking ahead of Anne, in the same direction as her.

Anne thought nothing of it. Lots of people walked in that general direction. But the woman kept throwing glances back at Anne, as if making sure she was still there. Anne picked up her pace, determined to catch up with her. She had never seen this person, but the woman seemed interested in her. Anne was curious to find out why.

As Anne walked faster, so did the woman, and soon they were speed walking past the turnoff for the bookstore, and continued into a narrow alley.

Anne now found herself in a dark tunnel. The grand palazzos that lined the lakefront, and behind which the alley ran, threw it into deep shadow. As Anne entered the alley, the woman ahead of her started to run. *That's odd*, Anne thought and ran after her.

Under normal circumstances, Anne would not have done such a thing. But so many strange things had happened lately, Anne was sure the woman's quick glances back beckoned her to follow.

The alleyway weaved in an unbroken continuity between houses and gardens, climbing ever higher. Anne knew this path well. She had strolled here often. It led to a church on top of a hill. The path was usually peaceful, the ancient stone walls blocking out the sound of the promenade below. All Anne could hear now was the measured pounding of feet on the stone pavement.

Anne reached a set of stone steps. Her lungs stung. She could not get enough air. She stopped to catch her breath. But the woman kept running. Despite her sandals, held on by two thin straps to her feet, she was sprinting effortlessly on the uneven gray stones lining the path. Anne needed to catch up with her before the next corner where the alley forked in opposite directions. *Why is she running?* wondered Anne between quick intakes of breath. *If she wants me to catch up with her, why run? Is she leading me somewhere?*

Anne pushed herself to continue running uphill. Her head pounded with the rush of blood. Anne looked ahead. At the fork, if the woman turned left, she would circle back to the lake and Anne would lose her in the crowd. But if she went right, they would end up at the church–a dead end. The woman turned right. *She's taking me to the church. Why?* Anne wondered.

Following her, in a moment Anne was at the church courtyard.

In the middle of the courtyard, the woman was doubled over, painting. Anne heard her curse something under her breath.

Perched on a hill, steep slopes of rough rock

and cacti ran down each side of the church's courtyard. From here there was nowhere to go.

So this is the end, Anne thought.

11 A secret revealed

The woman straightened, and, between breaths, cried out something in Italian to Anne. Her voice got amplified by the layers of stone surrounding them–the stone church facade, the stones paving the courtyard, the low stone wall surrounding it. The echo emphasized that Anne and this stranger were the only two people up here.

"Non parlo Italiano," Anne said, "solo Inglese." It was a phrase she had memorized, and often used, to let people know she didn't know Italian and spoke only English.

"Why are you following me?" the woman said, with a slight Italian pronunciation, moving back to keep her distance from Anne.

Anne was caught off guard by the question. "Following you? I wasn't following you," Anne said, confused. "Well, okay, I was following you," she corrected herself, "but I thought you wanted me to follow you."

"Why would you think that!" the woman yelled, exasperation in her voice.

"I don't know," Anne said, unsure now what had made her follow the woman. "You were acting like you wanted me to follow you, like you were leading me somewhere. You kept looking back, checking if I was there. Every time I tried to catch up with you, you started running faster."

"Yes! Because I wanted to *get away* from you," the woman emphasized her words. She took a deep breath, "*Basta*! Enough. There has obviously been some misunderstanding. Now let me go. You are blocking the only way out," she motioned to the alley behind Anne.

Anne stepped to the side to make way, but then a thought crossed her mind and she moved back to block the exit. "No, wait," Anne said, "why were you watching by the lake?"

"I wasn't," the woman said, defensively.

"I felt your eyes on me."

"Oh, okay," the woman said, as if relenting, "I saw you on the island two days ago, and was curious about you. I saw you getting a coffee today and followed you," the woman said.

"But why?" Anne asked, failing to see why the woman was interested in her.

"I'm Daniel's girlfriend, Julia," the woman said. "Well, ex, actually. The day we arrived on the island, Daniel broke up with me most unceremoniously. I had just received a call from work that I needed to go to Hong Kong for a valuation. And suddenly he went insane. Yelling, and telling me that this is not working out and that if my career was more important to me than him, then I should just go to Hong Kong. He knows how to push my buttons. He knows how important my career is to me."

Julia paused, looking towards the lake.

She turned to Anne. "He's wanted me out of the way before, when he's been on the verge of an affair, but he's never been so vicious. And he's always come crawling back. But not this time." Julia searched Anne's face.

"I don't know why I'm telling you all this," she continued, and turned her gaze towards the church, "but if you are planning to be his lover, I just wanted to tell you that you are ruining my life," Julia wiped her eyes. "I've stuck with him for so many years. Hoping that he would finally decide to start a family."

She took a deep breath and turned back to face Anne. "I was so devastated. But on the way to the airport, I called in a favor with a colleague who took over my trip to Hong Kong. I've just been hanging out in the area since then. I wanted to see what was going on."

Anne wasn't sure exactly how to respond. All this information was so strange to her. "But I'm not having an affair with Daniel, nor do I plan to have one," said Anne.

Julia let out an embarrassed laugh, "Oh. Ugh," she sighed, "sorry, I must be going crazy."

"Let's go sit over there," Anne led the distressed woman towards the low wall of the courtyard.

Anne herself was dealing with some of the same issues and felt sorry for Julia. She knew what it was like to plan your life around a man–*hadn't she just moved continents for her husband?* Julia's mention of wanting a child touched her. Anne and her husband had had many discussions about children, but he always insisted that now was not the time. Anne had hoped that moving to Switzerland and staying at home would change his mind, but he now insisted that Switzerland was too expensive to bring up a child. The years were rolling by. Anne worried that soon she'd be too old to have a child. But she pulled herself out of her own thoughts and focused on Julia.

"Why would you think it's me he wanted to have an affair with?" Anne asked.

"I don't know. I came back to the island the other day to talk to him, but then I saw you arrive, and I saw him sitting by you. You're his type, you know. He goes for the whole cute, wholesome, bookish librarian type sometimes." Julia threw Anne a sideways glance.

Anne couldn't help but compare herself to Julia. Dressed in a cream dress, with strappy flat sandals, and her hair in a stylish blonde bob, Julia exuded elegant minimalism. Anne, on the other hand, wore an old pair of jeans, a striped shirt, a pair of Converse sneakers, and her hair pulled back in a ponytail. Anne didn't have low self-esteem, and knew people found her attractive, but at 37 she still dressed like she did in graduate school. The contrast between the two women was visible.

Anne felt a strange affinity with Julia. They were both women in their thirties, longing for a child, and hindered by their significant others. And although Anne was happily married, she did sometimes feel abandoned by her husband, because of his many business trips.

"Well, it's not me he was planning to have an affair with. What about the other women on the island, do you think could be one of them?" Anne asked.

Julia let out a genuine laugh. "No, he can't stand either of them." Then catching herself, she lowered her voice, "Poor Poppy. You know, she always tried so desperately for Daniel to like her. But he wasn't into her. I'm sure of that."

A realization suddenly hit Anne. "Julia," she began cautiously, "how did you get to the island? And how come no one saw you lurking around?"

"Oh, that. I've been staying in a village down the lake and borrowed a dinghy. That way I could get to the island unobserved, without a loud motor or a big white sail. I was on the Oxford women's rowing team. I moored on one of the wilder corners of the island and then hid in the bushes to spy. Everyone thinks I'm in Hong Kong. They are all so self-absorbed, I was pretty sure no one would see me," Julia said.

Anne prepared for her next part of her question, "You didn't see any of the accidents happen, did you?"

It had crossed Anne's mind that Julia might be the killer. She had the opportunity for both accidents–no one suspected she was around, so no one had checked her whereabouts. Anne couldn't think of a motive for the first accident, but what if Julia was lying, and in reality was jealous of Poppy, and blamed her for Daniel breaking up with her?

And before her brain could catch up, Anne heard herself ask Julia, "You weren't involved in those accidents, Julia, were you?" Anne didn't know what to expect next. What if Julia was the killer?

Julia looked shocked at the implied accusation. "No! Of course not!" she said.

Well, of course a killer would say exactly that, Anne thought. But somehow she didn't really think Julia was a killer. Anne wasn't even sure there was a killer. Everyone seemed so satisfied with the explanation that these were mere accidents. But Anne had discovered threads that others might not have.

She wrestled with herself for a moment,

whether to talk to Julia about her suspicions. Anne had no one else to talk things over with, and Julia knew all the people involved, so she gave it a go.

"You know," began Anne, searching Julia's face, "don't you find these accidents strange?"

"I guess," Julia said with a shrug.

Anne pressed on, "It's just that, both Paolo and Poppy stopped by the store where I work looking for information out of diaries that belonged to Cecilia, the woman who started the art colony in the 1900s."

"Oh, yes, I know of Cece. My great-great grandmother," she counted out on her fingers, "had her first season at the same time as Cece," Julia said casually.

Are all these people related, wondered Anne.

Outloud Anne continued, "Well, both of them had deadly accidents after asking for the diaries. Don't you think that's spooky?"

"I guess," Julia said. "But there is the curse," she looked at Anne as if that explained everything.

"Do you really believe that?" Anne asked. "Don't you think there is another explanation? Something that we are not seeing? Poppy came to the store looking for a reference to John Sargent, the painter, in the diaries. She wanted to see if there was a mention of his stay on the island in the summer of 1912. Something to do with the book she was planning to publish on Carl Jung. She had seen a note about Sargent in Jung's papers."

"Yes, he must have stayed on the island," Julia said. "And not just in 1912, but also in 1911, because there is a painting of his hanging in the hall, dated 1911. It's the one everyone calls 'Cece's painting'. I'm not sure why–it is definitely a Sargent. I knew it the moment I saw it. It's the one with the little girl. Did you get to see it when you were on the island?" Julia turned to Anne. "Of course, it would have to be examined properly. But I haven't had time to let anyone know yet, since I'm here incognito."

"So no one knows about the Sargent painting on the island?" Anne said.

"Actually, James was standing next to me when I saw the painting. He had come to say hello. We've known each other since children. My father is an Italian film director, but my mother is British, distantly related to Barbara, a cousin, several times removed. I spent my summers in Gloucestershire, near Barbara's estate, and often visited. I told James, since his mother should know. There was an auction a few years ago in Lucerne of Sargent watercolors from his Swiss trips. The watercolors fetched just under a million dollars at the auction. But the one on the island is more valuable because it's an oil painting. Those sell for two million and above. More, if a museum wants it."

Anne's mind raced. A Sargent painting was a big deal. And very valuable. And it was just hanging on a wall on the island. How many people knew about it?

"Did anyone else hear you tell James?"

"Let's see, Elain was on the island, but not there, in the hall. Somewhere outside. And Daniel was up in our room, unpacking. That was before he went ballistic on me. Nick and Maude hadn't arrived yet," Julia said. She looked at her watch and jumped up. "I'm sorry, I have to go. I have a cab to Lugano, a train to Zurich, and then a plane to Los Angeles to catch," she counted out on her fingers. "Another art auction. Don't want to lose my job, now that I've lost my boyfriend. I've got to keep at least one of them." She headed towards the alley. Spinning back to face Anne, she said, "It was nice talking to you!"

Julia disappeared down the hill.

12 A night of bonfires

Before Anne could call after her, Julia was gone. Thoughts swirled in Anne's mind. She sat on the quiet hilltop by the church. It was quiet. A good place to collect her thoughts.

So, Sargent had not only stayed at the island, but painted there as well. And the painting was now hanging in the hall of the art colony. How many people knew about it? Anne's thoughts traveled to the day she visited the island. Certainly everyone acted as if they had no idea. The painting was discussed, but everyone referred to it as 'the painting by Cece'. James definitely knew about the real provenance of the painting. Did his mother? Did Elaine? Elaine was there at the time, maybe she overheard. And so was Daniel– up in his room unpacking.

A multi-million dollar painting by one of the greatest artists was a solid motive for murder. But why? What was the killer trying to achieve? Why kill Paolo and Poppy?

Things were beginning to crystalize in Anne's mind. It had to be about the Sargent painting. It all fit. The two dead people were looking for information about Sargent in the diaries. Paolo hadn't mentioned exactly what he was looking for that day in the store, but he had suggested to the others to get Cecilia's painting examined and valued. Poppy, on the other hand, didn't seem interested in the painting itself. Just the artist. But it all connected back to Sargent and his painting.

But who had the motive, Anne wondered. *James*. He was the one who was going to be disinherited by his mother. And he knew the painting was valuable. Maybe Paolo and Poppy were both getting too close to the truth about the painting, and he eliminated them. *But why? What was he planning to do with the painting?* Anne still couldn't see what he had to gain from their deaths.

Who else could know about it? Nick and Maud had not arrived yet, so that ruled them out. Elaine and Daniel were both on the island when Julia told James about the painting. Could one of them have overheard?

Anne couldn't work it out. But she was sure there was no curse involved. The curse was just a way to distract people from the actual cause of the deaths.

Lost in thought, the vibration of her phone in her back pocket startled Anne. She took her phone out and saw a text from Marco–he was heading out for the day. Anne hadn't realized how much time she had spent up here by the church. It was close to six o'clock. *Time for the bonfire*, Anne thought.

Anne stood up and walked to the other side of the church courtyard. The full expanse of the lake below unfolded in front of her. The island of the art colony, in the middle of the peaceful lake, was clearly visible from here. So many of her thoughts today had been occupied by the island. Anne needed to tell someone of her suspicions. She felt it was urgent. *I'll start with Marco*, Anne decided.

She sat down on the low wall; her back to the lake, she took out her phone again. She dialed Marco, but the call went to voicemail. *He must have turned his phone off for the physical therapy session.*

Anne wanted to call her husband, but he was in a completely different time zone, and the international phone rates would be exorbitant. And he was probably somewhere without cell phone reception, anyway. So that was not an option.

I could call the police, Anne thought. But she immediately talked herself out of it. What would she tell the police? She had no solid proof of anything. Just a bunch of hunches based on diary entries from the 1900s and a brief conversation with Julia. Plus, Anne knew her Italian was insufficient to convey even the simplest story, let alone one based on so many speculations and suppositions.

What if I call Elaine, Anne wondered. *Just to get a feel for what she knows, or maybe to let her know outright that there is a Sargent painting worth probably millions hanging on the wall in the hallway.* Anne debated with herself on how to proceed. Should she warn Elaine that James might be a killer? *But what if he is in this together with Elaine?*

Elaine was her only option at the moment. Anne decided to play it by ear and feel out if Elaine knew something. But her call to Elaine went to voicemail as well. *Great*, Anne thought. Anne didn't want to leave a message in case someone heard it, who shouldn't. So she just hung up.

With no one to call, Anne decided to make her way down to the bonfire on the promenade. She looked one last time towards the art colony island. She noticed a thin column of smoke rising from the island. *I guess they are doing their own bonfire celebration,* Anne thought. *Maybe that's why I can't get a hold of Elaine.*

Anne started walking down the alley, back towards the bookstore and the promenade. As she walked, she tried to put the day's events out of her mind. It would all have to wait until tomorrow when she could speak to Marco.

And then James' words floated up in her

mind. What had he said? Something about 'fire bringing things back to nature', wasn't it? And what had Daniel said? That the only way to break the curse was through a cleansing fire?

Her mind started spinning as she started running down the cobbled path. What if James had decided that fire is the only way to purge the island? The accidents hadn't done their job of driving the art colony residents away, so maybe he set fire to the island to fulfill the curse? As Anne gathered speed downhill, her thoughts raced. What if the fire reached the house? No one, except James, knew there was a Sargent painting in the house. What if the painting got damaged? *Plus, let's not forget that there was probably a killer loose on the island*, she reminded herself.

❖ ❖ ❖

Anne fumbled with the keys Marco had given her. *Why did he have so many keys!* The fourth key finally fit in the front door of the store. Anne closed the door behind her. In the evening twilight, the bookstore looked odd, as if the white walls glowed from within. Anne shook off the feeling and turned on the lights.

She phoned Elaine a second time. No answer.

Maggie ambled into the front of the store and jumped on the counter next to Anne. She started purring and rubbing her head on her arm. Anne was toying with the idea of calling the police. But she hesitated. Although her ideas made sense to Anne, she worried the police wouldn't see it that way. She had been on the island only once; she didn't really know these people, and she had no idea what their plans for bonfire night were. There could be a perfectly innocent explanation for the smoke she saw. But Anne's instinct told her there was something more going on.

Struggling with her indecision, unsure of what to do and how to find a way to communicate with the island, Anne jumped at a thud coming from the back of the store, followed by breaking glass.

Anne's first thought was a break-in, but there was no glass door in the back of the store. She grabbed Maggie for courage, and went to the back to investigate. She walked among the stacks, but couldn't find the source of the thud.

Maggie wriggled and jumped out of Anne's hands. Once on the ground, she rotted forward, leading the way. *Do you know where to go?* Anne followed the cat to Marco's office.

With disbelief, Anne stared down at Maggie. She was sitting right next to what must have been the source of the noise–a picture in a frame lay on the floor. Anne had noticed a group of photos hanging in his office, but never looked at them closely. It had felt like snooping to her. She picked up the broken frame, the glass on its front shattered, and looked at the photo. It was a photo of Marco and friends on his boat.

Of course, Anne thought, t*he boat! I can take the boat to the island.* But then she stopped herself, *I don't know how to drive a boat, and even if I knew, I don't have keys to it.*

At that moment, a key bunch clanked against the tiled floor at the front of the store. *What is going on today,* Anne thought, and hurried to the front.

Maggie–*how did you get here so fast!*–was sitting towards the edge of the counter, looking down at the floor. The keys to the store that Anne had left on the counter when she came in, were now on the floor. Anne picked them up. In addition to the keys to the store, there were a few others hanging on the bunch. Anne thought back to the day that she went for a boat ride to the island with Marco, and she now remembered that one of the keys on the bunch was actually a key to the boat. *How uncanny!* Anne thought.

"I guess I have to go try out the boat," Anne said to Maggie. "Everything in this store is pointing me to the boat," she shook her head in disbelief. As she thought a bit more about it, taking the boat to the island was the only way to see that everything was okay there.

"I wish I could take you with me," she said to the cat. And she really did, because she didn't want to go alone. But alone she must go. Her husband was not here, neither was Marco. And she couldn't take Maggie on the boat. *Could I?*

"Wish me luck!" Anne said to Maggie and locked up the store. Anne knew Maggie would be okay. She had a cat door in the back and could make her way to Marco's house whenever she felt like it.

Anne joined the stream of people down towards the lake, but as people turned left toward the promenade, and toward the bonfire, she continued forward and broke into a run towards the Old Port.

Anne located Marco's boat and started to untie the rope. She didn't know how to tie and untie boat ropes, but as she wriggled the thick rope and tugged on it, and the rope loosened free. She carried the loose end to the boat. Her hands trembled.

Jumping into the boat, Anne realized she faced another problem. She couldn't start up the boat in the port. She didn't know how to maneuver it among all the boats snuggled together in the tight space of the Old Port. If she wasn't careful, she could cause expensive damage.

She would have to do it without the motor. She grabbed the oars and plunged them into the waters. Pushing on one and then the other, she tried to maneuver the boat out. It was heavy. She was going to start up the boat when she got to open water, but first she had to get out of this tight port. She forced her weight onto the oars, pushing against the water to make the boat move back and out. Slowly, the boat slipped out between the two boats flanking it. Anne pushed against the water a few more times and fully backed out the boat.

Now she had to turn the boat and make it go forward. She was sweating and her hands were trembling from exhaustion already, but also from worry. She didn't really want to think that she was in fact stealing Marco's boat. What if she ruined it? Or someone else's boat? But she pushed those thoughts out of her head.

Anne thought she probably looked ridiculous to any onlookers. But she didn't have time to think about all that now. She wanted to get to the island and save it from whatever fate it was experiencing at the moment. Because even if the smoke was only from a bonfire, she had to let someone know about the Sargent painting and about her suspicions about a killer, *probably James*, on the island. She would never forgive herself if there was another death on the island.

She managed to move the boat forward, pushing the oars into the water, and slowly threaded the boat through the narrow entrance of the harbor.

Anne gave a little thanks to the forces in the universe that had helped her get this far and hoped they would continue guiding her as she placed the key in the ignition. She turned the key, and the boat started. Encouraged, Anne pressed the lever forward, as she had seen Marco do, and the boat started gliding slowly forward.

Anne pressed harder to make it go faster. The boat was now slicing through the water and bouncing off little waves. She let out a breath she hadn't realized she had been holding.

The boat was now making its way to the island, and Anne tried to turn the wheel to make it go in the right direction. She realized the boat didn't turn like a car. The water and wind made the boat much more difficult to turn in a precise direction. As the island moved closer and closer to her, Anne realized with a panic that she could never maneuver the boat to the dock. As the dock came into view, she killed the engine and let the boat coast. She decided to row to the dock. The dock was now so close, but also so far away, as Anne tried to row the heavy boat with arms already tired from the exercise at the port. She also had to fight against the waves her boat had created as it traveled through the water.

After what had felt like a long time, Anne reached the dock and the boat bumped against the wooden platform with a thud. *Hopefully not hard enough to cause damage*, Anne thought. She wedged an oar in the deck planks to steady the boat and jumped out onto the dock holding the rope. She had no idea how to tie the boat, but made several knots, as tight as she could, to the wooden post at the end of the dock and hoped the boat wouldn't untie and float away.

From here she could smell the smoke. She ran up the dock and she now saw that the construction area was on fire. This was definitely not a bonfire. But where was everyone? *Why is no one fighting this fire!* She pushed up the hill and hoped she was not too late.

13 To save a treasure

Anne ran up the hill towards the house. She could smell the fire in the air. As she rounded the corner, she saw flames coming out of the first floor. *So it was James all along. He was responsible for the accidents, and now he is bringing down the villa to make sure that the art colony never returns to this island.*

Anne got a sinking feeling in the pit of her stomach. *Where is everyone? Why is no one fighting the fire?* Her knees weakened. What had James done?

Just then, Anne heard voices in the distance, yelling. She ran towards the voices, past the house, towards the walled garden. As she got closer, she heard people yelling "Daniel!" at the top of their lungs. The voices were definitely coming from the walled garden. She could hear banging against the door. Anne ran to the door and tried to open it, but it was locked.

"It's Anne," she yelled to make her voice heard over the wall. "What are you doing in there? The house is on fire! Has anyone called the police and the fire department?"

"We're locked in! We don't have our cell phones–" It was Elaine.

"–we left them in the house. We were supposed to do yoga–" another woman's voice yelled, probably Maude.

"–no one has a cellphone in here–" *Nick*, Anne thought.

"What happened? Who is in there?" Anne asked.

"–Daniel is not here. He went back to the house for something. Someone locked us in–"

"I hope Daniel is safe–" Elaine said.

"Did you see Daniel?" Nick asked.

"No! Can't you try to climb the wall?" Anne yelled.

"We've tried, but it's too high," said Nick.

With all the yelling, Anne couldn't think straight. What was to be done first? She couldn't help them get out of the garden. And the fire was probably out of control by now. She couldn't fight it alone.

"Please help us!" Elain cried.

"Okay, I'll see what I can do," Anne said and ran back toward the house, panic rising inside Anne.

As she ran, her feet strangely heavy and slow, a question popped up in her mind each time one of her feet hit the ground. Had James locked them in? Or Daniel? Where was Daniel? Were they in this together? They were cousins, after all. What was their plan? To steal the painting and run away? But why the fire? Why burn the art colony? Was that just an awful coincidence or part of James' plan for revenge? Why would Daniel leave his friends to burn to death on the island? That was just evil.

Anne ran inside the house. There was no one there. Every door on the ground floor was open, and flames were spreading out of some of the rooms. She couldn't fight this fire alone. A thick layer of smoke slithered across the ground. But the hallway was big and lined with marble, so the flames of the fire had not reached the paintings. And the Sargent painting was still on the wall. Anne had been sure Daniel and James had made off with it by now.

I have to save the painting. And then I'll go back to rescue the rest of them somehow.

The painting was too high for Anne to reach without a chair. She looked around for something to use and saw a table in one corner.

Anne ran across the hallway and started pushing the table towards the painting. A sharp pain split her skull. It felt like a burning knife plunged into the base of her head. Everything went black. In the distance, through the blackness, she heard a crumbling sound, like a sack of potatoes coming undone. Somewhere in the depths of her consciousness she realized that the sound she was hearing was herself falling.

She didn't feel herself hit the ground.

❖ ❖ ❖

Anne regained consciousness, unsure of how long she'd been out. She started coughing and choking; the smoke on the ground enveloped her. She forced herself to lift her arm and bring it to her pocket. Everything was moving in slow motion. She brought her phone to her face and pressed the emergency number. Her addled brain registered a thanks to her husband who had programmed the police phone number. It was different here, but right now she couldn't think what it was. Someone on the end of the line picked up. Anne tried to lift her head above the smoke. Sputtering and coughing, she said, "Aiuto. Isola Caresio. Fuori. Morte. Help, there's a fire. I'm dying." A fit of coughing overtook Anne as smoke filled her lungs. She was suffocating. And with that final thought, her entire world went black.

❖ ❖ ❖

Somewhere far away, in what sounded like another dimension, Anne heard coughing. Her consciousness was trying to swim up to the surface through deep murky water and place the sound. She heard the cough again, this time closer. *So I'm not dead yet*, she thought. Formulating that thought made her realize how much her head hurt. She wasn't sure if it was the hit on the head or the smoke. *Both*, she thought. Her eyes stung with the acrid smoke and she didn't dare open them.

Now she was floating. No, her feet were dragging, but her body was floating. Fresh air hit her lungs and choked her. She started coughing. She could hear sirens in the background and felt a jolt of happiness that help was finally on the way.

She willed her senses to get a grasp on what was going on. She felt she was now on the ground, sharp jabs of gravel under her legs. But her upper body was propped up against someone. She could feel someone's arms around her. She forced her eyes open. A pair of clear blue eyes looked down at her. She couldn't remember where she had seen them before. Her head hurt too much. Her eyes were watering and stung, so she closed them again.

Cece, the thought popped into her mind. Those were Cece's eyes. How strange. *Maybe I am dead after all. And in her hands.*

She resigned to just let go and relaxed into the arms that held her. She was thankful to whoever had called the fire department and saved her.

14 In a meadow

Anne was sitting in the meadow at the art colony. She looked at the people sitting around here–Elaine, Marco, and Alex. Anne's husband, Ben, was sitting next to her, holding her hand. A woman Anne had seen only once, at the hospital, was sitting across Anne, next to James. She had come to the hospital to visit Anne and to thank her for all she had done to save the painting.. The woman stood out from among the rest of the group. Everything about her was oversized–her eyes were hidden behind large reading glasses with thick black frames, chunky jewelry rested on her breast, and her body was wrapped in a linen tunic and pants with the sartorial complexity of origami. But this bohemian ensemble was somewhat disrupted by a large orange Hermès bag in her lap. In contrast to her clothing and accessories, her silver hair was cut short and spiked. This was Barbara, James' mother.

It was two weeks after the fire and the breeze still carried a smell of burned wood. Or was that just Anne? She still couldn't get the smell of fire out of her lungs. The doctors had said it would take a while for her to make a complete recovery.

Ben leaned in towards Anne. "I just can't understand what made you come to the island," he said, quietly.

"I don't know," Anne said, truthfully.

This was Anne's first weekend out of the hospital, and the first time everyone involved had gathered together. Anne had heard bits and pieces of what happened, but not the complete story from beginning to end. She knew Nick and Maud had gone home, too distressed by the recent events.

"–I'm not actually sure how the confusion started, but that painting has always been called 'Cece's painting'. Even my grandmother referred to it that way. When Daniel first arrived on the island, it was for a romantic getaway with Julia. But he was on the stairs, unobserved, when he overheard Julia tell James that the painting everyone thought was by Cece was actually a painting by Sargent. So Daniel hatched a plan. It was all a spur-of-the-moment thing. An opportunistic crime that spiraled out of control," Barbara said.

"His initial plan was to make a copy of the original painting, hang the copy in the hall, and sell the original to a private collector. He even had tracked one down though some contacts he had made though Julia," Elain said.

"His breakup with Julia was just a way to get her away. He couldn't make a copy with her around. She would be on to him," Barbara said. "Initially, he never intended to kill anyone, but once his scheme got on the way, people started getting in his way.

"First Paolo proposed a valuation. Daniel couldn't have that, not before he had finished the copy and had disposed of the original. But Paolo was proving to be like a bulldog with a bone. He wouldn't let it go and started digging for information on Sargent, perhaps because of some hints that Poppy dropped. We'll never know," Barabara said, shaking her head.

"Daniel lured Paolo with some excuse to the dock that fatal night and attacked him. Daniel thought there would be no more interference," Elaine said, "but along came poor Poppy, who stumbled upon the truth. She didn't know much about art, but through her research she happened on the fact that Sargent indeed had stayed at the island at about the same time as the painting. Ever thirsty for Daniel's attention, she probably shared that tidbit with him, thinking that it would win her some of his approval. He asked her to meet him at the renovation site with a promise of an escapade, but smashed her head in instead," she said, shuddering.

"Daniel intended the blame for the murders and fire to go to James," Barbara picked up the story thread. "The idea came to him from James," she turned to her son, who sat with his head in his hands, and put her hand on his leg, "who was always going on about the curse." Barbara turned back to the group. "Daniel decided to use the curse to his advantage. The two of them were very close as children, and I believe James still regarded Daniel as a good friend. So it was easy for Daniel to manipulate James and egg on his obsession with the old curse. Daniel had convinced James the accidents were a retribution from a higher power. And that a cleansing fire would be the ultimate manifestation of the curse. Of course, Daniel's intention the entire time was to make people think James was crazy enough to kill and to set the island on fire," Barbara said. She sat quietly for a few moments. Then she reached her hand and ran it gently down James' back.

"Daniel needed the fire to complete his scheme, to put James under suspicion and hopefully to cause enough damage to the copy that no one would bother getting it valued," Elaine said. "He suggested the yoga in the garden and locked everyone in. He didn't really want to kill anyone else and hoped the thick walls would protect us until the fire department came." She turned to Anne, "He had forgotten about you, because you had been to the island only once. He didn't know you had put all the facts together–"

Barbara looked towards Anne, and added, "Daniel admitted that the first day you came to the island, he flirted with you because he wanted to see how much you knew about the painting. He was worried you had discovered something in the diaries. But as you didn't seem like a threat, he put you out of his mind," Barbara said, and smiled at Anne.

"–as he was leaving, he saw you rowing towards the island and followed to see what you would do. When he saw you go in and try to rescue the painting, he hit you over the head to get rid of you," Elaine said. "Daniel was losing time and needed to get away before the police and fire department came. Daniel was relying on James being at vespers and noticing the fire only when it was too late."

"But James smelled the fire and came out to see what was going on. He saw you go into the house and not come out," Barbara said. "He dragged you out."

The clear blue eyes, Anne thought.

"And what happened to Daniel and the painting?" Ben spoke up for the first time.

"They caught Daniel trying to cross the border into Italy with the real Sargent," Barbara said.

"But who called the police and the fire department? No one had a cell phone on them," Anne said.

"That was you," Marco said.

Anne felt a jolt of pride for having overcome her fear of communicating in Italian when it really counted.

Barbara's bag buzzed. She reached in and took out a large phone with a geometric cover. "Excuse me a moment," she said, and took the call. When she got off, she said, "That was Julia. The results of all the tests and analysis are now back, and it's beyond any doubt that the painting is a Sargent."

Everyone cheered, and Marco clapped. Barbara laughed.

"What will happen to the painting?" Anne asked. She hoped the painting wouldn't be sold. "Will you have to sell it? I mean, how do you plan on restoring the house, or are you not planning on doing that?"

"Oh, insurance will take care of the house," Barbara waved a hand towards the house. "I'm lucky in that regard. And once the house is fully restored in a few years, the painting will go back in and be displayed with pride."

Anne wondered what would happen to James, the house and the art colony, but didn't think it was appropriate to ask. She looked at mother and son. It was clear that they were on speaking terms again, so that must be a sign of positive things to come.

As they were leaving the island later that evening, Anne walking beside Marco, Alex guiding her husband's wheelchair down the tricky slope, Ben bringing up the back, Anne thought of something and turned to Marco. "You know, there is something strange going on with your store and your cat," Anne said to him.

He smiled up at her and said, "We'll talk about that on Monday."

Out Of Print Author's Notes

While the events described in this book are the product of the author's imagination, some elements are grounded in historical fact, and all of the events are historically plausible.

Brissago Islands

The Brissago Islands are a group of two islands on Lake Maggiore, off the coast of Ascona. They are easily accessible by boat and open to the public. In addition to the luscious botanical gardens on the larger island, the island has its own palazzo that now serves as a hotel and a restaurant. The Brissago Islands are a must on any visit to the region.

Isola Caresio and its Art Colony

While the Brissago Islands and their beautiful botanical gardens are real, the Caresio Island, its curse, and its art colony are the author's invention. In the beginning of the 20th century, however, there was an art colony–Monte Verità– in the hills above Ascona. Monte Verità served as the initial inspiration for the art colony on the Caresio Island, but is in no way related to the fictitious events described in the book.

John Sargent

Beginning in about 1900, the painter John Sargent spent summers traveling with his family and friends through Switzerland and Italy. He produced many vivid watercolors during those trips. They are distinguishable from the artist's famous portraits by their energy and unmistakably Impressionistic style. The artist, however, never visited Ascona, or the fictitious Caresio Island.

Book 2: Murderous Misprint

Old Bookstore Two-Hour Cozy Mysteries Book 2

By Isabella Bassett

Copyright © 2021 Isabella Bassett
All rights reserved. The moral right of the author has been asserted.

Murderous Misprint
(Old Bookstore Two-Hour Cozy Mysteries Book 2)
Kindle Edition
Published April 29, 2021

ASIN: B08W56LG58

This book is a work of fiction. Names, characters, places and events portrayed in this book are the product of the author's imagination or are used fictitiously. Any similarity to actual persons, living or dead, businesses, companies, events or locales is entirely coincidental and not intended by the author.

No part of this book may be reproduced,

or stored in a retrieval system, or transmitted in any form or by any means, electronic, mechanical, photocopying, recording, or otherwise, without express written permission of the publisher.

1 Scaredy-cat

Maggie, the store's black cat, hissed and arched her back.

The man standing in front of Anne was something out of a gothic novel. Greasy hair hung around his face like wet tentacles of a sea monster in a medieval rendering. The face–unshaven for days–resembled that of a prisoner cast away in the deepest dungeon. A rough linen tunic, spanning the color wheel of mud drying in the sun, long threads unraveling from its frayed raw edges, hung off the man's back. The stench he gave off reminded Anne of the smell that lingered on her fingers after slicing off the rind–the crust of hardened mold and yeast protecting the ripening innards–of aged Alpine cheese.

In his hands, the man held a cloth-bound book, its color long ago weathered to an indistinguishable shade of beige. Oily stains and water damage–discernible by the ombre edges of its wavy outlines–were soaked deep into the cloth. Faint gold letters, once embossed firmly into the cover but now worn away by the passing of time, and numerous inquisitive fingers, were the only relics of the once-glorious beginnings of this book.

Anne noticed the man's thick fingers–skin cracked along the tips and black dirt settled in the deep furrows, and under his nails–running over the embossed lettering, as if trying to wipe away invisible tarnish and reveal the hidden gold below, but in reality just adding to the gradual wearing away of the letters' gold-leaf.

When he finally spoke, the man's words conjured up visions of ancient barbarian tribes of Goths and Vandals attacking the gates of Rome. He spoke, in a word, German. But in his mouth the language was modulated by an unhealthy dose of phlegm, which made Anne recognize it as Swiss German–a form of German spoken only in Switzerland, distinguishable by its guttural pronunciation.

Anne didn't speak any form of German.

"I'm sorry, I don't speak German, only English," Anne told the man, who, she hazard a guess, was a medieval beggar.

He looked up and searched Anne's eyes with slow apprehension. Perhaps because they were both standing in a store located in Switzerland, and perhaps because Anne was an assistant at the store, he probably assumed she spoke German. *Not an unreasonable assumption,* thought Anne.

But not only did Anne not speak German, she

also did not speak Italian. Or French, for that matter. In fact, she only spoke English. For most of her life that had not been a problem, but now she found herself living in Switzerland, in the Italian-speaking part of the country, and working in a bookstore, where customers expected her (*quite rightly*, she thought) to speak at least one of the four official languages of Switzerland: German, French, Italian or Romansh (although that official language was only spoken in an isolated mountain region).

While her language deficiency was a constant struggle for Anne in her new life, she reminded herself that she was only a recent transplant to Switzerland, and an even more recent employee of the bookstore, where she had been hired as an English-speaking assistant. She was trying to get a handle on the language situation and had been taking Italian classes–for adults and recent newcomers–almost since arriving in Switzerland nine months ago. But her efforts on the language front, sadly, were not going swimmingly. She wondered if she was missing a language gene.

Customers, however, didn't care about her language struggles; they just wanted to buy books.

Her one saving grace was that the Swiss were often multi-lingual and usually spoke excellent English. And if all else failed, and she ever found herself in a language difficulty at the bookstore, she could always direct customers to Marco.

"The copy is stained," the man in front of Anne said, switching to English, accented with a hard Germanic intonation, as if to confirm her theory about the Swiss, "but the pages are in good condition. I would like to purchase it." He handed the book back to Anne, to complete the transaction.

While wrapping the book, Anne's eyes slid down the counter to where Marco sat behind the counter, hunched over a crumbling book, head to head with the pointed tip of a black hat; the witch, whose head the hat sat on, leaned over the book from the opposite side of the counter.

Anne rang up the man in the medieval beggar's getup and looked around the store.

The pathetic creature in the linen rags moving towards the exit, with the book now tucked under his sweat-stained armpit, was by far not the most interesting visitor to the store at the moment. Waiting politely for their turn were a Lord and Lady in resplendent Renaissance outfits, dripping in gold-thread embroidery, crisp white lace and layers of brocade fabric. Figures of other time-traveling oddities–a knight in shining armor, and a Druid high priest in a white cassock–were silhouetted against the store's two gothic windows.

The presence of these historic personalities was strangely fitting with the interior of the bookstore. Surrounding them on all sides were tall antique glass-fronted apothecary shelves, their dark wood frames carved with botanical details, now used as bookshelves. Old books with weathered spines crowded the lower shelves. On the upper shelves, just out of reach, white porcelain apothecary jars, with intricately painted colorful labels, jostled for attention. The jars looked as if they had been swept off the lower shelves and stuffed hurriedly on the upper ones to make room for the books, and then just left, forgotten. Which was probably very close to the truth.

Beyond the shelves, soaring high above their heads, was an unlikely vaulted ceiling. Thin ribs traveled up the white stone walls, above the apothecary shelves, and met in a symmetrical rosette at the center. Together with the two gothic windows that marked the store's front, the thick stone walls, and the geometric mosaic on the floor, the vaulted ceiling gave the store the appearance of a place of worship.

Today, the store was more crowded than usual. Since yesterday afternoon, the bookstore had had a steady stream of visitors–witches in layers of black, warlocks in embroidered robes, even a group of troubadours, complete with lutes. This constant flow of foot traffic, as Marco would call it, was also the reason Anne was working at the front of the store, despite her linguistic shortcomings, and not in the back as usual.

The startling costumes, makeup, and accessories of the recent customers also served to unnerve Maggie, and she patrolled the counters protectively, hissing periodically for good measure, and inserting herself between Anne and any new customer that approached the counter.

Anne scooped the cat in her hands and gave her a scratch behind the ears. She felt warmth radiating off the cat's body against her chest, and a sense of peace washed over her. She snuggled in Maggie's soft fur for a few moments longer and placed the cat on the floor.

Anne sent a silent thanks to Marco for having a cat in the store. In the short time Anne had worked here, Maggie had provided moral support more than once.

Marco gave Anne a sign that he can handle the customers, and she walked to the back of the store to take care of some shipments.

Marco had hired Anne a little over a month ago to digitize and index a set of English diaries from the 1900s. Those diaries had helped uncover a secret on a nearby island. The discovery had made the front page, above the fold, in the local, and even some national and international newspapers, and transformed the store into a local celebrity, for a few days. But as news stories cycle out, and are replaced by fresh gossip or scandals, life at the store quickly went back to its normal rhythm–days filled with reading books and occasional conversations with Marco.

Found on the cobbled pedestrian shopping street of the Old Town of Ascona, the bookstore was usually ignored by the town's regular visitors. Surrounded by colorful stores selling shiny things, the store's gray stone front faded to the background, and tourists' eyes slid past the bookstore's gothic facade to the jewelry store further down the street. Plus, being an antiquarian, aptly named 'Out Of Print', the books sold by the store–old ones, on long-forgotten topics–excited few of the visitors to Ascona, who were interested in less esoteric pastimes. So on most days, the bookstore sat quiet and content–just like its owner, Marco, and his single employee, Anne–with the store's business coming from email enquiries by academics and researchers.

But over the past few days, the local newspapers had started lamenting over a new breed of visitors that had descended on their small town. And the store's gothic windows and gray broodiness drew those visitors to it like a beacon.

Southern Switzerland's Pagan Festival had arrived in Ascona. Held annually in a farm field just outside town, it attracted attendees from all other Switzerland and beyond. The newspaper articles ran the full gamut of journalistic emotions. Some were breathlessly recommending attending the colorful show with its variety of family-friendly entertainment and historic reenactments. While others were decrying the clash of cultures between the costumed attendees and the quiet, luxurious lifestyle that the town of Ascona offered. The latter bemoaned the heathens and drunks who spoiled the quaint image of the charming lakeside town.

Anne couldn't deny that Ascona was special. Nestled in the foothills of the Swiss Alps, in the southernmost part of Switzerland–a part that actually protruded into Italy–the town was well known for its Mediterranean climate and exotic gardens crowned by palm trees. The cobblestoned pedestrian Old Town, marked by the tall bell tower of *Chiesa dei Santi Pietro e Paolo*, attracted tourists with its candy-colored houses, Italianate villas and palazzos, and a lakeside promenade dotted with cafes overlooking the calm expanse of Lake Maggiore, and Italy beyond. Bordering Italy, and having been part of Italy until quite recently–historically speaking– the town of Ascona, and the whole southern region of Switzerland, spoke Italian, ate Italian food, and was steeped in Italian culture.

Catering to rich retirees of any age, Ascona attracted tourists, and residents, of a certain income bracket who wanted the *dolce vita* lifestyle without leaving the clean efficiency of Switzerland. Retiring to Ascona was a status symbol among well-to-do northerners looking to escape the snow. Anne knew she was generalizing a bit, since she was one of many residents and visitors who didn't fit this specific demographic, but people like her were the exception.

Anne preferred avoiding the crowded promenade, and usually chose to get around town using the back alleys that wound in narrow cobbled paths among the ancient stone houses and stone-walled gardens, but this morning she had walked to the bookstore right through the center of town.

Walking to the store, Anne had taken a secret pleasure in the uneasy coexistence between Ascona's regulars and the festival's attendees. Middle-aged men, dressed in a uniform of faded boating shorts, candy-colored polo shirts, and boat shoes, and thus signaling to other middle-aged men that they also liked sailing and golf, sat elbow-to-elbow for their morning coffee–thanks to the intimate arrangement of tables at the lakeside cafes–with New Age hippies, Wicca enthusiasts (judging by the prominent displays of pentagram jewelry), and an array of brown-hued medieval denizens.

Held on the sprawling green fields of a local farmer, the festival was part renaissance fair, part pagan fest, part New Age and alternative-living gathering. Anne was surprised by the vibrant neo-pagan culture that seemed to thrive in Switzerland. The country had a reputation for being serious and practical, but the festival was evidence that a strong counter-culture existed. Judging by the licence plates, people traveled down from northern Switzerland, Germany and Austria, and up from Italy, to attend the festival. And attendees came from as far away as the Netherlands–the Dutch instantly recognizable on the roads by their yellow license plates and the ubiquitous caravans attached to the back of their cars.

Anne knew that her assessment of the man that had left the store a few minutes ago was a bit unfair. While he undoubtedly had been going for painstaking authenticity with his medieval beggar's costume, the smell, Anne had to admit, was probably only *raclette*–a traditional Swiss dish of pungent melted cheese typically served at outdoor events.

Walking back to the front of the store, Anne was surprised to find it suddenly empty.

"You better lock the door before anyone else comes in," Marco said.

Seeing a figure approaching the store, Anne lunged across the front and shot up the three stone steps leading to the front door. She reached for the deadbolt and heard it click in place just as another pagan character reached for the door. She flipped the store sign to '*chiuso*'–closed–and flashed an innocent smile at the confused face staring at her through the glass.

2 The sorcerer's house

Anne and Marco left the store through the back. Marco headed away from the bookstore in such a hurry that a casual observer would have thought he was running away from it.

The alley behind the store was one of the few in Ascona that was asphalted. As Anne walked next to Marco up the sloping street, away from the lake, she thought about how difficult it must be for Marco to get around the Old Town's cobbled streets in his wheelchair.

They made their way towards an underground parking lot just outside the pedestrian zone of the Old Town to meet Marco's wife, Alex–short for Alexandra. The crowd in the store this morning had held them back, and now they were running late for an auction in Locarno.

A mere ten-minute drive from Ascona–the two towns separated only by a river–Locarno too sat on the northern shore of Lake Maggiore, facing Italy, with Italian heritage permeating to its very core. But while Ascona was exuberant and colorful, an old fishing village frothing with tourists, Locarno had an aristocratic elegance and grace. Anne enjoyed going to Locarno.

Anne's favorite places in Locarno were the ones that made it so different from Ascona. A leafy lakeside park, with mature trees, manicured lawns, and geometric flower beds–happily devoid of crowded cafes–ran quietly along the shore of the lake. Further in from the lake, Italian-style palazzos in muted yellows and oranges, accented with white friezes and white windows, lined the streets. The same style of Italianate buildings, with wide stone arches supporting shopping arcades running underneath the buildings, encircled the Piazza Grande, the town's main square. In the arcades, large department stores and grocery store chains sat side-by-side with intimate cafes and restaurants.

The vast square of Piazza Grande, paved with rounded river stones, which created the illusion of an undulating gray sea of rocks, usually sat empty, except for a few brave souls taking shortcuts through it. The sharp sun typical of this region, intensified by the pebbled paving and compounded by the lack of shade, made the square's center an uncomfortable place to linger. Most people preferred to walk its periphery and escape to the cool shade of the arcades.

But once a year, this gray-stoned expanse filled with people, and Locarno shed its noble respectability to become an epicenter of celebrity culture. Held each August, the Locarno Film

Festival attracted actors, directors, and fans, and 8,000 people gathered nightly under the stars in Piazza Grande to watch movies on an outdoor screen set up in the square. Anne's enthusiasm for the festival had increased since reading that one of the inaugural movies shown at its opening in 1946 was *And Then There Were None*, an adaptation of Agatha Christie's famous novel.

Away from the grand square, cobbled alleys ran straight up and away from the lake, like the spokes on a wheel, to the upper parts of town. Like all the towns surrounding the lake, Locarno sat at the foothills of the Alps and was built in a series of terraces, each progressively higher.

In the past, during floods, when lake water rose dramatically due to heavy rainfall or meltwater from the surrounding mountains, and the low-lying parts of the town, like its lakeside park and the Piazza Grande, were submerged in several feet of water, the alleys provided escape routes to higher ground. While floods still happened occasionally, now these side alleys had been turned into attractive shopping streets with cool boutiques and quirky cafes.

Alex had parked in the upper part of town and the three of them proceeded to *Casa del Negromante* for the auction. A plaque outside the house–one of those placed by historical societies–announced, tantalizingly, that the house name translated to 'the house of the sorcerer'.

The name intrigued Anne as much as the house itself, but the sign provided little information beyond that it was 'the oldest secular building in Locarno'.

Like with most Italian medieval houses, the interesting bits were on the inside. The outside facade was plain stucco, with larger windows running only along the second floor–for security. An arched doorway with heavy wooden doors, their function suited more for keeping people out than welcoming them in, led into an inner courtyard enclosed on all sides by the house. A wooden balcony ran along the second floor and overlooked the courtyard. The auction took place in one of the rooms on the second floor.

A tiny restaurant, concealed under a canopy of green vines, huddled at the far end of the courtyard. Metal lanterns hung from the vines, and under each, wrought-iron chairs circled a round metal table, that barely fit three people.

Marco, Alex, and Anne now sat at one such table waiting for lunch, the vines above them filtering the strong midday sun to a dappled green. Anne could imagine that on fall evenings, the brilliant yellow vine leaves set ablaze by the setting sun, and the lit lanterns giving off a soft glow, the place would feel enchanting.

A laugh pierced the low lunchtime hum in the courtyard, its sound vibrating off the stone walls of the ancient building surrounding them.

Anne looked up at a woman seated a couple of tables away from them. She had her back to Anne and all Anne could see was a cloud of brown, bushy, slightly frizzy, curly hair. Although Anne couldn't see her face, she remembered the woman, and her hair, from the auction.

The auction, which had preceded lunch, was much like what Anne had imagined. She had seen antiques auctions on TV, so knew what to expect. This, having been a book auction, had been a bit quieter, with prices not reaching the astronomical heights Anne had sometimes seen on TV. Marco had explained that most of the books auctioned were from the collection of a recently deceased professor of botany, a certain Professor Grewald.

Marco had attended the action because he was interested in acquiring some 17th century illustrated botanical volumes in the professor's collection. Such books, and their botanical drawings, were much in demand among Marco's customers.

During the auction, Anne's attention had been drawn to the woman with the bushy hair by the jingling of the woman's numerous silver bracelets and bangles. A cascade of jingles announced the woman's bids every time she raised her hand. Anne could now see that an extensive collection of stacked David Yurman and John Hardy bracelets adorned the woman's right hand. They continued to jingle while the woman gesticulated animatedly to her lunch companion. The silver glints that kept time of the woman's hand gestures were matched by a flash of gold underneath the blazer of her lunch companion, each time he made a point.

It had struck Anne as odd that out of all the books at the auction, the woman had only been interested in the late professor's field log. The auction catalog mentioned that the log books were from Prof. Grewald's field trips to collect samples from his research. In her exquisitely tailored skirt suit, the woman looked to Anne more like an executive than a botanist. *But you should never judge a book by its cover*, Anne thought, and returned her attention to Marco and Alex, who were discussing the merits of a book Marco had purchased.

Anne was working through her plate of gnocchi with gorgonzola sauce, when the heavy wooden doors opened with a bang and a woman stormed through them into the small courtyard. It took her only a moment to get her bearings, and she proceeded towards the table of the bushy-haired woman with the speed, and probably the destructive force, of a tornado.

"What are you doing here with him?" the newly arrived woman said in a loud hiss, directing this question at the bushy-haired woman, while pointing to her lunch companion.

Marco and Alex, with their backs to the table, were too polite to turn around, but Anne had a clear view of the drama unfolding in front of her.

The newly arrived woman lowered her voice and proceeded to talk animatedly in hushed tones, probably now aware of the intimacy of the enclosed courtyard.

The snippets of English–some clearly American, some with an Italian accent–made it hard for Anne to tune out. She didn't really want to hear what the two women were talking about, but was intrigued by what a fellow American was doing at an obscure auction of botanical books.

The bushy-haired woman got up, and through her hand gestures Anne guessed she was trying to calm the other woman. The two women went towards the wooden doors and exited. The doors now sat open. Anne could see the women silhouetted against the light, framed in the arched doorway. They continued their animated conversation. Each of the women, in turn, pointed to the man sitting, now alone, inside the restaurant.

A lover's tiff, Anne thought.

She turned her attention to the man, the alleged object of the women's desire. He was concentrating on cutting his meat into the smallest slices possible. Undoubtedly he wanted to look busy and ignore all the concealed glances that came his way from his fellow diners. Anne thought that most people in his situation would turn to their phones. But maybe he was too polite to take out his phone at the table. Or maybe his generation was not in the habit of checking phones constantly.

The only word that came to Anne as she looked at the man was *distinguished*. His longish wavy hair, streaked with silver of varying intensity, was swept back. He had a tan, which Anne had noticed men of a certain age here wore, probably to hide wrinkles. He was dressed in a well cut navy suit and a heavy golden watch peeked out from under his white shirt cuff. And while he looked like he'd rather not have the whole restaurant staring at him, there was a smugness about him. A tiny smile played upon his face. Anne wondered if he was enjoying having two women fight over him.

Anne didn't see the attraction, but she knew a lot of women were attracted to rich or powerful men.

As she looked back to the two arguing women, still visible through the open door, she decided that he must indeed be rich or powerful. Both women were younger than the man over whom they were arguing, and both radiated a polished sophistication.

Despite her bushy hair, his lunch companion had something regal about her, in the way she had walked and the way she held her head when she spoke, shaking her lion's mane when she made a point.

The second woman was younger, tall and slender. She had a delicacy about her, but seemed to be holding her own during the argument. *Tenacious,* Anne thought.

Anne pulled her attention back to her own lunch companions. She laughed at herself for getting so caught up in someone else's drama.

Anne enjoyed spending time with Alex and Marco. Both in their late 50s, they radiated a calmness that made Anne feel as if everything was right with the world. She wondered if their serenity came from doing for a living what they clearly enjoyed. Marco had his bookstore. And Alex ran a yoga studio. Alex had the agility of someone half her age and moved with the grace of a dancer.

When Anne got up to leave with Alex and Marco, she noticed that the bushy-haired woman, whom Anne now thought of as 'the American', was again sitting with the man. Anne hadn't noticed when the woman had returned to her table, or when the willowy woman had left.

Alex touched Marco's shoulder. "Look who's here," she said quietly, but with a smile. Anne noticed that Marco's eyes traveled in the direction of the table where the bushy-haired American and the distinguished man were sitting. At lunch, Alex and Marco had had their backs to the table, and only Anne had been able to see the table's occupants.

A look passed between Alex and Marco, which Anne couldn't decipher.

"I'll just go say hi," said Alex, and walked over to the table. Marco continued moving towards the exit, and Anne followed. They stopped at the end of the courtyard to wait for Alex.

From where she was standing, Anne could see Alex lean in and greet the man. Alex looked excited to see him. The man got up and looked just as happy to see Alex.

An animated exchange followed. Anne noticed that Alex pointed in the direction of Marco, and Marco nodded a curt greeting, which the other man returned. But Marco didn't move to join Alex.

A change had come over Alex. Her demeanor was effervescent. Her face glowed as if from within, and her animated gestures, the flips of her golden hair as she spoke, and the smile that lit her face when she laughed, melted the years away, and Anne felt like she was catching glimpses of Alex as a young woman.

Anne wondered if the man was an old friend, or maybe even an old boyfriend of Alex's.

"Who is that man?" Anne asked without thinking.

After the words had tumbled out of her

mouth, Anne shot a glance at Marco, and regretted her impulsive question. In contrast to Alex, a darkness had settled over Marco's face.

Anne couldn't be sure, but she thought she could guess his thoughts. Everyone had a past, and old lovers, before their current partner. Anne wondered how she would feel and act if she met an old boyfriend, or worse, if Ben ran into an old girlfriend.

Marco interrupted her thoughts. "He's an old friend of Alex's. Both Australian. Alex knows him from before she met me," Marco said, and his face darkened further. "He's some sort of venture capitalist. Lots of investments in lots of different things. We move in very different social circles, so I've only met him a couple of times." Marco paused. "I don't know, he doesn't strike me as a good person. Alex insists on being nice to him whenever their paths cross. I'm not sure why."

Anne didn't ask more.

"Can you believe it," Alex was saying as she walked up to them, "to run into Patrick here." She paused and looked at Marco, her smile unwavering. "Oh Marco," she swatted him playfully on the shoulder, "he's not so bad."

Alex leaned towards Anne as they made their way through the doorway and onto the sidewalk. "Marco doesn't like him because Patrick is quite flashy with his wealth," she said, with a note of teasing in her voice.

"There's something fake about him," Marco said.

"Oh, that's just his tan," Alex laughed.

So much of Anne's attention during lunch had been preoccupied with this Patrick and his lunch companion, that Anne couldn't resist asking Alex about him.

"How do you know him?" Anne said.

"Oh, I know him from back home. We used to surf together on the beaches of Sidney. We weren't in the same group of friends or anything, just knew each other from running into each other on the beach in the mornings." Alex paused, as if trying to recollect the details of those days. "Uff, that was such a long time ago," she shook herself off.

"And then our paths diverged. Imagine my surprise when I ran into him here in Switzerland and found he was living here as well. By then he had become quite successful, so we moved in completely different social groups. But the number of Australian expats is much smaller than the Americans, or the Brits, or the Canadians, so we tended to run into each other at Australian events. Australia day celebrations and such. He is Zurich based, but has a vacation home here in the south, in Lugano. It's actually been years since I've seen him, now that I think about it."

Marco had been quiet during the entire exchange, and Anne decided not to pry further. The three of them proceeded in silence towards the parking lot where they'd left the car.

3 Death of a witch

On Saturday mornings, while Anne made coffee, Ben went down to get newspapers so they could familiarize themselves with local news and events. They would sit at the kitchen table and Ben would read out interesting local news and tidbits. Unlike Anne, Ben's Italian was good, and he kept improving it at work.

Anne had moved to Switzerland with her husband less than a year ago. He was an executive in a coffee company, a job that took him–sometimes for weeks at a time–to Africa, South America, and Asia, anywhere he could find good coffee beans. They had moved to Switzerland so that Ben's career could continue to grow. Counterintuitively, Switzerland was one of the biggest producers of roast coffee in the world.

The decision to move had been an easy one for Anne–she loved Europe and had always dreamed of getting the chance to live here. She had jumped at the opportunity to travel, to live in a historic town, and to immerse herself in a new culture. She enjoyed exploring the towns around Ascona and their history whenever she got the chance.

But she was struggling with Italian, hadn't made any friends, and on some days even missed her old job.

Actually, the thought of not going back to pharmaceutical research, or working another day in a lab, did not bother her. She had been stagnating in her old job in Boston, and had begun to find it boring. But she realized that at 37, she may have a hard time switching careers. Anne found it emotionally difficult giving up a career she had worked on building her whole adult life. There were plenty of opportunities in the pharmaceutical industry in Switzerland, but for now Anne wanted to see where working in the local antiquarian bookstore, and following her passion for books, and reading, would lead her.

What she missed most was having friends. She had tried socializing with the women from her Italian class–like her, they were all here because of their husbands' jobs–but they were often busy with their families and children, and nothing permanent had come out of it. And living in a tourist town, where visitors were transient, and most residents lived here only a few months out of the year, made it next to impossible to make local friends.

Anne had hoped that moving to Switzerland would finally give her and Ben the chance to start a family, but that hadn't happened yet either. Although 40 years old, Ben looked and felt younger, and he thought they still had plenty of time for kids. But Anne worried about being what they called a 'geriatric mother'.

"You'll never believe this," Ben said as he walked in through the door, pulling Anne out of her thoughts. "There has been a death at the pagan festival."

He spread out the front page of the newspaper on the kitchen table. A word stood out to Anne from the headline–'*strega*'. Witch.

"What does the headline say?" Anne asked. She read the headline in her halting Italian and translated it to herself. "Something about a dead witch?" she asked Ben.

"Yes. I just glanced at it and haven't read all the details, but it seems a woman dressed as a witch was found drowned at the festival," Ben said.

He sat down and read for a while. Then he translated. "So, it says that a woman was found drowned in a barrel of mead. It's not an accident. Someone must have pushed and held her head under. The newspaper is speculating about the way she died. They think the drowning was ritualistic. Witch drowning."

Anne's mind wandered to the uneasy coexistence between the festival's visitors and Ascona's residents and more typical tourists.

Leading up to the festival, the local press had been full of objections to the festival. Although the festival brought a lot of visitors to the area, and their cash, some local residents were opposed to the type of tourists the festival attracted. These opponents wanted Ascona to preserve a certain atmosphere of refinement and gentility. Their list of grievances was long. They resented: the caravans clogging the local roads; the alternative lifestyles of the festival goers, which clashed with the values of the upper middle class that normally frequented Ascona; and the people in ridiculous costumes who spoiled the elegant vistas of the lakeside promenade, and tarnished the gloss of the pedestrian streets.

Could one of the more zealous objectionists to the festival have taken matters into their own hands, Anne wondered.

"Ha!" Ben exclaimed from behind a newspaper. "The *Zurich Observer* has a piece on the death as well." He continued reading. The *Zurich Observer* was an English-language newspaper that came out on the weekend and contained news relevant to expats–like Anne and her husband.

"It seems the woman was a cosmetic industry executive. A big shot in the research of new cosmetic ingredients. Kathleen Price. She doesn't sound Swiss. Oh, yes, here it is. She was American. But had worked in the Swiss cosmetic industry for over 20 years," he said.

"Let me see," Anne reached for the newspaper. While not missing her old job, Anne was still interested in science and research. Plus, pharmaceuticals and cosmetic had a lot of common touch points. Anne found the job of the dead woman intriguing.

"Here they use the word 'witch' as well," Anne looked up from the article. "They say that her nickname in the industry was 'The Witch', attributed to her uncanny ability to find new ingredients, usually by investigating folk remedies and recipes. And to her witchy personality. Apparently she was not well liked. Ruthless, it says."

Anne thought it was a bit ironic that a cosmetic industry executive was interested in witchcraft and folk remedies. *Old versus new quackery,* Anne thought.

Anne took a closer look at the photo accompanying the article. "No way!" she said. Although the hair was tamed into careful waves, and she was younger, there was no mistaking the woman on the page. "I saw this woman at the restaurant, and at the auction, yesterday." Anne couldn't believe it. *What a coincidence,* she thought. "She was sitting at the table next to us yesterday at *Casa del Negromante*. She was having lunch with an older man. Quite dapper. And then a woman came in and they seemed to have an argument over the man. It looked like a love triangle. So strange..." Anne trailed off, thoughts racing through her mind.

But why would this woman be dressed like a witch? At lunch she had worn a business suit. And what was she doing at the pagan festival? Maybe she was into pagan things, given that she was into old remedies and folk knowledge? Maybe she liked living up to her nickname, embraced it, and turned what was meant as an insult into a badge of honor.

But why was she killed at the festival? Was the location significant? Her costume certainly made it seem so. Was this a planned killing? Was the killer sending a message with the method and the location? Or was it more of a spur of the moment killing, something that couldn't wait, and the location, method, and costume were just a coincidence? *Too much of a coincidence*, Anne thought.

Anne went back to reading the English article. Based on the article, Kathleen Price had many enemies in the industry. She had stepped on a lot of toes on her way to the top.

But would any of her colleagues from Zurich travel all the way here to kill her? Or maybe some of her colleagues were here with her? *For the pagan festival? Unlikely,* Anne thought.

So maybe the motive was something more personal. Something linked to the argument

Anne witnesses yesterday. A lover's triangle gone fatal. Maybe the other woman at lunch was the killer.

"Well, the police have definitely ruled it foul play, but they don't have any suspects yet," Ben cut into Anne's train of thoughts. "I'm sure the newspapers will be full of this story for days."

"I bet those opposed to the festival will use this as an excuse to shut it down next year," Anne said.

"And Switzerland was supposed to be quiet and boring," Ben said, sarcasm in his voice. "First deaths on a cursed island, now a dead witch. What next?"

Anne caught his reference to the mystery at the island she had been involved in a few weeks ago, but she didn't respond. Her thoughts were still with the dead woman and the pagan festival.

4 A book out of place

Anne tried not to work on weekends when her husband was home, but this weekend was an exception. With the store more busy than usual, she wanted to help Marco. Plus, tomorrow was Sunday, and all stores were closed on Sunday in Switzerland, so she'd get to spend time with Ben tomorrow.

Walking down the promenade toward the store, Anne could see groups of people huddled together over the small coffee tables at the outdoor cafes, clearly reading the same news Ben and Anne had read this morning. Anne wondered if there were any witnesses that the police were not making known. *Would they close down the festival early,* Anne wondered. *There's only one day left.*

When she got to the store, the first thing Anne wanted to do was ask Marco if he had read about the murder. But now was not the time; several people were already hanging about in the store, looking about them, as if at a museum, peering at the jars on the topmost shelves, as if trying to make out the words on the labels, while

Marco served a customer.

While the store's selection of historical books, documents, and maps usually attracted scholars and collectors from all over the world, over the last few days, Anne had discovered another group of target customers–those interested in pagan history, historical reenactments, and renaissance festivals.

"Anne, can you locate this book for me," Marco handed a piece of paper with the book's location to Anne.

Anne took the paper and walked to the back of the store. *Good thing customers can't see the back,* Anne thought. While the appeal of the front of the store lay in its dark wood bookcases, polished wood countertops, apothecary jars, and pointed gothic windows–giving it an appearance akin to a potent mix of gothic novel, alchemist's lab, and monastic library–the back of the store was all Swiss efficiency of cold steel at right angles. Rows of gleaming metal shelves housed faded antique books, manuscripts in flat cardboard boxes, and all other manner of rolls, maps, and stacks of yellowing papers bound with jute string.

The piece of paper in Anne's hand guided her to the precise location of the book Marco wanted–down to the isle and row. *Almost like Ikea*, Anne thought.

She took down the book and looked at the

gothic lettering on the front cover. *Something in old German,* Anne thought. The book had a thick embossed leather cover and she could see from the edging of the pages that they had been hand cut. She wanted to sneak a peek inside to look at the lettering and any images before taking it to the front.

At one end of the stacks was a table with a cloth pedestal designed specifically for examining books. Marco had shown her the proper way to look through old books. While Anne had thought that you have to use white cotton gloves to leaf through the pages, to protect them from the oils on the skin, she was surprised when Marco had explained that the newest theory in book preservation was not to use gloves. The fibers in the gloves had the tendency to get caught in the rough edges of old books and create minor, and not so minor, tears in the pages.

Anne noticed that there was a book already on the pedestal of the table. *How odd,* she thought. Marco usually put books away and did not leave antique books laying like that on the table. She looked at the book more closely, and it was not an antique book after all. It was some sort of a ledger.

Anne heard Marco's wheelchair rolling on the smooth concrete floor. "Have you located the book?" he asked, moving towards her.

"Yes, sorry. Here it is," she handed the leather

volume to Marco. "I'll just put this book away," she said pointing to the book on the table. But Marco was already moving to the front.

Maggie jumped up on the table and sat next to the book. Anne gave her a gentle scratch under her chin.

"So what is this doing here," Anne asked the cat. "It's not an old book. It's not a book at all." Anne closed the book and checked the cover. *No title*. Anne wondered if it was part of the inventory. She leafed through its pages. It was clearly a ledger. There were dates, names, titles of books. Anne wondered whose ledger this was. She knew the bookstore had an electronic inventory and a customer order system.

And how did the ledger get on the table? Did Marco put it there? The table had a lever on the side to lower it and raise it, so that Marco could use it at a convenient height. But it was raised to full standing height. It wouldn't be Marco. He would have the table at sitting level.

Is the store at it again, Anne wondered, her stomach doing a little flip. Her mind slipped to her first week at the store. While several strange things had happened at the start, like unexpectedly locked doors and books appearing as if out of nowhere, life in the store had been completely uneventful over the past few weeks.

Anne had approached Marco about what she had thought were strange phenomena in the store, but he had dismissed them as a coincidence. And she had to agree. They all seemed innocuous–a book left here, a door locked there, a cat jumping at an opportune moment. *But that is a lot of coincidences*, Anne had thought at the time.

As the weeks passed, however, even Anne had started doubting her original impression of the store and by now had brushed off everything as her overactive imagination, fed by the gothic atmosphere of the store.

And while a ledger left on a table was a harmless enough thing, its appearance brought back to Anne all of her initial feelings about the store with the force of a tidal wave. Anne could hear the blood rush past her ears.

She walked to the front of the store, carrying the ledger slightly away from her body, as if it could attack her. A customer was just walking up the stone steps to exit the store, so Anne saw her opportunity to approach Marco. She placed the thick book on the counter. "Hey, Marco, do you know what this is?" she asked.

Marco looked at the book and leafed through the pages. "It's one of the ledgers from the store, from about eight years ago. Where did you get it?" he asked, turning to Anne.

"It was sitting open on the table at the back. I thought you'd put it there."

"No, it wasn't me. That's strange," Marco said,

looking back towards the corridor and the stacks beyond.

You see, another strange thing, Anne thought, her stomach squeezing tighter. Outloud, she said, "You used to keep a written ledger? Not an electronic one?"

"Yes," Marco smiled. "I enjoyed the feeling of writing the orders in. I still do. It's so much easier to leaf through the ledger and find something, instead of searching that infernal database. It's like the difference between leafing through a book and reading one on an electronic reader. With a paper book you have an instinctive feeling of where a favorite passage, for example, or a quote you're looking for, might be–towards the front, the middle, the back." He paused, as if thinking back to the good old times. "It's like that with paper ledgers, I knew exactly where to look to find the information I needed, like previous orders, or leafing through to see a customer's buying pattern, and so on. But Alex convinced me I needed to move into the modern world and set up an electronic database and customer management system. It makes it much easier to do inventory, and accounting, and taxes, I'll give her that. But I feel like I've lost touch with what customers order exactly," he said, leafing gently through the pages. "Do you mind putting it back its place?" he asked Anne.

"I'm not sure where that is," Anne said, taking

the book.

"The bookcases that run along the wall on the right side of my office. You'll see other ledgers there as well."

Anne went to the back, but before putting the ledger away, she decided to look through it. If the events last month were anything to go by, she had learned that she shouldn't ignore randomly appearing books. They tended to give her clues. *But clues to what,* Anne wondered. *I'm not searching for anything.*

Maggie was waiting for her at the table, just where Anne had left her.

Anne leafed through the ledger aimlessly. Since she didn't know what she was looking for, she hoped that the store would give her a sign. Maggie flicked her tail from side to side, measuring each flip of the page like a metronome. The cat was getting bored. She walked towards Anne, butted her head and started purring. Anne was also getting bored with flipping through the ledger. She stopped and petted Maggie's soft fur. Clearly enjoying the attention, the cat got closer to Anne and sat on top of the book.

"Oh, don't do that," Anne spoke to the cat. "I'm sure Marco won't appreciate your bum on his ledger." Anne scooped up the cat and placed it on the floor. She straightened up and was about to close the book, when a word caught her attention. *Price.*

It wasn't 'price' as in the cost of something. It was a name. *K. Price.* At first Anne thought the name caught her attention simply because it was short and English, and stood out from among all the other long, Germanic, Italian, and French names. But it was something else. *Of course! It's the name from the newspaper this morning,* Anne thought.

Anne started looking through the book more carefully. She saw the name appear several more times in the ledger. Had Kathleen Price been a customer of this bookstore?

Anne started writing the names of the books the woman had purchased. A lot of them were in Latin, some in German, but a few English titles stood out to Anne, mostly because those were the titles she could understand: *The Green Witch Apothecary; Alpine Healing Herbs & Herbal Cures; The Swiss Witch Dispensary; Magical Herbs of Europe; Witch Herbs & Magic Plants: The power of plants; Herbal Magic Spells; Botanical Folk Medicine; Encyclopedia of Medical Botany; Herbal Book of Shadows; Alpine Witchcraft; Healing Alpine Plants.*

If nothing else, K. Price had consistent reading interests.

But it all fit. Hadn't one of the newspaper articles mentioned that Kathleen Price was indeed nicknamed 'The Witch' for her interest in folk remedies?

The more Anne thought about it, the more connections she saw. Wasn't the cosmetic industry a bit like witchcraft–an industry of modern-day witches, concocting potions through science and biochemistry. In essence, the cosmetic industry was doing exactly what witches were purported to do–extracting wondrous ingredients from plants. Plus, the cosmetic industry resembled witchcraft in another way; the cosmetic industry used its fair share of magical thinking in its advertising to shift billions of dollars worth of potions each year.

Pulling her thoughts back to the ledger, Anne wrote the names of the books. She hoped that at least some of them would still be available. Anne admitted to herself that she was more than curious to see what could have interested a cosmetics executive among books on folklore and magic.

But when she put the titles into the store's database, none of the books came up as available.

Anne looked through more ledgers. She pulled down ledgers from the years before and the years after the ledger she had.

And sure enough, the name K. Price came up several more times. Anne continued to write the book titles and look them up in the system. And at last, there it was, flashing on the screen in front of her, one title. She got a hit: *Collected Folk Remedies of the Alps: Healing Herbs of the Lepontine.* Anne slid her eyes to the right hand side of the screen. *Three copies*, she read to herself. But she didn't recognize the location–*AN*.

Anne had hoped to be able to locate the books herself, without Marco's help. She guessed he might not appreciate her snooping around his old ledgers. *And why am I snooping,* Anne asked herself. *What am I trying to find?* But Anne had to admit that the dead woman's reading selection made her curious. What was Kathleen Price searching for? Was it some ancient and forgotten wisdom, some lost truth?

In addition to her natural curiosity about witches, the reading list had piqued Anne's professional interest in pharmaceuticals.

There was no way around it, she'd have to ask Marco about the book's location.

"I was wondering where you'd disappeared to," Anne jumped at Marco's voice behind her. "I see you've been looking for something in the old ledgers. Did you find anything interesting?"

Anne was not sure what to say. She felt like she'd be caught doing something illicit, but Marco didn't seem upset. So Anne decided to share her findings with him.

"Did you read about the death at the pagan festival?" Anne asked Marco.

"Yes," he paused, as if choosing his next word carefully, "tragic. My friend Davide is one of the organizers. I spoke to him this morning, after I read the news. The death came as a shock to them. They've had nothing like it at the festival before. Apparently it'd happened yesterday evening during the main act. Everyone was at the concert stage to see a band 'Aire Melodikoa' from Basque perform. It's a big band in the community. Quite popular. Some sort of ethereal world music fusion band. Neo-pagan Gnostic music, or something like that. The death, a drowning, I think"–Maco looked up at Anne for confirmation of that detail, and she nodded in agreement–"happened out of the way, behind one of the food tents on the edge of the festival. No witnesses."

"Did he tell you anything about the woman?" Anne asked, curious for more insider information.

Marco shook his head. "No, I didn't want to pry."

"I don't think the local newspapers mentioned it," Anne said, "but the English-language newspaper from Zurich said the woman was Kathleen Price, an American. And I found her name in your ledgers. Or at least, I think I did. I think she used to be a customer of your store..." she trailed off, still unsure if Marco was upset about her intrusion into the store's ledgers.

"Was she now?" Marco said. He paused for a moment, looking at mid-distance. "Yes, I remember her now, very clearly, actually. She was a researcher, a biochemist from Zurich. She used to email me every week searching for books on folk remedies, herbs, witch lore, old wives' tales…I'd forgotten about her. Her enquiries stopped as suddenly as they'd started. At the time, I just assumed she had located whatever she'd been looking for. But I remember I found it strange that someone who is a scientist would be so interested in witchcraft–"

"I know, me too," Anne interrupted him. "But it kind of fits. She worked in the cosmetic industry, and cosmetics are not that far removed from magic potions and magical promises. Don't you think?"

"I guess," Marco said. "So, what have you found?"

"Well, I looked up all the books she had ordered from you to see if you had copies of any of them in stock. I was just interested to see what she was reading. A professional interest," Anne said, not wanting to reveal that it was actually the witch aspect that had lured her in.

"Yes, you were a researcher as well. I can see the attraction," Marco said.

"But I found only one book still in stock, three copies. But I don't recognize the location. What does 'AN' stand for?"

Marco rolled closer to the computer screen. "That's '*annesso*'–annex I think you call it in English. It's up there," he indicated the gallery at the back of the store.

The gallery was an area at the very end of the store. A metal staircase led up to a second floor gallery. It was always plunged in darkness, and Anne had never had the opportunity to go explore it. It had seemed abandoned to her. Plus, she had no idea how Marco could get up there with his wheelchair. Maybe he never had to. Or maybe Alex got the books located there for him.

"What's up there? Can I go get this book? I'm interested in reading it," Anne said.

"Sure, you can. But that book is the only book of value you'll find up there," Marco said, his eyes fixed on the dark abyss that was the gallery.

Anne waited. She felt like there was a story behind the remark.

"Stored up there are publications from a defunct publishing house–Celestial Press. It was operated by a friend of mine. Not a very successful one, and he went bankrupt in the late 1990s. I think it was 1997. Right about the time I opened this bookstore, actually. I bought his entire inventory and now keep it in the annex."

"Are they all in English?" Anne asked. It hadn't escaped her notice that the book was in English, unlike most of the books in Marco's store.

"Yes, he published mostly in English. English being the current *lingua franca* and all, he thought he would find a larger audience for his publications if they were in English."

"You don't have any of the publications listed online," Anne said. While they had been talking, she had clicked around the inventory and noticed that while the books from Celestial Press were listed in the inventory, they were not live in the bookstore's online shop for customers to see and purchase.

"No, they are not right for my customers. I sell mostly historical materials. I don't want to confuse my customers," Marco said. "Celestial Press published mostly new-age things, revelations, ancient visits from aliens, occult stuff…"

"We should set up a stall at the pagan fest next year with those books," Anne joked.

"It might not be a bad idea," Marco laughed. "But the *Healing Herbs of Lepontine Alps* book you found is probably one of the few genuinely good books that he published. It contains lots of valuable folk wisdom."

"It says we have three copies of it. Can we put them up online?"

"Okay. But let's also make a digital copy of the book to keep," Marco said.

5 Last-minute customer

Adding *Collected Folk Remedies of the Alps: Healing Herbs of the Lepontine* to the online store was easy. The book was already in the inventory, so all Anne had to do was to make it live. She spent the rest of the afternoon sitting in her office, digitizing the book.

"Do you mind locking the front door?" Marco called out from the back, from among the stacks. "It's five minutes to closing. Let's lock up before any more customers come in. It's been a busy day."

"Okay," Anne called back.

Anne walked to the front and as she came up the three stone steps that led to the front door, the front door swung open, almost hitting her in the face.

The man at the door excused himself and rattled off something quickly in Italian.

"I'm sorry, but we are just about to close," Anne answered in English, hoping he would catch the drift that they were closing.

"Pardon me. I understand you are closing. But I wonder if you could keep the store open for a few more minutes," the man said in English, with strong German overtones. "I would like to purchase all your copies of *Healing Herbs of the Alps*. I saw you have it listed as available. I hope I am not too late to make my purchase?"

"Oh," Anne said, surprised. *That was fast,* she thought. She had just listed the books online a few hours ago. No more than four or five hours. How did he find them so fast?...And why was he in such a hurry to buy *all* the copies?...Yes, the store was closed tomorrow, because it was Sunday, but couldn't he wait until Monday?

"I'm sorry, but can you come back on Monday? We're just in the process of digitizing the book–"

"Digitizing them?" The man yelped, as if surprised. "No, no. I can't wait. I'd like to buy them now," he said, with a note of determination in his voice.

Anne realized how funny they probably looked to any passers-by, perched on the store's threshold, with the door between them as a shield. An impasse. What could Anne say to make him leave?

"If you are leaving Ascona today," Anne said, trying to be accommodating and not sound rude, "we can ship the books to you, if you leave us your address. I should be done with the book by the end of Monday."

The man stood there, with his hand planted

firmly on the door handle. He was clearly thinking and going over his options.

Why are the books so important to him, Anne wondered.

"Very well, if you will not let me into the store, here is my card," the man said, handing a business card to Anne. "Please put the books on reserve for me and send them to me on Monday. Please take the books offline, so no one else can purchase them. You may send an invoice to the address on the card."

Asking to pay by invoice was normal in Switzerland, as Anne had learned. In the US only businesses paid by invoice, but in Switzerland even regular people could request to be invoiced for a purchase, especially when purchasing through websites.

Anne looked down at the man's business card. It listed Orselina as his address. She actually knew where that was. It was a community in the hills above Locarno. She had driven with Ben through there in the fall, on their way to Cardada, a mountain just above Orselina. The views of Lake Maggiore from there were breathtaking.

"Well, I look forward to receiving the books. Good evening," the man said, interrupting Anne's thoughts.

As he walked away, he abruptly turned around. "Did you say you were making a digital copy of the book? For what purpose do you plan to use the digital copy?"

"Ugh," Anne said, unsure if that was any of his business. "Just to keep a copy for our records. Some of the books we sell are quite rare and they only pass through our store once."

"But you do not plan to put that copy online for all to read?" the man asked.

"I don't think so," Anne answered. "We'll ship the books to you when they are ready," she said, and closed the door before he could reply.

❖ ❖ ❖

"You'll never believe this," Anne said when she found Marco in the back. "Someone just came in and requested to buy *all* the copies we have of the *Healing Herbs* book."

"That was quick," Marco said, and raised his eyebrows. "Maybe he had a Google alert set up on the title. I knew it was a good book, even so," he shook his head as if in disbelief.

Anne looked at Marco for a few moments, trying to figure out why someone would be so interested in an old book as to set up a Google alert on it. But maybe that's what book collectors did.

"He wanted to take all the copies right now. But I wouldn't let him. He gave me his card to ship them when we are done digitizing. On invoice," Anne said. "That's okay, right?"

"Yes, that should be fine. Let me see," Marco extended his hand for the card. "A local man. Gunter Keller. That is a Swiss German name. Probably from the northern part of Switzerland, originally. Doesn't list his profession, though. I wonder what he wants with the book. And you said he wants all three copies?"

"Yes," Anne said.

"Maybe he will resell them. Maybe he has specialized buyers looking for it. The print run of that book was not big to begin with. I don't know how many copies are on the market now, but the book could be valuable," Marco said, and sat silent for a few moments. "Oh well, let's go. See you Monday, Anne."

"See you Monday, Marco," Anne answered.

6 Witchwort

"What are you reading?" Ben asked Anne.

They were sitting on the couch. Their apartment was small by American standards, but Anne loved its thick stone walls–the stones' roughness still visible under the whitewash–and exposed dark wood beams. The apartment was on the second floor of a renovated medieval stone house, a *rustico*, typical for the Ticino region, built from the same gray Ticino granite visible everywhere in the Old Town. From houses to church bell towers, to bridges, to garden walls, the gray stone was ubiquitous in the region.

Ben was flipping through the TV channels and not finding anything. Even with channels in English, German, Italian, and French to choose from, they still had trouble deciding what to watch in the eveting. Anne could always fall back on the continuous reruns of *Midsomer Murders* on the British channels, or on one of the Italian channels (where the show was called *Inspector Barnaby*), but Ben didn't like murder mystery shows. So they usually ended up watching one of the nightly shows on the British channels about train journeys through the UK. Ben and Anne joked that, with so many train programs–from scenic train routes, to train station architecture, to shows about the history of Great Britain told through train journeys, to documentaries about heritage steam train lines–there should just be a British channel devoted entirely to train programs.

"It's a book of recipes and remedies using herbs and plants found in the Alps," Anne said. Before leaving the store, Anne had slipped a copy of the *Collected Folk Remedies of the Alps: Healing Herbs of the Lepontine* book she had been digitizing into her purse. "You know the murdered woman we read about this morning? Well, it turns out, she was a customer of the bookstore. Can you believe it? And this is one of the books she had ordered from Marco. Plus, and this is where it gets strange, as Marco would say, we had three copies of the book left in stock, listed them online today, and within hours, a man came asking to buy them all."

"Let me see," Ben reached for the book. He flipped through it. "I don't see what is so special about it. It's not even old." He handed the book back to Anne.

"Marco said it's a good book. That there was a lot of valuable information in it. I want to see if something jumps out at me. Maybe there is a recipe in here that is special. You know, Kathleen

Price, the dead woman, she seemed to have been interested in old folklore recipes and green witch stuff, nature-witch type of recipes. I bet she was looking for old wives' remedies and ingredients she could examine for use in cosmetics. I just don't know why that man today was so interested in this book. Marco said the copies were probably worth a lot to the right buyer." Anne flipped to the cover again, "Do you know what 'Lepontine' means? I feel like I've seen that word somewhere else, but can't put my finger on it."

Ben typed on his phone and read through the results. "Lepontine refers to the Alps that are in our part of Switzerland, in the Ticino canton, plus a couple of neighboring cantons. But basically it's the name for the Alps here in our region."

"So it's healing herbs found in our region. Interesting," Anne said. "Let's see what the book says."

Most of the recipes in the book turned out to be various teas and tinctures to be taken internally for digestion problems; internal maladies, such as liver problems or kidney stones; headaches.

Anne's professional interest was piqued. She was familiar with the powerful ingredients that could be extracted from plants. Pharmaceutical companies spent significant chunks of their budgets going to remote corners of the world, looking for plants with unique properties and compounds.

And then she saw it. She knew that that was the recipe Kathleen had been looking for. It was a remedy for healing the skin. The text accompanying it claimed the salve could heal anything from a skin rash to sun and wind burns, to speeding up healing of cuts and wounds, and reducing old scarring. *Quite a tall order,* Anne thought.

"Listen to this, Ben. There is a recipe here for a skin ointment that sounds pretty miraculous. It claims to heal all sorts of skin issues and wounds. The book says it's a plant that 'the people of the region call *witchwort*–a reference to its miraculous curative powers known to the shepherds and residents of high altitude Alpine villages. Spending months–from early April to late October–isolated high in the mountains, grazing their flock of sheep or herds of cows, living in stone huts, *rusticos*, with little contact with others, and no means to call for help, shepherds had to treat maladies themselves, and passed down, from generation to generation, intimate knowledge of the healing powers of various plants. None as powerful as witchwort.' And it's found only at high altitudes in the Alps, above the treeline. I bet this was what the woman was interested in. If these properties are true," Anne looked up from the book to Ben, "then that would probably have made it a very valuable discovery to Kathleen Price."

Anne spent the rest of the evening looking up witchwort–*Saponaria venefica*, to give it its proper scientific name–online. It was a member of the soapwort family of plants, but other specific information about it was scant.

Anne got only one direct match–an article published in 1978, in the journal of *Plant Ecology*. In addition to being the only direct match for witchwort, the article caught Anne's attention for another reason. The author of the article was Prof. Grewald. *So that's where I've seen the term 'Lepontine' before,* Anne said to herself.

She went to get her bag and pulled out a copy of the auction catalog from yesterday. She flipped through the pages, looking for one auction item in particular. And there, among the exquisitely illustrated, and sometimes even illuminated, botanical books on offer at the auction, was Prof. Grewald's field log. The catalog description listed it as a 'field journal of Prof. Grewald's specimen collecting expeditions in the Lepontine Alps, 1975-1980, with dates, locations, and inventory of specimens collected'.

This was what Kathleen Price had bid on so enthusiastically. *But why did Kathleen Price want this field log?* Anne wondered. The article in Plant Ecology already listed the exact location of the witchwort plants Prof. Grewald had located.

Anne had more success looking up 'refugia plants', a term she had discovered in Prof. Grewald's article.

Witchwort was what botanists called a refugia plant–plants that had survived unfavorable conditions, conditions that had wiped out a lot of other plants and organisms, by retreating to isolated areas. The term was most often applied to plants that had survived during the last ice age by retreating to ice-free refuges, called Nunataks, at the very tips of the Alps. Several such plants were still found in the Alps today.

Witchwort had escaped the destructive sweep of the glaciers by retreating to the top of the Lepontine Alps. *It's an ice-age relic,* Anne thought.

Digging deeper into refugia plants, Anne discovered they were of special interest to the cosmetic industry.

An article published just four years ago, in the cosmetic industry trade journal *Advances in Cosmetics*, talked about the special chemical compounds and repair mechanisms of refugia plants that made them resistant to UV damage at high altitude. Those same compounds made them ideal candidates for cosmetics. The compounds that protected the cells of refugia plants from UV damage, high at the bare tops of the Alps, and repaired their cells, had skin regenerative properties in humans.

This was groundbreaking stuff. The plant's stem cells protected it from UV damage and promoted cell regeneration when damage occurred.

Through the use of biotechnology, cosmetics companies were able to extract and cultivate these plant stem cells. But they need raw material, the plants themselves, to harvest the stem cells.

None of the cosmetic industry articles she found on the topic, however, mentioned the witchwort plant. Had it gone extinct since the professor had located it?

And how did all this information fit together? Prof. Grewald's article from 1978; his field log that Kathleen Price purchased at the auction; the *Collected Folk Remedies of the Alps: Healing Herbs of the Lepontine* book sitting in Anne's lap, that Kathleen had purchased from Marco many years ago; and the articles about recent research on refugia plants, and their stem cells, for use in cosmetics. Anne couldn't work it out, but she thought somehow all of these were connected.

Whoever wrote the *Healing Herbs* book knew about the witchwort, and so did Prof. Grewald, and so did Kathleen Price. Anne flipped to the first pages of the *Healing Herbs* book–it was published in 1983.

All of these publications are separated by decades, Anne thought. *Is that significant?*

Could Prof. Grewald have also been killed? Had his death been natural, or did he die under suspicious circumstances? And if he was killed, was his murder connected to Kathlee Price's murder?

Stop it, Anne told herself. *The professor was not killed. He was just an old man.* But she made a mental note to look into it further.

And maybe Kathleen Price's murder had been unrelated to her work and research. Maybe it was something personal. Anne's mind jumped to the lunch after the auction in Locarno. Anne was sure the argument she witnessed was personal in nature.

She pushed the murder out of her mind and spent the rest of the evening reading the various recipes in the book and looking up the plants mentioned in it online. She wondered if she could go foraging and recreate some of the recipes in her kitchen.

7 The witching hour

Anne had a restless sleep. In her dream she kept trying to remember something, she kept repeating it, re-reading it, but then when she tried to remember it, it was gone. She had to say a short text, she was sure of it, to perform a poem in front of an audience, but she couldn't remember her lines. She kept getting the dates wrong. Was it dates? Or was it a text? She couldn't remember. And she couldn't remember the title of the poem. But was it a poem? Or was it now a science paper on which she had to do a presentation? She was at a science conference and everyone was staring at her. She was sure her boss would be mad if she didn't make a good impression. She desperately tried to remember what it was she was supposed to say.

Anne woke up with a start. Her still sleepy brain slowly realized that it was just a dream. She was not a science researcher any more. There were no more presentations and conferences to worry about. In the soft darkness, she looked over at Ben, sleeping on her right, and listened to the slow, steady breaths marking his deep sleep.

She got up slowly and quietly, snuck out of the room, and closed the door softly behind her, so as not to wake him up.

In the living room, soft gray light slipped in from the windows. The faint light visible at the horizon announced that dawn was breaking somewhere far away, but not here yet.

Four in the morning. *The tail end of the witching hour*, Anne thought.

Her thought traveled back to her disturbed sleep. She was glad it was only a dream. Lately, she kept having dreams about her old job, always worrying about something she'd forgotten or something she'd missed to do. She explained it to herself as her subconscious letting go of all the stress she had internalized over the years. *And reading all those science articles yesterday probably just reminded me of my research days,* Anne thought.

She felt relief pour over her tense muscles at the thought that she didn't have to go to a lab in the morning. Just a bookstore. And it was Sunday. *So no work until Monday*, she reminded herself.

Anne didn't feel like going back to bed. She looked out of the window. She had never explored the town this early in the morning. It would be magical to see its streets right at dawn, before anyone woke up.

She pulled on a pair of yoga pants, put on a

jacket and her running shoes, and slipped out of the house. With any luck, Ben wouldn't wake up before she was back and worry about where she was. She checked to make sure she had her phone, just in case.

Outside, all was in darkness. As safe as Switzerland was, Anne decided that she would avoid the dark alleyways. They didn't have any light and she might trip on something. She turned left to head to the promenade.

Ahead, the smooth surface of the lake looked like a sheet of dark silver, little waves undulating on its surface. The silver glow of dawn reflected in the dark lake. A faint glow behind the mountains outlined their dark peaks against the sky.

As she walked, the pre-dawn air enveloped her, and a damp chill seeped through the layers of her clothes. Anne shook off a shiver. She had rarely experienced such stillness. It was as if the air was still sleeping.

But as her senses adjusted, she noticed that although there was no breeze, the air was filled with the chirps, and calls, and early morning songs of birds. Hundreds of thrills and crescendos. As if each bird was trying to outdo the other in its call. All welcoming the coming day. Anne had never noticed birds being so loud during the day. Maybe their songs were drowned out by the hum of modern life. Or maybe they just sang loudest at dawn.

Small waves lapped softly against the paved shore and the stone steps leading down to the water. Anne looked at the windows of the hotels along the promenade. Most of them were black, but a few, on the ground floors, were lit. *Probably staff getting ready for the day*, she thought.

Anne turned the corner and found herself on the shopping street. Up ahead was the bookstore. In the cold blue light of the morning, all colors were muted and the gray store didn't look as out of place as during the day, when the bright stores surrounding it displayed their vivid colors.

Anne walked up to the store windows and looked inside. She was not sure what she was looking for. Maybe she wanted to recapture that feeling of wonder she had experienced the first time she had discovered the old store and had looked through its windows to see the apothecary shelves lined with books.

All was dark. But as her eyes adjusted, she saw a faint luminescence. It reminded her of a similar glow she had seen emanating from the store's walls one evening. But that had turned out to be just her imagination, and the walls had glowed in the golden light of the setting sun.

But this light was different. The light moved. Anne's heart skipped. Someone was in the back of the store. She was sure of it. Was it Marco? Maybe. *But what would he be doing here so early*, Anne wondered.

Anne didn't have a key for the front door. Marco, because of his wheelchair, and the steps leading down from the front door of the store, always used the back entrance.

Anne retraced her steps, and hurried back down the street, turned right, and took the narrow path that ran behind the stores and served as an access to the back entrances.

The bookstore's back door was slightly ajar. She touched it gently, to open it. But something pale caught her eye. Slivers of light wood jutted out from the dark door. Even in the faint morning light Anne could see that there were splinters around the lock, where the door had been forced open.

She wasn't sure what to do. Should she phone Marco? Why would anyone break into the store? *Because there are so many valuable books here*, Anne answered herself. Her thoughts leaped to all the books that Marco had in the store. She hoped the most important ones were locked behind that fireproof door below the gallery, and that whoever was in the store could not break through it as easily as the entrance door.

Anne pushed the door slowly and slipped into the darkness of the store. She planned to sneak in silently and see what was going on. She'd take something heavy and hit whoever it was over the head if needed. Then she'll call Marco and the police.

In the dark, she could clearly see a light dancing around in Marco's office. And she could hear the person rummaging and books falling on the ground. She walked softly, winding her way among the stacks, waiting for her eyes to adjust to the darkness.

And then it happened. She bumped into a cart stacked with books and it gave off a traitorous squeak. The sound was amplified by the metal bookcases and the concrete floor, and reverberated with a deafening ringing in the complete silence among the stacks.

The rummaging in the office stopped. Anne saw the light move fast from the office toward the back door. She heard feet running. She ran after the light and the dark figure behind it. But the person had a head start. The back door slammed with a bang against the wall as the person opened it with force and slammed back again against the door frame as it closed. Anne ran after the thief, but as she got to the back alley, she couldn't see which way the person had gone. She listened to hear running, but there was only silence. The person was smart enough to hide in the shadows.

❖ ❖ ❖

"This is my grandmother's book," Marco said, leafing through the copy of *Healing Herbs* Anne had taken the previous evening home with her.

After losing the thief in the darkness, Anne had decided not to waste her time chasing after shadows. Plus, all of a sudden, fear had overtaken her. She didn't want to be attacked in a dark alley.

Instead, she had called Marco to tell him about the break-in. He arrived with Alex, and the three of them had gone through the store to determine what was missing.

But after about an hour, the only thing that seemed to have been disturbed were Marco's and Anne's offices. Marco's office was completely ransacked. It was as if the thief was looking for something specific. But Marco couldn't identify anything in particular that might be missing from his office.

None of the valuable books, which Marco inexplicably kept out in the open, in the stacks, were touched.

Going through her own office, Anne had realized that the two copies of the book she was scanning the previous day were missing. Her thoughts jumped to the impatient man who had visited the store at closing time. And she immediately suspected him of the break-in.

She shared her theory with Marco, who said they needed to keep an open mind until the police had had a chance to investigate.

Anne had texted her husband to let him know what was going on, and to ask him to bring the copy of the book to the store. When Ben arrived, slightly bewildered about being summoned to the store at such an early hour on a Sunday, Anne had extracted a small piece of paper from among the book's pages. On it were the name and address of her suspected thief.

If Anne was right, the person–Gunter Keller, she had looked at the name on the card–who had wanted to buy the books so desperately the previous afternoon, had come back during the night looking for the copies.

Anne had used his business card as a bookmark. *Good thing I took a copy home*, she thought. If he had stolen all three copies, with his business card inside one of them, they would never have known who he was.

Eventually they had called the police, but since it was Sunday, and no one was hurt, the police came only for a cursory glance around the store. The two policemen told Marco to make a full statement, and to report any missing items for insurance purposes, at the police station on Monday.

"My grandmother arrived from England in the 1930s. The lakes of Northern Italy and Southern Switzerland were quite popular summer destinations," Marco continued. "She might have even socialized with the art colony on Caresio island...My grandmother was the one that taught me English," Marco said.

That surprised Anne. She had always assumed that Marco had learned English from Alex.

"My grandfather and grandmother found each other one summer. Maybe my grandmother had heard about my grandfather, or his accomplishments. Or maybe it was the other way around, but it was like the pot finding its lid.

"My grandfather was a chemist, pharmacist you would call him, but also an experimental chemist. He came from a long line of physicians, apothecaries, and alchemists. He claimed to be a descendent of Paracelsus, the noted 16th century Swiss physician and alchemist, credited with the invention of laudanum, an opium-based pill used for relief of dysentery and many other illnesses. A Renaissance physician in any sense of the word, he was one of the first to use chemicals and minerals in medicine. And to use specific chemicals to treat specific illnesses. Like in modern medicine. From what I've read about him, Paracelsus was a fascinating man and well ahead of his time. He anticipated antiseptics and the germ theory. We're lucky to have some of his books and writings in our possession. And like your Kathleen Price, he investigated folk medicine because he believed it served as a repository of ancient wisdom and knowledge."

Marco paused and let his gaze linger over the apothecary shelves. "This store had been in the family for generations, before I turned it into a bookstore.

"While Paracelsus would have to be one of my most illustrious ancestors, my family had always included successful healers. Some were so successful at curing the ill that they were accused of witchcraft. But the family was well off enough to buy their way out of any tight spots and avoided any serious persecutions or prosecutions. Not so for the many innocent people who were burned at the stake."

A chill passed over Anne. She knew what Marco was referring to. Since working in the bookstore, she had started reading more about Swiss history. Most of it was a complete jumble in her head of dates, cantons, and wars. But one part of the Swiss historical record stood out clearly to her–Switzerland's zeal for persecuting witches.

On a per capita basis, Switzerland's fervor for witch hunting surpassed even that of Germany or Scotland. From the first execution in 1428, until the last, of Anna Goeldi, in 1782–long after witch hunting had gone out of fashion in the rest of Europe–the Swiss killed over 5,600 people for witchcraft. Witch-hunting mania reached a fever pitch during the reformation and counterreformation of the 16th century, when Protestant and Catholic churches competed to attract new members. Witch hunts, trials, and executions demonstrated to the masses, in no uncertain terms, each church's ability to protect their members from evil. Fiery sermons by pious preachers, like John Calvin, who urged officials to wipe out the race of witches, fanned the flames of fear and retribution.

"While my grandfather was a skilled chemist," Marco's voice pulled Anne back to the present, "my grandmother was a gifted herbalist. After marrying my grandfather, she devoted years to collecting traditional knowledge of folk medicine and cures from around Switzerland. This book," Marco indicated the volume in his hands, "was a sliver of her collected knowledge. I still have so many of her notes and unpublished manuscripts.

"She spent time with shepherds in the Alps, learning about the different plants that grew there. She taught me that cows that graze on different pastures produce different tasting cheese. Each pasture high in the Alps has its own unique microclimate, from the amount of sun it gets, to the composition of the soil, to the amount of wind. So each pasture has its own unique combination of plants, flowers, and herbs growing. That gives the milk, and then the cheese, unique flavors."

Anne nodded. It reminded her of the time last fall when she had gone with Ben to a local cheese festival and had been surprised to find that each stall sold seemingly exactly the same cheese–a small wheel of yellow cheese with a gray, moldy-looking crust. It had taken her a second pass through the market to notice that each stall displayed a sign with a photo of a mountain hill with a name under it, such as 'Alp di Lorezzo' or 'Alp Ostalia'. The name always included the word 'alp'. It was only after Ben had searched online that they had discovered that in Switzerland 'alp' meant not only the tall mountains that traversed the country but also referred to the mountainside pastures where cows and sheep grazed during the summer. And each pasture had its own name. So each stall at the cheese festival listed the exact mountain pasture–*alp*–from which the milk and cheese came. And while Anne couldn't tell apart one gray cheese wheel from another, she noticed that some stalls had more customers. She had decided that the locals were able to taste the difference in cheese and had their own preferences.

"How come you didn't follow in your family's footsteps and become a pharmacist or a doctor?" Anne asked, curious about why Marco had transformed the apothecary into a bookstore.

"Oh, that's a long story. A story for another day," he said, dismissing her question with a gentle shake of his head. Disappointment washed over Anne.

Marco stood looking in midair for a few moments and then continued. "I think my mother was the reason I didn't. Despite being born into a long line of practitioners–from alchemists to doctors–the subtle art of healing, in any of its forms, didn't grace her. She just didn't have the talent for it. She wanted to be good at it, but she wasn't. And it became her obsession.

"Since the time of Paracelsus, my family had always relied on experiments, research, and empirical data for their success. But my mother threw herself into the occult. It ruined her family life, drove away my father, and it probably led to her early death.

"It put me off wanting anything to do with the family legacy. I went the opposite direction. I made the army my career. In the army, there was no room for ethereal matters and the occult."

Marco paused again. Anne stood still. She wondered what had brought on this intimate family revelation. But she was fascinated by his story and didn't want to break the spell. So she didn't dare move. She hadn't realized she was holding her breath until Marco spoke again.

"Within a few months of my mother's death, I had a freak accident during a training exercise that left me partially paralyzed. So I had to think of a new career. I had this store and a lot of valuable family books, writings, and diaries, so I set up an antiquarian."

Anne didn't know what to say. But she also

suspected that Marco wasn't looking for sympathy. That was not the reason he had opened up to her.

Marco's story of rebellion and breaking with family tradition reminded Anne of the art colony she had visited a few weeks ago, where a son had joined the church as an act of rebellion. Anne sent a silent thanks to her parents, Penny, a science teacher, and David, a medieval history professor at a small liberal arts college in New England, for being so ordinary and solid.

"The store is actually not as old as it looks. It's not medieval, that is. A great uncle, several times removed, built it to look like a gothic apothecary, influenced in the design by images of alchemical laboratories he had seen in books. It makes for quite a good bookstore, don't you think?" Marco said, turning to Anne with a smile.

8 The coven

"Have you seen the newspapers?" Marco said, startling Anne.

He had been gone all morning, at the police station, filing a report about the break-in. Anne, sitting at the counter, in case a customer should come in, absorbed in a murder mystery book, hadn't heard him come in at the back.

"No," Anne said, and wondered what news Marco might be referring to. With the pagan festival over–it had ended yesterday evening–Anne didn't think the local newspapers would have anything interesting. Plus, she'd have to rely on the translation app on her phone to understand the articles. And reading a whole article with an app was a painful experience.

"There's been another murder," Marco said, and paused, it seemed to Anne, for effect.

"Another *witch*," he said. He tapped a folded copy of a newspaper in his lap. "The newspapers are having a field day with it. They are calling it a modern-day witch hunt. Two murders of witches, or at least women dressed as witches, in as many days."

"At the festival?" Anne asked.

Marco nodded.

What is going on, Anne thought. *It does sound like a witch hunt.*

"How did she die?" she asked. "When did they find her?"

"They found her early in the morning on Sunday, when opening the festival. She was killed at some point during the night. They have a suspect in custody, it says."

A chill passed over Anne. In the early hours of Sunday she was walking the streets of Ascona and then trying to apprehend a thief. Maybe Switzerland was not as safe as she thought.

"That is strange, you have to admit," Anne said. "I wonder if it was random. Some crazy person attacking women who are dressed as witches? Maybe some crazy local who hates the pagan festival or hates witches?"

"Actually, it doesn't seem random at all." Marco said and spread the newspaper on the counter. "This woman, Olivia Rossetti, was a botanist. The article says that the police have established that she knew Kathleen Price." Marco pointed to a word in the newspaper. "In fact, and here comes the exciting part, they were part of the same *coven*."

"*Coven*?" Anne asked, unable to suppress the surprise in her voice. "What do you mean *coven*?"

"Remember how Kathleen Price was nicknamed 'the Witch'? Well, it turns out that the research department she ran at–" Marco leaned over the newspaper, looking through it, "–at Rubrum Biocosmetics, was staffed by mostly women. And that, coupled with her nickname, earned the department its own moniker in the industry–'the Coven'. But I don't know if that explains why she was dressed like a witch and why she was killed."

"Can I see?" Anne leaned over his shoulder to look at the article. "Sorry, can I take a closer look at this photo?" Anne looked closer at the headshot of the victim. It looked like one you would find on an online career profile. *It's so easy to get pictures of people nowadays with social media and the internet,* Anne thought. She studied the picture for a few moments. She wasn't absolutely sure, but she thought the woman in the picture could be the woman from the restaurant the other day.

"Marco, remember our lunch in Locarno after the auction?"

"Yes," Marco said.

"And remember how a woman came in and started an argument with Kathleen?"

"I heard some commotion, but I didn't see any of it. I had my back to that table, remember?"

"I think that's her. That's the woman who argued with Kathleen Price that day," Anne said, pointing to the picture in the newspaper.

"You're sure?" Marco said, examining the photo. "It's possible, if they worked together. Maybe it's something to do with corporate espionage gone wrong. Those things happen. There's a lot of money at stake. Especially in the cosmetic industry."

"Or," Anne said, wanting to run her theory by Marco, "it could be a lovers' triangle gone wrong. Remember how upset the second woman was, assuming it was this Olivia, to see Kathleen and Patrick at lunch together?"

"It's possible…But now both women are dead. Are you suggesting Patrick killed them both?" Marco said, sounding unsure.

"Well, what if this Olivia killed Kathleen out of jealousy, because Olivia wanted to be his girlfriend, because he's rich? But then Patrick, who was really in love with Kathleen, killed Olivia…" Anne said, trailing off. That theory sounded like a lame soap opera even to her.

Marco laughed.

"Nah. And it seems that the police have their suspect," he said, glancing at the newspaper. "And it's not Partick."

"Does it say who it is?" Anne said. Marco shook his head. "Then how do you know it's not Patrick?" She smiled at Marco, as if that proved her point. But with this second murder, the lovers' triangle theory had lost its sparkle.

A thought popped into Anne's mind.

"Marco, what sort of things does Patrick usually invest in? I mean, does he invest in biomedical and pharmaceutical stuff?"

"No, that's not shiny enough for him," Marco said. "He usually invests in real estate developments, new marinas, new golf courses. Places where he can meet important people. Developments that will get him into newspapers and keep him invited to the best parties. That sort of thing. Now, enough about Patrick," Marco said, with some finality in his voice.

"How did your police report go?" Anne said, changing the subject, and kicking herself for asking about Patrick.

"I told them about the missing books, explained about the man who had shown a great interest in them. I gave them his address," Marco said, and handed the business card back to Anne. "Here, you can go back to using it as a bookmark. Plus, if he's not the thief, we'll need his address to send him a nice letter of apology." Marco winked at her.

Anne froze. *What if this man is innocent*, she thought. All of a sudden she felt so bad for suspecting him without any evidence.

"But is the police going to follow up on him?" Anne asked.

"They took notes, but told me that since nothing really valuable was taken, not to hold out great hope that they'll recover the books or that they'll even arrest this man, assuming he's even the thief. They'll follow up, but if there is no other evidence against him, or if he doesn't confess, there is nothing really they can do–."

At that moment, Marco's phone rang, and he took the call. He wheeled towards the back and Anne remained at the front to give him some privacy.

After the excitement of the previous week, with the pagan festival attendees, and the store break-in, today seemed quiet. There had been only a few customers. Maggie was lounging on the tiled floor, basking in a spot of sun. Anne walked up to the tall gothic windows and looked at the shopping street. *Good thing the thief had the sense to use the back door,* Anne thought. *And that he didn't break these beautiful windows.*

What are these murders about, Anne wondered. Was it all about witches and secret covens? Were the murders connected to the pagan festival? They had to be. Both murders occurred at the festival. Both murders were of witches, or women dressed as such, belonging to a coven. Was Marco's grandmother's book significant somehow? Or was the break-in just a coincidence?

Would Marco's grandmother have called herself a witch? Anne's thoughts jumped. *She was certainly a gifted herbalist interested in folk remedies, and probably would have been called a witch in pre-*

vious centuries.

"Ha!" Marco exclaimed from the corridor, interrupting Anne's thoughts. "You'll never believe this!"

Anne turned to face him, curious to hear what about the call could get him so excited.

"They've caught our thief."

"That's great! So quick?"

"Yes, exactly, but here comes the exciting part," Marco paused for dramatic effect. "The thief is, as we suspected, Gunter Keller, who came in on Saturday to ask about the books. But the reason they were able to locate him so quickly, was that he was already in police custody. He was arrested for the murders of the two women," Marco paused again, as if to give Anne time to process this information. "From the little the police on the phone said, Gunter used to work with Kathleen Price, years ago. They were both in the cosmetic industry."

Anne's mind was spinning. *What did this all mean? How was this Gunter implicated? Was it some old rivalry?*

"But they are letting him go," Marco continued.

What? Anne thought.

"They didn't elaborate, but the person on the phone suggested that the break-in at the store clears Gunter of the murders, somehow," Marco said, and paused again.

There was something in the expression on his face that Anne couldn't read. Was there something he was not telling her? He was smiling like a Cheshire cat.

"The police asked me," he picked up his thread again, slowly, "if I want to press charges against him." He looked at Anne. "But I told the police that instead of pressing charges, I want to talk to him in person. To understand his motivations, so to speak."

Comprehension dawned on Anne and she gave Marco a big smile.

Marco smiled back at her. "He strikes me as a man who can give us some clues. There seems to be some mystery surrounding my grandmother's book, and I wouldn't mind joining you in finding out what that is. So, I've arranged for us to go see this Gunter Keller this afternoon. It will be a nice sunny afternoon in Orselina. Judging by his address, we can expect some wonderful views of the lake," Marco said, and turned his wheelchair in the direction of his office.

9 The thief's story

The road to Orselina wound its way up the side of the mountain, switching back and forth in sharp u-turns. Anne was glad Marco was driving. Used to wide American highways, these narrow mountain roads, sometimes not wide enough for two cars to pass, still made her uneasy.

With each turn, the car climbed higher, and with each turn, Anne could see more of the expanse of the lake below. Colorful houses crowded the steep slopes, as if each jockeying for a perfect view of the lake.

Walls of stacked gray stone paved the sides of the hills and kept them from collapsing onto the road. The slopes on this side of the lake received full sun, from sunrise to sunset, and created the perfect environment for heat-loving tropical plants. Here and there mature agave rosettes clung perilously to the stones, their fleshy leaves overhanging the road. And tale-tale banana leaves swayed in the afternoon breeze.

In the distance, a glimpse of blue among the green trees caught Anne's attention. The funicular from Locarno to Orselina was making its slow ascent. It traveled in an almost straight line up the hill, along a high stone viaduct bridge that traversed the valley below and climbed up the mountainside. Cog teeth on the bottom of the funicular car gripped each step up the bridge with a click as the small train made its way along narrow rails.

Anne loved the shape of the blue funicular car. It leaned forward, like a rhomboid, as if stooping headfirst in an effort to cling tight to its rails over the precipitous valley. The funicular worked like a pulley, with two cars pulling at opposite ends. As one descended, it pulled the other car up. The cars moved along a single track, which split in two in the middle of the course so the two cars could pass each other.

The funicular's final destination in Orselina was the Sanctuary of the Madonna del Sasso. The pilgrimage complex, perched on the edge of a hill, overlooked Lake Maggiore below. In the afternoon sun, the sanctuary–its pale ochre walls and vivid orange tiled roofs illuminated as if from within–appeared to be floating among the green hills.

Marco drove further into Orselina and parked in the wide driveway of a single-storey, mid-century modern house.

Anne got out first to get Marco's wheelchair out of the trunk and unfold it.

Gunter Keller greeted them at the front door. As they entered, the reflection off the black marble floor pulled Anne's eyes towards the vast surface of windows that made up the opposite wall of the house. They walked through an open concept living room, its minimalist decor emphasized by the straight lines of two long leather couches positioned at a right angle to each other, flanking a low square coffee table. The only adornment in the room was a small stack of books at one end of the coffee table.

While the ride up to the house had been beautiful, Anne was not prepared for the view that greeted them as they walked out through a sliding glass door that opened in the wall of windows and into the garden.

Below them, the whole vista of Lake Maggiore opened up. The silvery mirror-like surface of the lake expanded on all sides to the mountains–enveloped in a bluish haze–which marked its shores.

They sat on a large, stone-paved patio, a sail providing triangular shade on the table and chairs underneath. A tall glass pitcher of lemonade, its sides perspiring in the heat, stood on the table. The clear sun brought into a high contrast the intense green of the gardens and palm trees in front of them.

Gunter's garden was a terraced garden typical of the region, if much larger than any Anne had seen. To make gardens on such steep slopes possible, terraces were cut into the hills. Beyond the patio, an azure rectangle, sparkling in the sun, announced a pool on the terrace below. Beyond, Anne could see the tops of trees, flowering bushes, and palm trees on the terraces below.

"I have to begin by apologizing for my behavior," Gunter said. "I have never behaved like this in my life. I don't know what possessed me to break into the store. I can only blame the events of the last few days for my delinquency. But I've made it my life's mission to protect the fragile ecology of alpine plants from unscrupulous cosmetics and pharmaceutical companies. I had to protect that plant."

Anne glanced at Marco. He was nodding as if he understood and agreed with what Gunter was saying. She turned her focus back to Gunter. She was not exactly sure what he was talking about.

Gunter must have noticed the strain on her face because he said, "Maybe I should go back to the beginning."

He adjusted his chair to get the sun off his back and moved under the shade. "I used to be a Marketing Director of a cosmetics company. The same one that Kathleen worked for at the time. She was brilliant, but ruthless. The newspapers communicated that part of her character correctly.

"But she was also very charming. When she

wanted something she turned on a charm that was blinding, and you didn't realize you were being run over by a bulldozer until she was done with you and achieved what she wanted.

"The cosmetic industry is a cut-throat business. Millions go into developing new ingredients, and then you have only a few years to make back your money, before your patent expires, and your competitors are copying your formula and ingredients.

"Kathleen had a knack for discovering new ingredients. She was intelligent and well-read. While most researchers were focused on lab work, she loved exploring old texts for novel plants or forgotten ingredients. That's how she came across this book..." Gunter got up and went through the open glass doors and came back holding a book. Anne recognized it right away as the *Collected Folk Remedies of the Alps: Healing Herbs of the Lepontine* book. *Another copy,* she thought.

"I have my own copy," Gunter said, following Anne's glance and guessing at what she was thinking. "The reason I wanted all the copies was because I wanted to protect the plant...But I'm getting ahead of myself."

Anne sat quiet, unsure where the story was leading. She glanced at Marco again, but he sat patiently, his glance traveling over the surface of the lake, his face not revealing any emotion.

Gunter leafed through the book and came upon the witchwort balm recipe. "Kathleen came up to me one day, some years ago, she had bought this book, from your store I assume, and had found the balm recipe with witchwort, *Saponaria venefica*. She was so excited.

"The cosmetic industry was just starting to research these refugia plants and was discovering that their stem cells were very beneficial to skin regeneration. So this plant sounded very promising. Before coming to me, she had already done her research, and had found an article from a botanist about the plant and its location."

Gunter put down the book and took a sip of lemonade.

"But it turned out that the location in the article was wrong. She couldn't be sure if the author of the article gave the wrong location coordinates in the article on purpose, to protect the plant, or if it was done through an oversight. Either way, it was a misprint that drove Kathleen crazy. She began hounding the professor, but he wasn't swayed by her charm. He was an old man, even at the time, and was only focused on his plants.

"Unable to locate the plant based on the misprinted coordinates in the article, Kathleen even broke into the professor's green house to steal one of his specimens of witchwort...I think that was a warning bell to the professor, and he stopped publishing about refugia plants and began working on other research.

"She was able to extract potent compounds from the stolen specimen. But when she tried to grow and propagate more plants from that one specimen, they didn't produce the exact compounds she needed. They weren't as effective. It turned out that the plant only produced those compounds in its natural habitat. Only the correct combination of sun, wind exposure, and temperature made it exhibit the correct combination of compounds. She couldn't recreate the conditions in the lab, and the plants were not producing the chemicals she needed.

"It became clear that she would need to be a natural supply, a supply from the plant's native location to produce these compounds. So finding the location of the witchwort became paramount. Kathleen employed a talented local botanist, Olivia Rossetti, the woman that was just killed–" he shifted in his seat, "–to help her with the search. But season after season they were not able to locate the right mountain peak. It was like looking for a needle in the proverbial haystack. By then, I had retired from the cosmetic industry and instead focused on preserving the ecology of rare Alpine plants."

Anne glanced around. *Not before you made millions*, she thought.

Gunter followed her glance and said, "Yes,

I had made a lot of money from plants and cosmetics"–*his perception is uncanny*, thought Anne–"and I might have been at times unscrupulous in my marketing claims and techniques, but now I'm using that same money to protect the fragile ecosystem of the Alps. I think of myself as an environmentalist."

Gunter paused. *Is he looking for praise,* Anne wondered. But since none came, he continued. "Kathleen and I had lost touch. Our paths diverged. And then, she was fortuitously murdered."

Anne gasped.

"I'm sorry, I didn't mean it that way," Gunter corrected himself. "I just meant...I would never hurt another human being. I've devoted these past few years to preserving life, even if it's only plant life, not destroying it."

"Where do the books from my store fit in?" Marco interrupted.

Anne could see that he was irritated. She wondered why that might be. Perhaps none of what the avid environmentalist had said so far explained the reason for his break-in at the store. But Anne had to admit that she'd found Gunter's story fascinating. Especially because it corroborated some of what she had discovered on her own.

"Yes, my story has wound its way to that shameful moment. I knew that with Kathleen dead, the search for the witchwort would probably stop. So I wanted to make sure that no one else discovered the plant. I hadn't come across another reference to the plant, except in that article I mentioned. And the misprinted location coordinates meant that the plant was safe–"

Anne was sure that he was referring to the article by Prof. Grewald she had found online. It was the only article that referenced witchwort directly. She turned her attention back to Gunter.

"–so if I could get a hold of every copy of this book–" he lifted his copy of the *Healing Herbs* book, "–on the market, I knew I would be doing the lion's share of protecting the plant from other researchers. I was pretty sure Kathleen hadn't shared her research with any rivals.

"So you see, when you told me you were digitizing the book," Gunter turned to Anne, "I had to get the copies before you could do that. But one copy was missing and I couldn't find it anywhere in the store. And I wanted to find the business card I gave you...I apologize profusely," he now turned to Marco, "I will pay for any damages."

Marco nodded his head in agreement.

"What about Olivia, the second murdered woman? Do you know anything about her?" Anne asked.

Gunter shifted in his chair. Anne realized that her question was a bit forward and might have sounded like an accusation.

"If you mean to ask whether I killed her," Gunter said, with a sting in his voice, "no, I didn't. The police have already cleared me of any suspicion."

"But do you have any theory as to what all of this might be about?" Anne pressed. She didn't mean to be rude, but Gunter was the only person who had known both women and might have his own theory about the murders.

"I'm sorry, but I don't know what it might be all about. It certainly looks like it's about the plant. But that might all be circumstantial. Were they not both dressed like witches and killed at that pagan festival? I'm sure the police will discover that it's some fanatic on a modern-day witch-hunt, as the newspapers say."

A thought crossed Anne's mind, and she wondered whether Gunter knew about the field log Kathleen had bought at the auction. She wondered if Gunter knew anything about it. He hadn't mentioned it, but he seemed to know a lot about the plant.

"Did Kathleen mention anything about a field log?" Anne asked before she could stop herself.

Marco looked at her sharply. She couldn't exactly interpret his look, but instantly regretted asking the question.

"A field log? No, I'm not sure what you are referring to..." Gunter said.

I guess, it is possible that he doesn't know about

it, Anne thought. But she remained skeptical. She reminded herself that the only reason she knew about it was because of the auction. None of the newspapers had mentioned it. *Why have none of the newspapers mentioned it,* Anne wondered. *Maybe it has nothing to do with all of this.*

As there was nothing much left to say, Marco and Anne made their way to the car. Gunter followed them to the door, and as he passed the coffee table, he placed his copy of the *Healing Herbs* book back on top of the neat stack of books on it.

The police had the other copies and would be returning them to Marco after completing their report.

◆ ◆ ◆

"You should not have mentioned the field log from the auction," Marco said to Anne when they got in the car. "You don't know who this person is. He says he's not involved in the murders. But he broke into the store. You are exposing yourself to danger, Anne. Who knows how far he would go to protect this plant. And now he knows you know about it."

They continued their ride down to Ascona in an uneasy silence.

Anne was not angry at Marco for his remark.

He was right. She knew he was just worried about her. But she never actually considered that she might be putting herself in danger. And now there was nothing she could do. She had already asked the question and there was no way to undo it. If she really was in danger, then she would just have to be careful until the killer was caught.

10 Old friends

Anne looked up as the store's bells jingled. A man in brown boat shoes, sun-bleached navy sailing shorts, a pink polo shirt, and a yellow sweater tied around his shoulders walked in. It took Anne a second to recognize him out of his tailored suit. But this was undoubtedly the Australian man from the restaurant in Locarno– Patrick. Alex's acquaintance. The fake tan was a giveaway. And the gold watch.

"G'day," he said cheerfully as he walked down the stone steps. He paused a bit and then continued, pointing a finger at Anne, "I recognize you. That's right, from the restaurant the other day. I always notice beautiful women," he smiled, revealing expensive teeth. "You were with Alex's husband. I'm Patrick, by the way," he extended his hand towards Anne. He leaned to the side, as if to look past Anne and into the back of the store, still holding her hand. "Is he here?"

Anne pulled her hand away. She opened her mouth to say something, but Partick just continued. "I'm here for some old maps to decorate my apartment. Something big," he said, spreading out his hands. "And old. Ah, here is the man himself."

Marco wheeled to the front of the store.

"How are you mate?" Patrick asked, with the same cheerful voice.

Anne saw Marco flinch at the 'mate'.

"I was just telling this beautiful Sheila here, you don't mind me calling you Sheila, just a little term of endearment," he winked at Anne, "that I'm looking for some old maps." His focus had turned back to Marco. "Something old and impressive. And big."

Marco examined him for a few moments. "I'm not sure if we have what you need," he said.

"No worries, mate, see if you can rustle up something for me," Patrick said. Marco didn't reply, but just turned his wheelchair around and went to the back of the store. Anne wasn't sure if he would come back.

For a while Patrick and Anne stood without speaking, and awkward silence expanded to fill the empty space.

Patrick spun around slowly, looking at the store, and let out a low whistle, "Quite a place they've got here. I've never actually visited. Must be a treat working here."

Anne wasn't sure he meant that as a compliment.

He turned back to Anne, "Where is the beautiful Alex today? Is she here?"

Anne could feel her cheeks beginning to burn. She felt protective of Marco, but didn't know what to say except the truth. "She's at her yoga studio," she said quietly, as if revealing a closely guarded secret.

"Yeah, that's how she keeps her beautiful figure. You know, she hasn't changed a bit since she was a girl. What a looker. I should visit her there sometimes," Patrick said, with a faraway look in his eyes.

Anne felt herself getting hotter. *What is this guy doing here? What does he want? How could he be so cheerful,* she thought. *Didn't one of his girlfriends just get murdered?*

"My condolences," Anne said.

"What?" Patrick said, turning sharply. And then, as if recovering himself, he said, "Yes, tragic. What a loss. Kathleen was a brilliant woman. Great at finding new ways to make you ladies look more beautiful. Not that any of you need it," he winked again.

Anne stared at him and couldn't understand how this person could be as successful as Alex had said. And why did he have so many women fawning over him? He was repulsive. His behavior might have been acceptable in the 60s, or even in the 80s. But now it bordered on harassment.

"Yes, terrible loss," he continued. "You know,

I was one of the people most affected by her death."

Ah, thought Anne. *I knew they were an item.*

"We were about to become business partners," he said.

That revelation got Anne's attention, and she hoped he would share more.

"That day at lunch, we were just finalizing a new business venture. Kathleen had been working on a new ingredient. A newly discovered plant. Grows just here in your beautiful region," he swept a hand around the store. "We were going to make heaps of money. The whole plan was a beauty, no pun intended. So sad. She died before we could get it off the ground. Not that I care about the money. I was dead set on helping her out. She wanted to start her own company. Tired of working for someone else, you see. She really believed in that ingredient. Thought it was good enough to build a whole company on. Crikey," he shook his head and stared at the floor for a moment. "And then the beautiful Oliva got herself killed. So tragic."

For a moment Anne had forgotten about the second murdered woman, Olivia. Yes, of course, he knew them both. She had seen the three of them at the restaurant and thought it was a love triangle. So Kathleen was his business partner. *But how did Oliva fit in,* Anne wondered.

Patrick kept on with his monolog, "Without

them, I have no access to the plant. You know, it has a funny name. Something about the wart on a witch's face. Isn't that the funniest name you've ever heard? Ah, what a shame," he said and paused, as if thinking.

Here is a second person who knew both women, Anne thought.

"Do you know why Kathleen and Olivia were both dressed as witches? Do you think their deaths were random, I mean?" Anne asked, remembering only too late Marco's warning about asking strange men about the killings.

Patrick looked at her for a moment before answering. "Some weirdo, probably. One of those people who attended the festival. Such a waste of life. If I get my hands on the scum. The things I'll do to him...You know, that ingredient Kathleen spoke about? It wasn't just for cosmetics. She told me it could also be used for burn victims to regenerate their skin. She was a saint," he said.

Not what the press said about her, Anne thought. *What is taking Marco so long,* she wondered.

Anne stepped to the back to look for Marco. Through the stacks she saw him going through rolls of maps. *I wouldn't have bothered to accommodate a man like Patrick*, Anne thought, and she spun around to go back to the front. Marco would come when he was ready. No need to rush him.

As she walked towards the front, Partick

picked up something off the floor and put it back inside a book in his hand. It was Anne's copy of the *Healing Herbs* book. She had left it on the counter. He must have looked through it, and was now putting back Gunter Keller's business card. *It must have fluttered out*, she thought.

Patrick looked up as she walked in. He placed the book back on the counter and tapped its cover. "I see you know my good friend Gunter," he said, and gave her a dazzling white smile. "Listen," he looked at his watch, "Marco is taking his sweet time with these maps. Tell him I'll drop by another day to look at them," he said as he headed for the door. "Cheers!" he said, jogging up the steps, and left the store.

Just at that moment, Marco came to the front with a stack of rolled up maps in his lap.

"Did he just leave?" Marco asked, sounding incredulous.

"Yes, it looked like he was in a hurry. He said he'll drop by another day to look at the maps."

"I hope he doesn't," Marco said, darkly.

"Yes. He's such a repulsive man," she said. Anne's eyes landed on the book on the counter. "You know that he knows Gunter as well? What a small world Southern Switzerland is. He seems to know so many people. Kathleen, Olivia, Gunter, Alex…" Anne stopped herself. She wished she hadn't said Alex's name in the same sentence as the murdered women.

Marco looked up at her. "I need a bit of fresh air. I'll just drop by Alex's studio for a while," he said.

Anne was sorry she had brought up Alex's name. He seemed worried. Was it the murders? Or was he worried about Patrick? Anne thought Marco had nothing to worry about. Alex was in no way involved with the two murdered women. And from what Anne knew of Alex, she was too level-headed to be flattered by a guy like Patrick. But she didn't say any of this to Marco.

"No problem," she said instead, "I'll look after the store for a while. It's so quiet now without the pagan festival. Maybe I'll grab a coffee from Luigi's."

11 Who is lying

With Marco out of the store, and no customers at the moment, Anne ran across the cobbled street to 'Luigi's'–purveyor of expensive coffee to the rich and idle, as Marco called him.

Although his slightly old-fashioned name conjured up images of Italian grandpas, Luigi was actually a young hipster whose barista skills and showmanship eclipsed that of any celebrity magician. His look was a copy of the hundreds of other hipsters sauntering around town–hair short on the sides with a gelled bouffant on top, complemented by a long beard, and a mustache to rival Poirot's. He always dressed in a starched white shirt accented with black suspenders. The shirt's rolled-up sleeves revealed meticulously designed tattoos. But despite all his ostentatiousness, he served great coffee. He applied the same attention to detail to making cappuccinos as he did to his look.

Back in her office, Anne returned to scanning the *Healing Herbs* book. In the midst of all the excitement, she hadn't completed that project.

While there wasn't much thinking required

in scanning pages, she couldn't concentrate on her work. Her thoughts drifted back to the events of the past few days.

Something was bothering her, and she couldn't put her finger on it.

Anne leaned back in her chair, and Maggie jumped up in her lap. Anne hadn't noticed her come into the office, but Maggie had a sixth sense when it came to locating a free lap to jump into. Maggie wrapped her tail around herself and curled up in Anne's lap. The cat began purring as Anne stroked her.

So what do I know, Anne asked herself.

"Listen, Maggie, see if you can make any sense of this," Anne spoke to the cat. The cat just looked back at her with clear green eyes and continued to pur. With each stroke, it closed its eyes in pleasure.

"Kathleen was interested in a plant that she had found in a book written by Marco's grandmother, but she couldn't locate it, because a botanist who published an article about its location, put the wrong location. And no one is sure if he did that on purpose, or if it was an honest misprint. Kathleen bought the botanist's field log, presumably to find the correct location. Where is the log book now?"

Anne marveled at how the rhythm of Maggie's purrs helped her thoughts flow.

"Does the police know about this field log?

Do they have it? It all has to do with the plant and finding its right location. Because whoever finds it will make a lot of money. But why kill two women for it? It's clear that the catalyst for the murders, the whole chain reaction, started with the field log. Kathleen got the journal, and she was murdered. Or was it random attacks on women dressed as witches...No, it can't be. There are too many coincidences here. We have to look for the simplest explanation. Occam's razor and all."

Anne's thoughts traveled over all the things she knew. And all the people she thought were involved. And yet, something kept tugging at the back of her mind. She was sure someone had lied. Perhaps not exactly something they had said, but something they had not said.

"Oh, Maggie, I don't know where to begin," she said to the cat, stroking her soft fur. "We know that Kathleen, now that she had the location of the plant, assuming that it was correct in the field log, had planned to start a company with Partick. Was she killed to keep her from starting the company? By whom? By Gunter? But the police cleared him. Why? And what about Olivia, I'm always forgetting about Olivia. Where does she fit?"

And then Anne realized that while she had looked up Kathleen online, she had never searched for information on Olivia, or on Gunter, or on Patrick. It was time to look up all of them online.

"Do you want to sit on top of the keyboard?" Anne asked Maggie, playfully. Maggie had a habit of sitting on top of the keyboard, attracted, Anne assumed, to the heat given off by the laptop.

A few weeks ago, when Anne had searched for information about the mystery on the cursed island, Maggie's keyboard shenanigans had helped her find some crucial details. But today Maggie just stayed in Anne's lap, unphased by the clicking of Anne's fingers on the keys.

Anne searched for information on Olivia first, but there was very little about her beyond the recent news. *How odd,* Anne thought. It was unusual these days to find anyone with so little personal information online. *Especially someone who was younger than me*, Anne thought. It seemed Olivia avoided social media and social media profiles.

"Where does Olivia fit in?" Anne addressed Maggie again. "Why is there so little information about her? We know from Gunter that she was a botanist who was helping Kathleen locate the plant. But she was not successful. And she was killed soon after Kathleen. And in the same manner, so to speak. Wearing a witch costume at the pagan festival. Why were they both dressed like that?...Does it have anything to do with this coven? Kathleen seemed to have had a genuine interest in folklore, witchcraft, and herbal remedies. Magic potions, if you will. But what about Olivia? Was she influenced by Kathleen? Was she her protege? But she was no biochemist. She couldn't develop any cosmetic ingredients. She could only help her look for the plants.

"And why were they both arguing about Patrick? I had assumed that it was a lovers' triangle. But now we know that it was a business lunch. Did Olivia feel left out? Did she think she should have been included in the business deal? But why? What had Kathleen promised her?

"You know Maggie, when I first read about Kathleen's murder, I suspected Olivia as the killer. You know, out of jealousy. But now we know there was no love triangle. Just a business deal. And Olivia was left out of it. And then she was killed.

"So that just leaves Gunter and Patrick. Or another person that we don't even know about. Gunter had the strongest motive for murdering them both. He wanted to keep the location of the plants secret. And Patrick had the most to lose by their deaths, because now he has nothing to invest in. He stood to make the most money out of the whole deal. And where is the field log? I bet Patrick would pay a lot of money for it now that he knows what it's worth...And so would Gunter, come to think of it, because he wants to protect the plants."

Anne realized that she knew very little about Gunter and Patrick. All she knew about Patrick was what other people had told her about him. And all she knew about Gunter was what he had told her himself.

She typed in each of their names and read through all the articles she found.

It seemed both men were very socially active. Gunter was mentioned in a lot of cosmetic industry-related events from years ago. And now plenty of articles about his environmental protection and preservation work. Patrick had even more articles. He was active on two continents.

"I don't believe it. He was lying. He has had contact with Kathleen quite recently. Look, Maggie. Here is a picture of Kathleen and him at an industry gala last December. And there is Olivia in the background."

So Gunter had lied. But why? Why was he hiding the fact that he'd had a recent contact with Kathleen and Olivia? What else was he hiding?

Emboldened by having caught out Gunter so quickly, and with Maggie purring peacefully in her lap, Anne continued digging deeper into images and articles.

And then she saw it. It was a small local article. No more than a footnote. But it helped tie everything together. And she didn't even need to use a translator to read it.

The cogs in her brain turned slowly and her

thoughts began clicking into place, one click after the other, just like the funicular making its slow ascent. *I've been looking at this all wrong,* Anne thought.

"Oh, Maggie! I think I know who the murderer is. And I'm pretty sure he's going to him." Anne picked up the cat from the lap and placed her on the floor. "I think there will be a third murder."

12 Not so scenic drive

Anne gripped the steering wheel and stared at the road ahead of her. She slammed on the breaks as a car careened down the mountainside towards her. She shut her eyes, bracing for impact. But she felt only a slight blast of air as the car drove past her. The driver coming from the opposite direction had somehow squeezed between Anne's car and the sheer cliff flanking the road on the opposite side.

Anne hated these narrow mountain roads. She was never sure if there was enough space for two cars to pass. Where the roads were wide enough, road markings showed the two lanes. But on the narrower parts, there were no road markings, and you were on your own.

Anne slowed down again to navigate the tight u-turn, making her way up the mountain, retracing her ride with Marco to Orselina. Cars honked behind her, impatient with her slow and careful driving.

But she just had to ignore them. There was no other way around it. Normally, she would have asked Ben to drive, but he was at work. And there was no time to wait for him.

On the way to the car garage where her car was parked, Anne had called Marco to let him know about her theory and to tell him she was going to Orselina. But her call went to voicemail. Anne knew from Marco that Alex's yoga studio had a horrendous reception. There was only one corner, near a window, which received a descent signal.

Hopefully, he gets my message on time, Anne thought.

Anne estimated that Partick had left the store 20 minutes ago. If her hunch was correct, he was going to Gunter's place. She hoped she was wrong, but she would try to stop him.

With another u-turn ahead of her, Anne wondered why she hadn't taken the funicular. It certainly would have been easier and faster.

At last the ochre buildings of the Madonna del Sasso sanctuary floated up ahead of her, and she knew she was close.

When Anne got to Gunter's place, she saw two cars in the driveway. *I hope I'm not too late*, she thought.

She parked across the driveway, blocking the two cars on purpose. She was pleased with herself for having thought of that trick.

The front door was unlocked. It didn't surprise Anne. She had heard that the Swiss, with their low crime rate, didn't think of locking their doors during the day.

The inside of the house was eerily silent. Anne walked through the living room towards the sliding glass doors. The neat stack of books was now spread jumbled across the coffee table.

She went up to the table to check the books, but a loud splash cut through the silence.

They are in the garden, Anne thought. *I hope I haven't just barged in on two old friends having a pool party?*

As she made her way through glass doors, she heard strained yells and grunts, and knew that was no pool party.

She ran to the lower terrace, to Gunter's pool. And there was Gunter, his upper body soaked, sitting across someone's chest. She recognized the brown boat shoes.

Gunter had a large rock in his hand, probably pulled out of his garden wall, raised precariously in the air.

"Stop! Gunter, stop!" Anne yelled, unable to restrain herself.

Gunter turned around, startled.

Using the momentary distraction, the man under him pushed Gunter forcefully out of the way, and punched him in the stomach. Gunter rolled off him in pain, and the man got up clumsily. It was Patrick, as Anne had thought.

Patrick's pink shirt was also splashed with

dark water stains. He was breathing heavily and staring at Anne. Anne noticed that in his hand he clutched a brown notebook.

Gunter coughed and got up gingerly.

For a moment the three of them just stood. But in the next, Gunter lunged for Patrick. Partick jumped out of the way, and Gunter stumbled. With two leaps, Patrick was almost at Anne with Gunter a step behind him.

Panicked, Anne grabbed the pool chair next to her and put it up like a shield. She blocked the men's way.

"Stop! I know it was you," Anne said, trying to make her voice sound scary and menacing. "I know you killed them and I know why. Give it up. You can't kill all of us. There are so many people now who know about the plant and can sell the information to other investors." Anne was bluffing here a bit, but she wanted to distract the killer.

"And I've called the police." This last one was an outright lie, but he didn't need to know that.

Partick moved to pass Anne, but she shoved the chair's legs towards him. The distraction gave Gunter the opportunity to grab the notebook out of Patrick's hand.

Patrick stared like a trapped wild animal, unsure which way to go.

"You're bankrupt. I found an article. Kathleen didn't know about it, that's why she approached you. You had no money to invest in her idea. But once you'd heard about it, you couldn't let anyone else have it. You wanted that idea for yourself. You needed a good business idea desperately. You hoped it would make you back the money you'd lost in a series of bad investments." Anne kept speaking to stall for time. She wasn't sure if she was right, but it sounded right.

In the distance, she heard the wails of a police car. *Thank you, Marco,* Anne thought.

13 Under a cherry tree

Ben and Anne were in Marco and Alex's garden. An old cherry tree, its branches spread like an umbrella over a granite stone table and two stone benches, filled the tiny yard. A sloping vineyard took up the rest of the garden.

Sitting under the shade of the cherry tree, Anne thought their garden was perfect.

"So it did all begin with my grandmother's book," Marco was saying.

It was a couple of days after Patrick had been arrested for the murders of Kathleen Price and Olivia Rossetti.

"That's right," Gunter said. He had agreed to join the group for afternoon coffee. "Kathleen discovered the witchwort recipe in the book and thought the plant sounded promising. More than promising. Harnessing the power of its stem cells would have made Kathleen a very rich woman.

"But she couldn't locate it. The professor's coordinates were wrong. So Kathleen had to put that ingredient on the back-burner. But she never forgot about it. It was a stroke of her genius that she guessed that the professor–like any good botanist–had kept a detailed field log, and she bade her time. I was not aware of the field log coming up for auction. I somehow missed it. I didn't put two and two together.

"It wasn't until Olivia contacted me to sell it, that I learned about the auction, and that Kathleen had bought the professor's field log.

"Once Kathleen bought the log, however, the wheels were set in motion. There was nothing standing in Kathleen's way."

"But she picked the wrong venture capitalist to pitch her business idea to," Marco jumped in. While at the police station to fill out his report on the break-in, Marco had met an old army buddy, now working as a policeman. His friend had filled in some of the missing details about Kathleen's and Olivia's murders.

"Your hunch was right, Anne, Patrick was bankrupt. He couldn't invest in developing this new ingredient," Marco continued.

"How did you know Patrick was bankrupt," Alex asked, looking at Anne. "I had no idea."

"I came across an article from a local newspaper, from Kirribilli, I think it's a suburb of Sidney?" Anne asked Alex.

Alex nodded in reply.

"So, this local newspaper had a small piece of news about how the bank had foreclosed on the house of Doris McGinty, mother of the investor

Patrick McGinty," Anne said. "Well, it just got me thinking. Given what Marco had said about Patrick, that he was big on being seen with the right people and at the right parties, it just seemed to me that he would have never let his mother's house be repossessed by the bank, if he had the choice. Even if he hated her, he would be painfully aware of the bad publicity it would bring him. So I just reasoned that he simply had no money to stop the foreclosure.

"And that realization made all else fall into place. I'm sure the police would have come to the same conclusion once they'd had the chance to look deeper into his finances. He made such a big deal about losing out on a great investment. He was hiding behind that story, using that as his alibi, in a sense."

"But what about all these witches, and covens, and the pagan festival?" Ben asked. "Was that just a screen?"

"The police think it was just a screen," Marco said. "What a better way to disguise your true identity than at a festival where everyone is wearing costumes. No one would have recognized Patrick, even if they saw him. From what Patrick told the police, Kathleen was genuinely interested in the festival and was there dressed as a witch. Patrick followed her there, and had an argument with her, and killed her."

"But why kill her in the first place, what was

he trying to gain?" Ben asked.

"The police think it was because he was angry with her," Marco said. "Once she learned that he had no money to invest in her venture, we're talking millions of startup costs, research and development and marketing, she told him she was going to take her idea elsewhere. But Patrick saw this new ingredient as his way out. He begged her to let him in on the deal. She probably just laughed it off."

"And how did the field log end up with Olivia? And why did she sell it to you," Alex asked, directing her question to Gunter.

"Olivia was angry at Kathleen for cutting her out of the deal. Now that Kathleen had the correct location for the plant, she didn't need Oliva."

"So Oliva barged in on the business lunch," Anne added, "to voice her discontent."

Gunter nodded. "I'm not sure how Olivia came by the field log," he said. "She must have stolen it out of Kathleen's room while Kathleen was at the festival. But after Kathleen was killed, she contacted me to sell it. She knew of my interest in the plant. Maybe she was scared. Maybe she suspected Patrick of killing Kathleen. Or maybe she just wanted to cash in. She was no biochemist. She couldn't develop that ingredient. I bought the field log straight away. No questions asked. And then I saw that book for sale in your store. I had a Google alert set up on the title."

"I knew it," Marco interjected.

"Everything was coming together. I was so close to protecting the plant. Sorry again about the break-in. I was so wrong of me, but I wasn't thinking straight," Gunter turned to Marco. "And then, Patrick showed up at my house, asking if I knew anything about the field journal. Sorry I lied to you about having it," Gunter said to Anne, "I was actually sure you had seen it on my coffee table."

"No, I totally missed it," Anne said, shaking her head.

"But Partick saw it, and he was desperate to get it," Gunter continued. "He actually thought he could steal it from me, from under my nose. But he ran in the wrong direction, towards my garden. Or maybe he thought he could escape faster through the gardens and down to the lake. You caught us in the middle of our struggle."

"I'm sorry," said Ben, "I know I keep bringing up these witches, but why was Oliva also dressed as a witch and also killed at the festival?"

"I think I can answer that one as well," Gunter said. "Olivia was enamored with Kathleen. She wanted to be like her. She worshiped her. I'm not surprised she developed the same interests as her and even dressed as her. Patrick must have lured Olivia somehow to the festival. Or maybe she asked him to meet her there. I would not put it past Olivia to have tried to blackmail him, if she suspected him of killing Kathleen. There were some rumors about her in the industry. People whispered that she climbed the corporate ladder in a series of well-timed blackmails."

"I'd wondered why she had so little personal information on social media," said Anne. "I guess, knowing the power of blackmail, she kept her own personal life closely guarded."

"And why did Patrick kill Olivia?" Ben asked.

"I don't think even the police are sure yet. Maybe she was blackmailing him, as Gunter said, or maybe he was hoping to get the field log from her. Maybe she taunted him about having sold it to someone else."

"But it seems that Patrick didn't know who Olivia had sold the field log to. Not until he saw Gunter's business card in the bookstore," Marco said.

"Yes, the card must have jogged his memory. He must have made the connection. He knew I used to work with Kathleen. He must have assumed that I was a likely person Olivia would sell the field log to. I live in the area, I used to be in the business, it's an easy connection to make," Gunter said.

"And all this just from a misprint from an old botanist," Alex said, shaking her head.

"But tell me," Gunter turned to Anne, "how did you figure it all out?"

"I think it was because of Maggie, the store's

cat," Anne said, joking. She had meant to continue on and explain all the steps that had led to her conclusions, but Marco interrupted her.

"I'm not surprised. Maggie was my grandmother's cat."

Murderous Misprint
Author's Notes

Paracelsus

Paracelsus was a Swiss physician and an actual historical figure. His life story is fascinating and his discoveries, theories and achievements were well ahead of his time. Alas, he probably doesn't have any direct descendents.

Casa del Negromante

Casa del Negromante is an actual place in Locarno that is open to visitors. The restaurant, however, now appears to be closed. The translation of the house name is correct, but the author regrets that there isn't more information available about the house's history or the provenance of its name.

Southern Switzerland's Pagan Festival

While there are a lot of mediaeval and folk festivals around Switzerland, the one in this book is invented by the author.

Witchwort, refugia plants and Nunatak

Refugia plants, and their survival during the last ice age by retreating to Nunataks, are scientific facts. As are the regenerative capabilities of their stem cells. Several such plants are being studied by biomedical companies. Witchwort, Saponaria venefica, is not one of them. It's a product of the author's imagination.

The funicular from Locarno to Orselina

If you visit Locarno, the author recommends a ride on the blue funicular from Locarno to Orselina. The experience of riding through the valley over the old viaduct bridge is truly picturesque. And a visit to the Sanctuary of the Madonna del Sasso at the end of your ride is also highly recommended.

Book 3: Suspicious Small Print

Old Bookstore Two-Hour Cozy Mysteries Book 3

By Isabella Bassett

Copyright © 2021 Isabella Bassett
All rights reserved. The moral right of the author has been asserted.

Suspicious Small Print
(Old Bookstore Two-Hour Cozy Mysteries Book 3)
Kindle Edition
Published June 13, 2021

ASIN: B08W56Z3JX

This book is a work of fiction. Names, characters, places and events portrayed in this book are the product of the author's imagination or are used fictitiously. Any similarity to actual persons, living or dead, businesses, companies, events or locales is entirely coincidental and not intended by the author.

No part of this book may be reproduced, or stored in a retrieval system, or transmitted in any form or by any means, electronic, mechanical, photocopying, recording, or otherwise, without express written permission of the publisher.

1 A treasure map

'Treasure!' proclaimed the newspaper headline. The pit of Anne's stomach gave a tiny squeeze in response.

The whole of Southern Switzerland–perhaps all of Switzerland–was in the grips of treasure fever. Archaeologists in Bellinzona, a nearby town famous for its three medieval castles, had discovered Roman treasure, believed to be the largest haul in Swiss history. And tonight, a select group of local politicians, journalists, historians, and archeologists would be the first to glimpse the valuable discovery. Belonging to none of those vocations, Anne still couldn't believe her luck at being among tonight's invited guests.

Anne looked down at the newspaper in front of her. As any treasure was bound to, this one attracted its own controversy. The treasure had swiftly become a source of Swiss national pride, and the fact that a foreign expert–even if it was the world-renowned Sir Hubert Fieldchester– had now been invited to take over the excavation did not go over well with the Swiss press.

That a second Briton had been lurking about, namely Melinda Spencer, of the 'Society for Preservation of Roman Antiques', with an eye on the treasure, sent the press' nationalistic feelings into overdrive.

Anne's own excitement over the treasure stemmed not so much from the riches it contained, but from the fact that the old bookstore where she worked had supplied a crucial piece of the puzzle that had led to the treasure's location.

It had all happened–as most exciting things did–unexpectedly. While searching for old maps at the request of an ill-fated customer, who was now rotting in a prison cell, Marco, the bookstore's owner, had made the fateful discovery among the store's collection of maps.

A medieval map, one of a set depicting the Bellinzona castles, bore a faint footnote at the bottom. The Latin inscription, though difficult to read, had caught Marco's attention. The footnote alluded to something hidden at the base of the biggest of the three castles.

Marco had contacted the Ticino Ministry of Culture, and Emma Muller, lead archaeologist of the Bellinzona castles, arrived shortly to review the map. Anne had sensed that the faded footnote generated immense excitement in Dr. Muller, but the news of the actual treasure discovery, which came a few weeks later, had been a shock.

While Marco had kept the store's involvement out of the newspapers–the store had been getting enough press attention over the past few months–the grateful Ministry of Culture had extended tonight's hand-picked invitation to Marco, his wife, and the staff of the bookstore, of which there was just Anne.

Why the treasure had lain hidden for so long, and why the author of the footnote on the medieval map had not excavated the treasure himself, remained a mystery that the scholars involved planned to unravel next. For now, the archeologists had their hands full with excavating, cataloging, and cleaning the treasure.

News media vans lined the narrow streets of the usually sleepy provincial town of Bellinzona in anticipation of tonight's big reveal. The cocktail party was to be held at the *Castello Grande*, the largest of the three castles, and the castle where the treasure itself had been uncovered.

Anne was excited. Not only could she not wait to see the treasure, but she also had to admit that she was more than a little curious to see the unfolding drama of Swiss versus British scholars up-close.

Anne looked at her watch. *A few minutes to go*.

Just then, Maggie, the store's black cat, jumped up on the counter on soft paws. Hanging around her neck, on a new collar, was a shiny gold Roman coin–a gift from the archeology team to the store, as a memento of the treasure.

Maggie strutted down the counter, as though on a fashion runway–*a catwalk,* Anne laughed–clearly showing off her coin to no one in particular.

She made her way to Anne's newspaper.

"You have an unhealthy attraction to newspapers. And books, for that matter", Anne told the cat while giving her a gentle stroke. Maggie ignored her comment, laid on top of the article Anne had been perusing, and purred.

Anne looked at the cat intently. And then glanced back down at the newspaper. She had learned to be attentive to Maggie's choice of reading material. It wouldn't be the first time Maggie had given Anne a clue about a mystery.

Marco claimed Maggie was his grandmother's cat.

"I'm a man of facts and an ex-army man," he had told Anne. "How do you think it makes me feel to admit that Maggie resembles my grandmother's cat in everything–in the way it looks, the way it behaves? It even acts like it's been in the store before. The cat seems to know where everything is."

Both Marco and Anne had trouble accepting the unexplained, so mostly they avoided talking about Maggie's peculiarities. But just recently, Marco had told Anne the story of how Maggie had come to the store.

This Maggie had arrived at the bookstore two

weeks before Anne herself had started work. One day, it just walked into the store through the cat flap in the back door, through which the original Maggie had left many years before.

"Too long for it to be the same cat, unless cats do have nine lives," Marco had said. "The original Maggie left shortly after my grandmother died, and while I know, rationally, that it could not possibly be the same cat, this black cat resembled my grandmother's cat so much." Marco had done the only natural thing and named the new cat 'Maggie'.

Thinking of Marco's grandmother, Anne glanced at the surrounding store. For a moment, the light in the store dimmed. *A cloud*, Anne thought.

The dark wood bookcases that lined three sides of the store stood out in contrast against the white stone walls. A careful observer would notice that the bookcases were actually old apothecary cases with white porcelain jars still lining the top shelves. The bottom shelves were full of old books.

The store had been in Marco's family for generations. Originally an apothecary, the last person who had used it for its intended purpose had been Marco's grandmother–an English herbalist. Failing to follow in the family's footsteps, Marco had eventually turned it into a bookstore.

Seen from the outside, the broody gray stone

facade, with its two gothic windows, gave the impression that the store would be cave-like and dark. But walking through the door and down three stone steps brought the visitor into a cathedral-like space. Bright light streamed into the store through the windows, bounced off the geometric tiled floor, and reverberated off its walls. On a sunny day, the bright light traveled up the walls and illuminated the vaulted ceiling above. But few people ventured inside. *Especially on sunny days*, Anne thought.

It was the beginning of June and the beginning of the tourist season. While the town of Ascona never lacked visitors, over the past few weeks the stream of tourists past the store's windows had swelled. Marco had joked that the more tourists arrived, the less busy the bookstore became. Anne had to admit that there was some truth to that. But she attributed it more to the fact that summer also coincided with the time when academics and researchers, who made up the bulk of the store's customers, began taking sabbaticals and vacations.

The name of the bookstore was 'Out of Print', alluding to the antiquarian books the store carried. *'Out of Sight' would have been a better name*, Anne thought as she watched the stream of tourists flow past the store's windows towards the town's lake-side promenade and its cafes. She had the feeling that people truly didn't see the bookstore.

"Time to go and change", Marco's voice behind her brought Anne out of her thoughts.

"Great! See you later," Anne replied, and almost skipped like a little child on her way home. Waiting for her there, hanging on the closet door, was the most exquisite, and the most expensive, dress Anne had ever owned.

The promenade, overlooking the storied Lake Maggiore, was even more crowded than usual. Anne sidestepped couple after couple, holding hands and walking down the lakeside promenade, looking for a place to have dinner.

Anne felt a pang of sadness deep down. She wasn't jealous of the couples, but she wished Ben could go to the cocktail party tonight.

Anne tried to push down the feeling of disappointment. Her husband traveled a lot for work, but it was thanks to his job that she was now living in a European country. How many times had she dreamed of escaping to a quaint European town and living where others only vacationed?

Glancing at the sun-drenched cafes and candy-colored boutique hotels lining the promenade, Anne's mood lifted. Ascona was a gem in a Switzerland few knew existed. This was Switzerland with a Mediterranean flair–a land of sun, exotic Italian villas and palazzos, lush gardens, palm trees, and a never-ending dose of *dolce vita*.

A child walked by Anne, and the sight of a

stuffed cat in its hand jerked Anne's thoughts back to Maggie sitting on top of her newspaper. An uneasy feeling clenched her stomach, but Anne brushed it off as nerves about having to go to a party on her own.

2 A party at the castle

Often overlooked by tourists, Bellinzona was neither as glamorous as Lugano, nor as charming as Ascona. Being the capital of the canton of Ticino, it carried an air of administrative dullness.

Despite being the canton's biggest town, it felt sleepy and provincial. Driving into town, and seeing it for the first time from its outskirts, the impression was quite disappointing. Low apartment blocks in garish colors intermingled with concrete office buildings and industrial warehouses.

But Bellinzona had the capacity to surprise. Hidden in the middle of the old town, high on a rocky outcrop, sat a medieval castle. Its massive stone towers and battlements rose out of the granite rock on which it sat, among the pastel-colored nineteenth century palazzos that made up the center of town.

Aptly named *Castello Grande*, it was the biggest of three castles that traversed the valley in which the town of Bellinzona stood. A network of thick stone walls connected the castles and in medieval times essentially closed off the valley.

Anne had wondered why such a small town would need three castles to protect it, until she learned the castles were there not to guard the town, but to control something far more valuable–the traffic of goods and people through the valley.

The three castles visible today were from the middle ages, but the importance of the valley in controlling movement of goods from Italy to Northern Europe was recognized as far back as Roman times. In fact, *Castello Grande* was built on the ruins of a Roman garrison.

The castles' obsolete function was best observed after sundown, when floodlights illuminated the three castles and formed a path of light across the valley against the dark hills of Bellinzona.

As she drove closer to *Castello Grande*, Anne's thoughts turned to the treasure she was about to see tonight. Like most people in the region, she was excited to see a sliver of the innumerable coins and other valuables that had passed through the valley.

Anne parked in the underground parking below the castle. An elevator took her to the top of the castle's wall and to the castle's entrance. Through the battlements, Anne could see the roofs of the palazzos below and beyond them the Renaissance facade of the *Collegiate of SS. Pietro e Stefano*, a church which sat at the heart of old Bellinzona.

She smoothed her dress and turned her focus on navigating the cobblestone path up to the door in her high-heeled sandals.

Anne had decided it was time to buy a proper little black dress. At her previous job as a pharmaceutical lab researcher, back in Boston, she'd had no need for fancy cocktail dresses. The only occasion she'd had to dress up had been during science conferences, and then only in a knee-length skirt and a nice blouse.

At one of the many boutiques lining the narrow pedestrian streets of Ascona, Anne had picked a simple but expertly cut number. She had gawked at the price tag, but had to agree with the saleswoman that the dress really did fit well. It helped that Anne was slim, and regular hikes in the mountains on the weekend kept her in shape.

Clinging on to her invitation, Anne hesitated about going in. A doubt nagged at the back of her mind that she was overdressed and that the high heels made her taller than even most men.

But as she pushed open the heavy wood door and entered the reception room, her doubts melted away. A great medieval hall opened up in front of her: rough-hewn stone walls, a flagstone floor, and a high ceiling that disappeared into the shadows overhead. The hall was dark except for the light emanating from clusters of candles strategically placed around the room, which gave it a mysterious ambiance.

People mingled in small groups around tall cocktail tables, dressed in suits and elegant cocktail dresses, talking in hushed tones. Anne had to admit that the entire atmosphere was subtly glamorous. She was glad she had dressed up.

A server materialized in front of her, out of the darkness, and offered her a tall flute of champagne. Anne took a glass and glanced at the tiny bubbles as they sparkled in the candlelight, rising from the bottom of the glass.

She scanned the crowd for Marco and Alex, but her eyes were drawn past the crowd to the back of the room. There, glass cases illuminated from within sparkled like giant diamonds in the darkness. Anne assumed those cases held the treasure.

"I'm glad you could make it," a female voice said next to Anne. Anne turned, surprised. In the shadowy interior, she hadn't noticed Emma walk up to her.

"Hi!," Anne said, relieved to see a familiar face. "Of course. I would not have missed it!"

"Come, let me show you the treasure," Emma said, and with a gentle hand on her elbow, guided Anne towards the cases in the back of the room.

"There are Alex and Marco," Anne said. "Hi guys," she mouthed and waved as she passed.

On one side of the glass case displays stood

a lectern, and on the other a young man–Anne guessed around eighteen years old–dressed in an army uniform a little too big for him stood guard of the cases. Straight-backed and stiff, he tried to avoid eye contact. Anne could see he was really uncomfortable.

Her eyes turned to the glass cases. The treasure was breathtaking. Displayed on black velvet were a gold pendant, a bracelet, and a few gold and bronze coins. The black velvet absorbed the spotlight on the artifacts, and gave the impression the gold treasure was floating magically in the darkness.

"That's just a small part of what we've uncovered," said Emma, close at Anne's side. "But this is what we've been able to get ready for this cocktail party. The rest still needs to be cleaned and catalogued. The Board of Directors wanted to have something displayed as they welcomed Sir Hubert. But tonight's party is really for the press. To give them and the public a little taste of what we've discovered. That it coincides with Sir Hubert's arrival is an unhappy accident."

Anne and Emma had become friends over the last few weeks, ever since Emma had first come into the bookstore. During the excavations, Emma had come back regularly to go through Marco's archives, maps, and documents. And Anne had digitized the maps before taking them to Emma's office at the castle.

The two friends walked to where Marco and Alex were standing. Talking a sip out of her champagne, Anne scanned the room. Besides the three people next to her, she didn't know anyone else, but she recognized a few people by sight.

Sir Hubert Fieldchester, the Oxford University expert on Roman history, who was invited by the Board of Directors to take over the project, was standing in the middle of a large group of people, speaking with a booming voice. His graying hair was swept back, giving him the look of an orchestra conductor, and Anne got the impression that he expected an equal type of obedience from those facing him.

Standing at the opposite side of the room was a man who Anne recognized as Thomas Schmidt, the Director of the castles and Emma's boss. His short stature and sleek appearance were unmistakable. He reminded Anne of an upscale car salesman.

"Emma, that's your boss, Thomas, right?" Anne said.

"Yes, that's him. Little weasel. Trying to hide from Sir Hubert," Emma said with indignation.

Her remark surprised Anne, but ignored it for now. "Who are the two women with him?" Anne said.

"That's Sarah Graf, standing next to him," Emma said, indicating a young woman with light blond hair that, lit by the candlelight, almost glowed in the darkness. She reminded Anne of an elven queen. "She's my research assistant. And behind Thomas is his secretary, Ruth Weber." Anne's gaze turned to a woman about her and Emma's age, wearing a long cardigan that she kept wrapping around herself like a security blanket. O*r a shield*, Anne thought. Ruth looked as though she was trying to blend with the shadows. The occasional reflection of candlelight off the lenses of her glasses, however, gave her position away.

"It's a very big turnout," Anne said, scanning the room. She knew there were a lot of local dignitaries and press, but she didn't recognize anyone.

"The crowd around Hubert, or *Sir* Hubert as he enjoys correcting everyone,"–Anne was sure Emma rolled her eyes, but in the darkness she couldn't be positive–"is mostly Board members and their significant others. That young man is Adrian, Sir Hubert's own research assistant. I can tell you Sarah has been so unhappy since he arrived. We all have…" Emma trailed off. "Then there is a bunch of press scattered all around. Oh, and the woman over there, talking to some people I don't know, maybe more press, is Melinda, Melinda Spencer. She is the President of the 'Society for Preservation of Roman Antiques'. Ugh, don't even ask me what she is doing here. Some self-appointed crusader on a mission to repatriate Roman archaeological finds back to Rome. Her husband–"

Emma's description was cut off by a clink on a glass announcing that speeches were about to commence. "I'll go stand with my people. I think they all need some moral support," Emma said and was swallowed by the shadows as she walked towards Thomas and the two women.

The speeches, by various people in Italian and German, had been going on for at least twenty minutes, and Anne's shoes were hurting. She was not used to standing on high heels for such a long time, and blood was pooling in her feet. As Sir Hubert took the podium next to the treasure display case, Anne decided it was time to move a bit and get circulation back to her feet.

She leaned towards Alex and whispered, "Do you know where the bathroom is?"

Alex nodded and pointed to a corridor at the back of the room that Anne hadn't noticed before. Alex leaned in close to Anne's ear. "If these speeches go on for much longer, I'll be looking to escape to the bathroom as well."

Anne felt bad about walking out in the middle of speeches, but she was sure the shadows would hide her as she slipped away.

Looking for the bathroom down the corridor, Anne was surprised how well she could still hear Sir Hubert's speech. *Acoustics are so weird in the castle*, Anne thought. *Must be the stone walls.* He was going on and on about the privilege to take over such an important archaeological investigation and the world-class expertise he would bring to the project. *Pompous ass*, Anne said to herself.

Anne came out of the bathroom and realized that Sir Hubert was still speaking. She was glad she had taken a walk. As she made her way back, reluctantly, up the corridor, a voice caught her attention. It was coming from the darkness, deep in the passageway.

"...but that would mean Emma will have to go," said a cold man's voice out of the darkness. Emma's name caught Anne's attention.

"No!" protested a woman's voice. "You can't do that! I won't let you hurt her. You'll have to find another way...."

Anne stopped and pressed herself against the stone wall, hoping the shadows would conceal her. She waited to hear more.

"There is no other way, don't you see," the male voice answered, angry. Anne now heard that it was a man's voice with a British accent.

Anne heard footsteps and walked back to the reception room, not wanting to be discovered eavesdropping in the shadows.

Sir Hubert's speech had just ended, and the groups were reconfiguring. Anne wanted to find Emma, but couldn't see her in the room's gloom. She walked back to Marco and Alex. A server was passing with a plate of mini canapes and Anne grabbed a couple. She hadn't eaten, and the champagne was getting to her. She chatted with Marco and Alex about the reception and secretly wondered when it would be polite to leave.

Suddenly, a piercing scream echoed from the corridor and pulsated off the stone walls. For a few moments, everyone stood rooted to their spot. Then a second scream followed, this one filled with pleading, and people ran in the scream's direction.

Anne stayed behind with Marco and Alex. The rough floor and general darkness made it difficult for Marco to move around the reception room. But Alex nodded to Anne that it was okay for her to go, and Anne followed at the back of the crowd.

As she made her way to the tail of the gathered crowd, Anne heard more screams and gasps. In her high heels, Anne could see above and between people's heads. The crowd had made a large semi-circle around a spot on the floor.

An eerie glow of cell phones illuminated people's faces, and their heads floated in the darkness like insects drawn to the blue light. Anne stood on the tips of her toes. The first thing she saw was the young man in uniform who had been guarding the treasure. He had abandoned his post and was now standing, his face as pale as a ghost, to the left of the group.

Anne followed his gaze to a pool of blue light in the middle of the dark floor and saw that he was looking at the severed head of Thomas Schmidt.

3 Zweihander, a sword for two hands

"His head was cut off with a *zweihander*," Marco said.

Anne was sitting in Marco's office at the bookstore. Newspapers lay open across his desk. Anne was nursing a cup of tea. She couldn't face a cup of coffee. She was rattled enough.

He had been reading the newspapers and translating them for Anne. While Anne's Italian was improving, she preferred for Marco to translate the articles for her. The information was too important, and she struggled with terminology related to homicide and police procedure.

What was originally planned by the news media to be pictures of yesterday evening's reception, of treasure and dignitaries, had turned into articles with screaming headlines and unsavory details of Thomas Schmidt's murder. Anne was glad that at least the newspapers had not published pictures of the severed head.

She shuddered. She couldn't get the image out of her mind.

It had been a long night. After they arrived,

the police asked everyone to remain for questioning. Anne, Marco and Alex had been one of the last people to be interviewed. She assumed that was because they were the least important people there, but also the ones with the least connections to the victim.

Anne was still shaking and going over the questions from the police. She had told them about her visit to the bathroom, of course, and the voices she heard after.

The police were eager to establish everyone's whereabouts at the time of the murder. But as Anne tried to recreate the position of people around the room in her mind's eye, she discovered that the gloom and shadows of the reception room made that difficult. All she could be sure about is that she was standing next to Marco and Alex. She was not sure of anyone else's location.

Anne worried that her visit to the bathroom put her in the crime's vicinity. She wondered if she was on the police's list of possible suspects.

One of the voices she'd heard last night in the corridor could have been the killer's. A chill passed down her spine as she thought of being so close to such a grizzly crime.

Even though there were no pictures of the actual crime, with so many journalists present, the police seemed to have a hard time keeping details out of the newspapers.

"What's a *zweihander*?" Anne asked.

"It's a type of medieval longsword. *Zweihander* means you have to hold it with two hands," Marco said, illustrating with his hands how to hold such a sword. Anne nodded. It was the sword featured in every medieval or fantasy movie. "It's a type of sword used by Swiss and German medieval mercenaries. Apparently," he looked down at the article, "the castle museum has an entire collection of them, plus more in storage."

"Where did the one that was used to kill Thomas come from? I mean, from the museum display or from storage?" Anne said.

"The police are not sure. There is nothing missing from the museum. And it will take museum staff a few days to see if anything is missing from the storage room. The storage room can only be accessed by a keycard, so maybe that will give the police more clues. Maybe someone used it that evening."

"Does it say if the police have any suspects?"

Marco scanned the newspapers again. "No one specifically. They think it's someone connected to the castles."

Anne nodded again. "Does it say anything about Thomas? Maybe something in his past or behavior would suggest a motive. Do the newspapers mention anything about a motive?"

"Nothing concrete. Obviously it's murder. But

the police are not saying if they think it's premeditated or spur of the moment. It says that with so many guests and with the reception room being so dark, it will take a while to establish everyone's whereabouts and go over everyone's witness statements."

"I wonder what the motive is," Anne said. "I mean, it's such a gruesome way to kill a person. You would have to be really angry or really strong to do that. Do you think it's related to the Roman treasure?"

"It could be. It certainly looks that way. Maybe something happened at the party that triggered it. But it was so dark, I saw nothing out of the ordinary. And why would anyone choose to do it at the cocktail party? So many potential witnesses. It seems like a spur of the moment. But to use a large sword like that to decapitate someone, you'd have to be an expert, it seems to me."

Anne thought back to the previous evening. "You know, I've been thinking about that argument I heard. The man's voice definitely had a British accent. So it could have been one of Sir Hubert's assistants. But the two people were arguing about Emma, not Thomas. I hope Emma is okay. It must be such a shock to her," Anne said. She sat in silence for a few moments. "Do you know anything about Thomas, anything beyond that he was the Director of the Bellinzona castles?"

Marco thought for a few moments. "Not much. I have a friend who is on the Board of Directors. I could ask him for more details. But I didn't know Thomas at all. He probably wasn't happy Sir Hubert was invited to take over the project."

"Really?" Anne said, surprised. "I had assumed Sir Hubert was his idea. It's something Emma said last night. She was certainly very angry at him..." Anne stopped herself. She felt bad for pointing out a motive for Emma to kill Thomas.

Marco shook his head. "I don't know. It was the idea of the Board of Directors. Sir Hubert is a world-famous authority. I would look good for him to lead the project. The last time I spoke to Emma, she said there might be a lot more excavation to be done and a lot more artifacts to be discovered. They'll certainly need a bigger team. Plus, Sir Hubert's name could attract international funds to support the research. It will take years to excavate properly and catalog everything, and then as many years to work out theories of where the treasure trove came from, and how it ended up buried at the castle."

"But it's a little unfair that Emma is essentially being pushed out of her own project. She was the one who put all the clues together and made the discovery," said Anne.

"I agree with you," said Marco. "But we don't

know how archaeology works. It was probably the best decision."

Just then Marco's phone rang, and he picked it up. Anne left his office to give him privacy. She walked to the front of the store. They had decided not to open today. But Anne enjoyed standing at the counter and watching people walk by the windows.

The day outside was sunny, and the colorful polo shirts of tourists shone brightly past the windows. Anne's thoughts went over and over what she had seen and heard yesterday. But she couldn't make any sense of it.

Maggie leaped up on the counter and sat by Anne. She butted her head, as was her habit, and started purring. Anne's mind jumped to the time just before the cocktail party when she was standing at this exact spot with a newspaper, reading about the treasure, and remembered Maggie laying on top of it.

Not for the first time, Anne wondered how uncannily accurate the cat was. It was as if she knew something would happen at the cocktail party.

Anne's phone vibrated in her back pocket. '*I need a friend to talk to. I believe I'm in a bit of trouble. Can you stop by the castle for coffee?*' It was a message from Emma.

4 Voices among the shadows

Anne had agreed to meet Emma for coffee at one of the numerous cafes sprinkled around the old town of Bellinzona. This one was in a square with a fountain with a seal, just a short walk from the castle. Anne had always considered the seal-shaped fountain, shooting water out of its mouth, a strange choice for a square surrounded by serious buildings, and wondered if there was a story behind it, but now was not the time to ask. As her step quickened, she struggled to control her apprehension over what Emma had to tell her.

It was early afternoon, and the sun was bearing down on the square. Tall chestnut trees rustled in the warm afternoon breeze and provided patchy shade. The square was empty except for a few people sitting at the cafe. Anne noticed Emma. A palazzo building threw its solid shadow over the cafe, and Anne welcomed the shade.

"Thank you for coming," Emma said.

"No problem," Anne said as she took a seat across from Emma. "We didn't open the store today, and my husband is away, so it was not a problem at all."

"I just didn't know who to talk to. I can't talk to anyone at work," Emma took a sip of her coffee, and paused as though deliberating what to say next. "We're all suspects, you know? And I can't talk to my family about it. The whole thing is freaking them out. You were actually there. I would feel better talking to someone who was there and experienced the horror."

Anne was surprised that Emma had reached out to her. Driving over, Anne had wondered why Emma texted her. They knew each other, and Anne enjoyed Emma's company, but she didn't think the two of them were close enough to talk about the murder. *I guess sometimes it's easier to talk to strangers or near strangers*, Anne had decided. But what Emma was saying now made sense.

Anne leaned in closer to Emma. "You said you–" Anne stopped herself. The server had walked up to their table.

"*Un cappuccino per favore,*" Anne said in Italian.

As the server walked away, Anne continued. "You said you were in trouble."

Emma nodded her head. "Well, nothing specific, yet. But I've been going over everything in my head, and just from the way the police are behaving towards me, I can't make up my mind if

I'm their number one suspect or if they think I'm next." Emma's eyes were wide with fear.

"Why would they think that?" Anne said. She wanted to ask *'have you done something that you should not have?'* but thought better of it.

"I hate to speak ill of the dead, but Thomas was such an inept fool. I was so angry with him. You know, the reason the Board of Directors insisted Sir Hubert Fieldchester take over the project was because of Thomas. He was such a bumbling idiot. The only reason he had the post of Director was because he's the brother-in-law of someone high-ranking official in City Hall. Apparently being inept and really bad at your job is not enough to get you fired. The Board of Directors should have gotten rid of him years ago. But he had tenure. And short of doing something illegal, they couldn't touch him."

Emma paused. The server was back with Anne's coffee.

Emma watched the server go back inside and continued. "It's my project," she said with force. "I made all the discoveries. Do you know how it hurts to have such a project taken away from you?"

Anne could only imagine how angry she would be in a similar situation. She sympathized with Emma. "Did you talk to the Board of Directors to tell them how you feel?"

"Yes. I let them have a piece of my mind."

Emma shook her head, "But by then it was too late. By the time I heard about it, the wheels were set in motion, Sir Hubert had been invited to take over, and of course he had agreed, and everything had been decided. And Thomas knew all about it, but was keeping it secret from the staff. He was afraid, apparently, how we would react.

"You know, I feel so bad for Sarah, as well. This Adrian is taking over her duties. She was the one responsible for cataloging all the artifacts. But now Sir Hubert assigned his own assistant, of course, to do that. She's being pushed down the pecking order as well. Sarah is so angry, I can see it. But she keeps it all bottled up. The dear girl can't be in the same room as Adrian. She can't even look me in the eye. She probably blames me for the whole thing. I don't know." Emma took a sip of her coffee and stared out at the fountain for a moment.

Anne watched Emma as she pushed a flyaway strand out of her face. Her usually disheveled curly hair was even more messy today.

"And the police, with their probing questions, managed to get all sorts of information out of me yesterday. I felt so vulnerable. I didn't keep any of this information back. Well, actually I didn't tell them about Sarah, but I did let them know how I felt about Thomas…how could I be so naive?" Emma bit her lower lip, lost in thought.

Anne wasn't sure what to say. She wasn't sure

if she was required to say anything. She felt that Emma just needed someone to talk to.

But as the silence extended, Anne said, "I don't see anything incriminating in what you've said. Just because you don't like someone doesn't mean you'd kill him."

"Yes, but the police suggested that my motive was to get his position. Because now that he's dead, I will most likely be made director of the castles. Sir Hubert is here only for the Roman artifacts research. So I guess I do benefit from Thomas' death."

"But what about 'opportunity' and so on?" Anne said. "The way Thomas was killed is so particular. Not many people would be able to do that."

Emma shrugged. "Yes, and no. The police have established that the weapon was taken from the storage room. There is a keycard access. But over the past few days all of us–well, except for Ruth– had been in and out of that room. And there are so many artifacts there. No one would have noticed if one of the swords had gone missing. The police think that the sword could have been removed at any time and hidden somewhere."

"They think it was planned?"

"That's what they're suggesting."

"But where would someone hide such a weapon with no one seeing it?"

Emma shrugged her shoulders again in response. She went back to staring at the fountain. "You know," she pushed a hair strand back, "now that I think about it, for a while now I'd felt like stuff had been moved around in the storage room."

"Did you tell the police?" Anne said.

Emma shook her head. "I just thought about it."

"How long has it been going on?"

"I can't say. It just hit me one day. It could have been months, or it could have been days. I'm not sure if it's even significant."

"You need to tell the police," Anne said.

Emma nodded in agreement and sipped her coffee.

"But what about alibis? Anne said. "Do you have one? Sorry to ask, but it was so dark, I couldn't be sure where anyone was after I came back from the bathroom…It's funny, I was worried that I would be a suspect as well because I had been in that vicinity just before the murder was discovered…"

"I have no one to vouch for me," Emma said, staring out into the middle distance. "By the end I was all alone at the table, feeling sorry for myself. Ruth and Sarah had walked off somewhere. By that time everyone was hoping to go home. And the police think the murder could have happened at any time during the speeches. Thomas left at some point to make a phone call and didn't come back. And that corridor is so long, and the body was discovered a long way down it. If that journalist who discovered him hadn't wandered around trying to sneak a peek at the rest of the artifacts, Thomas' body might not have been discovered until this morning or even later. No one really uses that part of the castle. Except for receptions, like yesterday."

Emma paused and seemed to have retreated to her thoughts.

Anne's own thoughts trailed off to the voices she heard in the dark corridor. She wondered if she should share it with Emma, or if it would make her even more worried. She decided that keeping secrets in a murder investigation was not a good idea. "Emma, I heard something in the corridor that evening, just as I got out of the bathroom, that concerns you. I don't know if it has anything to do with the murder, but I think you should know."

Emma looked Anne straight in the eyes. "That was you?" Emma said. Anne was taken aback by the comment. *Is there a note of accusation in her tone,* Anne wondered. "The police told me that a witness had overheard a conversation about me, a threat, but didn't tell me who had given them that information." Emma searched Anne's eyes.

Anne couldn't interpret Emma's reaction and for a moment got a ping of regret in her stomach. Maybe she shouldn't have identified herself as the witness. What did she know about Emma? *What if she's the killer?* Anne shook off that thought.

Since Emma now knew what Anne had overheard, Anne decided to share with her the rest of her speculations. "The voice was definitely a man. With a British accent. Since Sir Hubert was still speaking at the time, it must have been Adrian, or another assistant. But I don't know who the woman was. He was speaking to a woman. Her English was accented. So maybe a journalist or someone from your staff. Sarah or Ruth? Does it make sense to you? Do you suspect someone wants to hurt you? Is that what you are afraid of?" Anne said.

Emma let out a laugh, which surprised Anne. "I don't know!" Emma brought her hands to her hair and let out a yelp, which scared some sparrows into flight nearby. "The treasure is valuable. But not enough to kill for. I have no idea who would wish to harm me. I don't know who would wish to kill Thomas either."

"Well, you told me what the police think your motive is, but what about everyone else's?" Anne said.

"Everyone else liked Thomas. Ruth certainly did. She hasn't stopped crying. She really liked working for Thomas. Ruth has been with him for nearly 20 years. She started out at about the same time I did. I got her this job. We met at university–we were both studying archeology, you know–and then I ran into her one day. She seemed a little lost to me at the time, and I told her Thomas is looking for a secretary. I'm not sure if she ever finished her degree. She certainly doesn't talk about it."

"She seemed so shy at the reception," Anne said.

"She is. She hasn't had the easiest of lives," Emma said, but waved it off as though warning Anne not to ask any particulars. "She's such a sweet person. I actually heard her talking to Thomas a while back, once we knew Sir Hubert was coming, begging him to prevent Sir Hubert's arrival. She actually stood up for me. I heard her. When he asked her why she cared so much, she said that it was because it was going to be such a big shock for me and ruin all that I had worked for."

Anne nodded.

"Do you think Sir Hubert could have killed Thomas? Or what about Adrian?" Anne asked.

"I don't know."

"What about that woman, Melinda Spencer?" Anne suggested.

Emma laughed again. "She is scary, for sure. But I don't know if she can wield a sword. Actually, that reminds me, something I meant to tell you, when you asked about the weapon earlier-...the police think it doesn't have to be an expert.

The sword was sharp enough that if someone just swung it with enough force, it could take anyone's head off. Oh Anne, I've been going over everything, over and over, all night. I don't see anyone else who could have a motive. It looks like I'm the only one angry enough to kill him. Everyone loved the bumbling, harmless fool. Well, harmless to them, not to my career. He was the ruin of my career." Emma looked down at her watch. "Thank you for coming, Anne. I really needed to talk things over with someone. But I need to go back to work."

"I understand. If there is any way I can help you," Anne said, "I will."

Anne stayed behind to finish her coffee. She felt sorry for Emma. She couldn't understand why Emma was so hard on herself and why she assumed the police would consider her a prime suspect. Was there something that Emma was keeping from her? Why was Emma so worried? Was it what Anne had overheard that made her so distraught?

As she walked towards her car, questions swirled in Anne's mind: Who was angry enough with Thomas to kill him? Was there something in his past? Why now, what precipitated the murder? What had changed recently to make someone kill him? Was it the treasure? Was it one of the newcomers from England?

Adrian was a dark horse, Anne was sure of it.

Especially because she suspected he was the one she had overheard in the corridor. Did he have a reason to kill Thomas?

5 A visit from the past

Anne reached for her old jean shorts. On second thought, she decided against the jeans, partly because it was going to be another hot day, but partly because she wanted to dress up for Wendy. So she put on a breezy summer dress instead.

Wendy, an old colleague from Anne's pharmaceutical lab research days in Boston, was in Milan for four days for an industry conference and had decided to visit Anne in Ascona.

Milan was just a two-hour train ride and Anne was picking Wendy up at the train station in Locarno. Anne had offered to meet Wendy in Milan, but Wendy wanted to see where Anne lived. *To tell everyone one in the office about it*, Wendy had joked on the phone.

While Anne looked forward to seeing someone from her old life, she had to admit that Wendy was not on the top of her list. They had been in the same circle of friends at work, and had sometimes eaten lunch together, but Anne never really warmed up to Wendy. Wendy always struck her as too competitive, even when she didn't need to be.

And Wendy was the personification of the rule of dressing for the job you wanted. Anne thought there might be some truth to the saying. She had never followed that rule at her old job, and had dressed casually, and now had a new job where she could wear jeans every day. *Is that a bad thing,* Anne wondered, but brushed away the thought before she could decide.

From what Anne had heard from her old coworkers, and from Wendy herself when they spoke on the phone, Wendy had managed to get a promotion, in large part due to Anne's departure. Anne still found the topic of giving up her past career in order to move to Switzerland for her husband's job a bit sore, so she hoped that Wendy wouldn't talk shop the whole time.

"Yippee!" screamed Wendy when she saw Anne walking towards her.

Even if Wendy hadn't screamed, Anne would have had no problem spotting her among all the tourists waiting in front of Locarno's train station. Unlike most of them–who looked ready for a day of hiking in twill hiking shorts, sturdy boots, and backpacks, which more often than not, had hiking sticks hanging off of them– Wendy was dressed in a long summer dress worthy of a fashion blogger and wore a big straw sun hat. She looked as if she was going for a modern reinterpretation of *La Dolce Vita. At least,* thought Anne, *she'll fit with all the other people trying to out-impress each other along the promenade in Ascona.*

"It's so good to see you!" Wendy screamed again and leaned in to kiss Anne on each cheek. People turned to see what all the screaming was about. Anne wished Wendy would tone it down.

"Good to see you as well, Wendy!" Anne meant it. It was nice to see someone from her old life. All of a sudden a wave of nostalgia hit her, and she decided to put aside her hangups about Wendy and have a good time. Wendy had made the trip from Milan to visit her when she didn't have to. The least Anne could do was appreciate the gesture.

"Let's go Wendy, I think you'll enjoy what I have planned for the day," Anne said, and led the way to the car.

As they drove the ten minutes it took to get from Locarno to Ascona, Anne could see that Wendy was impressed. She kept commenting about everything she saw. It was exactly the stuff that had impressed Anne when she had arrived– the palm trees, the luscious flowers and gardens, the verdant mountains surrounding them on each side, the snow clinging to the mountain peaks even though it was June, and the temperature felt like August, the clusters of villages scattered among the hills, each with a stone bell tower marking its center.

Wendy's praises got even louder as they drove into Ascona.

"Oh, Anne. I can't believe this is Switzerland. This looks like a cross between a tropical island and Italy. I mean, look at all these palm trees and cacti. And these houses!"–Anne let Wendy keep on gushing, hoping she would get most of it out of her system and wouldn't be tossing loud comments around as they walked through Ascona or had lunch.–"They are so adorable. Absolutely to die for. I can't believe you live here. Don't tell me you live in a mansion with a pool."

Anne laughed and shook her head. "No. We actually have a tiny apartment, but it's enough for the two of us. And real estate is so expensive here."

"So it's still just the two of you?" Wendy lowered her tone as though she was a highschool guidance counselor about to discuss drugs with a student. She placed her hand on Anne's forearm. "I half expected you to come meet me with a stroller." Wendy laughed.

Anne focused on finding a parking place. She had decided to park next to the lake, and finding a spot could be tricky. *Maybe today won't be as fun as I expected*, Anne thought as she squeezed into a tight parking spot.

"So what have you been doing with yourself?" Wendy said.

They were sitting under the yellow and white

awning of a small traditional restaurant on the promenade overlooking the sparkling blue lake. The lake was extra sparkly today, as though showing off.

It was eleven in the morning and the kitchen would not be open for another hour, but the day was sunny, the view was gorgeous, and the constant stream of tourists along the promenade provided enough of a diversion when the conversation lagged.

Wendy sipped an Aperol spritz through a white plastic straw. *Why do Americans always order that drink*, Anne wondered. Anne was having a chilled glass of Prosecco. *I guess I'm an American cliche as well*, Anne laughed at herself.

"Not much," Anne answered. "I'm taking Italian lessons–they speak Italian in this part of Switzerland–and I started working in a bookstore. It's actually just up the street there."

"A bookstore?" Wendy almost choked on her orange cocktail. "I mean, Anne, Switzerland is like the mother ship for the pharmaceutical industry. Someone with your experience should not have trouble finding work," Wendy said, sounding almost indignant at the missed opportunities.

Anne just shrugged. She didn't have a good answer for Wendy. She had wondered the same thing.

"It's a pleasant place to work. Low stress, and a

nice cat."

"A cat! Anne, you can't be serious!" Wendy laughed.

Anne smiled, unsure whether to defend Maggie or let it pass. She decided to just let it go.

"I mean, yes, you are living everyone's dream, living in Europe," Wendy said, between bites of breadsticks that the server had brought, "but what are you doing with your life? What are you doing with your career? At least have a kid..."

The rest of the afternoon continued in the same vein, and Anne soon checked out of the conversation. She gave the expected answers and asked the expected questions about her old co-workers and work. But she was glad that she'd have to stomach Wendy only until her train back to Milan this afternoon.

Walking home after, Anne thought about all the doubt that Wendy had managed to stir up in a few hours. But she knew it wasn't really Wendy's fault. All the thoughts that Wendy's visit had brought up to the surface had been doubts that Anne had been avoiding addressing.

Yes, her life is so different now, but was that a bad thing? She was happy and relaxed. She lived in a beautiful place and worked in a place that gave her joy. Did she have to be ambitious? Was she really throwing away all her education and hard work? Was a woman who wasn't pursuing a career expected to have kids instead? Was she getting too old for kids?

And what about the bookstore? Is that what she wanted to do? Well, yes, for now she did. She felt a strange fascination with it. So many mysterious things had happened since she started work there–the store had a knack for attracting customers who got up to strange matters, and Maggie was one interesting cat.

But was it all Anne's imagination? Was the novelty of it all going to wear away soon and Anne would wake up one day sorry for all that she let the real world–her pharmaceutical career–slip by?

If she didn't have a clear life goal right now, did that mean she was wasting her life?

Sitting alone at dinner in her apartment, Anne wished that at least Ben were here.

6 Sticky fingers in the treasure trove

The sound of text messages pinging on her phone startled Anne out of her sleep. She leaped out of bed to find her phone.

While she usually switched her phone to sleep mode during the night–her family in the US had not yet figured out how to calculate the six-hour difference–when Ben was away Anne left her phone on in case he called in an emergency.

Still blurry-eyed, she peered at the phone screen. Several messages were waiting for her. But not from Ben.

The messages were from Emma. For a moment, Anne wondered if Emma had been arrested.

Stacked one under the other, the brief messages didn't give away much: *Are you awake? We should talk! It's about Thomas! Call me when you get this!*

Anne dialed Emma.

"Hi Emma!" Anne said when she picked up. "What's up?"

"Have you seen the papers this morning?" Emma said.

"No, I just woke up. To the pings of your messages. What's going on? What's this about Thomas? Has someone been arrested?"

"No, not yet, anyway. But Melinda from the *Roman-Society-for-Whatever* dropped a major bombshell yesterday to the police. Prior to his death, Thomas had been involved in smuggling artifacts!"

"Wow!" was all Anne could say. Her brain was still waking up, and this was way too much information to process this early in the morning.

"Yes, I know!" came Emma's excited voice on the other end. "This is major! A major scandal. This complicates things even further. Do you have time to drop by today? I'd love to have a chat with you over coffee. I need to get out of my head and talk these things through with someone. I'm sorry to always ask for you to come up to Bellinzona, but it's crazy here right now and I need to be near the castle."

"Yes, no problem. Let me stop by the store first and see if Marco needs me today. I'll text you at around 9:00-9:15."

"Okay."

"Talk to you soon." Anne hung up.

The news about Thomas being a smuggler sent Anne's thoughts in all sorts of directions. But she didn't really know what to make of it. She didn't know what smuggling meant exactly in the archaeological world. Was a lot of money involved? Could smuggling be the reason Thomas was killed? Sure seemed like it. But how did Melinda know about all this?

Anne hoped Marco wouldn't need her today. She really wanted to go have coffee with Emma and get more information about the smuggling. On the way to the bookstore, Anne grabbed a couple of local newspapers, and sure enough, the major headlines all had to do with the fresh development in the murder–Thomas the treasure smuggler.

The door bells jingled as Anne pushed the store door open, and Maggie jumped up on the counter to greet her.

◆ ◆ ◆

As Anne left the bookstore to meet Emma for coffee in Bellinzona, she heard someone call her name. She looked around at the crowd of tourists to see who was calling her. But they all walked past her. She turned back to head up the street, thinking someone had called another woman named Anne, when she heard her name again. This time she noticed that Luigi, the hipster purveyor of expensive coffee for the rich and idle, waved at her.

Anne weaved through the tourists and came

up to his street-side counter, which was right across from the bookstore.

"Hi Luigi," Anne said. "What's up?"

"Who was that gorgeous girl I saw you with yesterday?" Luigi flashed her a white smile, and his manicured hipster mustache curled up.

Anne rolled her eyes. She couldn't believe he called her over just to ask about Wendy.

"She went back to Milan and then is going back to Boston," Anne answered dryly.

"No, listen, that was not the reason I called you over," he said, and made to run his hand through his gelled hair, but thought better of it at the last moment. "Marco told me you guys were at the reception at the castle when the murder happened."

Anne didn't think asking for first-hand details about the murder was a better topic than Wendy.

She looked to the side. A couple of people were waiting to place coffee orders.

"Luigi, I don't think now is a good time to gossip about it. I have to run to Bellinzona and you have customers waiting." She nodded towards the people hanging about. She turned to leave.

"No, wait, I actually wanted to tell you something," Luigi said.

"Sorry, I've got to go. I'll catch you later," Anne said, jogging up the street.

"Marco thought it was significant," he yelled after her, but Anne was too far up the street to go back and she just waved back at him to indicate that she'd heard him.

Whatever it was, it could wait. She wanted to get to Emma.

❖ ❖ ❖

When Anne arrived at the cafe by the fountain with the water spitting seal, it surprised her to see that Emma was not alone. Ruth and Sarah sat on either side of her.

Anne threw Emma a questioning look, and Emma replied with a barely perceptible shrug.

"Hi everyone," Anne said.

"Hi, Anne," Emma said. "You remember Sarah, my research assistant and Ruth, Thomas' secretary."

"Hi guys," Anne said, and joined them at the table.

Anne had so many questions for Emma, but didn't know if she could speak freely in front of Ruth and Sarah. She waited to get her cue from Emma.

Anne ordered a cappuccino from the server, who walked up to their table.

"The news that Thomas was smuggling museum artifacts hit all of us pretty hard this morning," Emma said, as if trying to explain why Ruth and Sarah had joined them for coffee. "All of us wanted to get out of the castle for a while. With the police and Sir Hubert and his team, the place is becoming unbearable."

Ruth wrapped herself tighter in her ever-present cardigan. That she was wearing one despite the heat surprised Anne.

Ruth looked miserable. Her brown hair, peppered with gray strands, hung limply on each side of her face. Her eyes, rimmed with red, looked as though she hadn't stopped crying since the murder. Anne thought Thomas' murder must have been the biggest shock for Ruth.

Anne turned to look at Sarah. She looked just as downcast as Ruth. She avoided eye contact and kept her eyes glued to her cup of coffee.

Anne wondered why the two women had come at all. But maybe they were scared to be in the castle with a killer about.

"So have the police made any progress?" Anne asked. "Does this revelation throw new light on the case?"

"The inspector in charge came to interview us yesterday evening, just as we were about to go home for the day. Apparently, Melinda went to the police with her *revelation*, as you say, yesterday afternoon. They asked us if we knew anything about the smuggling. But none of us had any idea." Emma looked at the two other women.

Ruth shook her head. Sarah avoided eye contact again by gazing at the plaza beyond the cafe.

"Sarah feels bad, because she is responsible for keeping a record of all the artifacts we've excavated or acquired over the years. But most of them go in the storage room, and short of doing an inventory, we wouldn't know if anything is missing. It could have been going on for years."

"*Dio*," Sarah sobbed softly.

"No one is blaming you, Sarah," Emma said, turning to her.

"But how did Melinda discover Thomas was a smuggler?" Anne said.

"She is friends with antique dealers in Italy, and whenever some interesting Roman artifact surfaces, they call her. Her husband has deep pockets, and she's willing to pay top price for items to put in the museum they are planning to open." Emma must have noticed Anne's questioning look because she added, "There is speculation that her retired investment banker husband is dreaming of opening a museum under his name in Rome, similar to the Peggy Guggenheim collection in Venice, and his tenacious bulldog of a wife is bullying dealers and buying up Roman artifacts on the cheap under the guise of returning them to their rightful place of origin.

"But anyway, apparently, Italian dealers have known for some time now of an illicit source of antiques from Switzerland. And when one of the items excavated here at the castle came up for sale just a few days ago, at a shady dealer in Italy, Melinda managed to get to the bottom of it, and traced the source to Thomas. Money can buy you a lot of information."

"Where is Melinda now?"

"She's making the rounds this morning at radio talk shows and interviews with journalists. I wouldn't be surprised if her husband bankrolls a news conference for her in the next few days. She's using this shocking news to shore up support for her organization. She's arguing that the best place for Roman artifacts is in Rome. Otherwise the plebes cannot be trusted and will smuggle or sell artifacts to the highest bidder, and the cultural treasures of the Roman Empire will forever disappear into private collections and away from the public, and so on, and so on." An emotion akin to disgust passed over Emma's face.

"The Board of Directors is desperate to stop her," Ruth spoke for the first time, surprising Anne. She didn't know Ruth spoke English, at least not so well. "She is ruining the reputation of the castles and the reputation of the whole Ticino archaeological and historical community with her rumors."

"I'm not sure if they're exactly rumors," Emma said. "That Thomas was selling museum artifacts on the black market is a fact."

"So does that explain the murder?" Anne said. "Was it related to smuggling? Does the police think the killer is someone involved with the smuggling?"

A loud sob emerged from Sarah, and suddenly tears rolled down her face.

"What is it, Sarah?" Emma said.

"It's Adrian," she cried out.

"What do you mean? What about Adrian? Do you think he's the killer?"

"I don't know," Sarah sobbed. And then she began to cry.

Everyone was silent, letting Sarah cry it out.

After a few moments, Sarah took a deep breath and said, "Adrian and I are an item."

Ruth gasped.

Sarah looked at Ruth and then around the table. "We started dating when I went to England, a few months back, for that conference," she turned to Emma, "but we had to keep it secret because Sir Hubert has forbidden Adrian and his entire staff from having relationships with other archaeologists. Says it's a perfect way for rivals to steal information on unpublished research. So we had to keep our relationship secret."

Anne noticed Ruth shaking her head in disbelief.

"And then," Sarah kept talking without a

pause, "when it became clear Adrian would move here for a while, I was so excited. But things got even more complicated. Adrian demanded that we continued keeping our relationship secret. He was afraid that Sir Hubert would fire him on the spot. But he told me he had a plan. On the night of the cocktail party we argued." Sarah took a deep breath and continued, "Adrian told me he had approached Thomas for a job, and that Thomas was willing to give a job to him, but in return Adrian, who is not in charge of artifacts, had to agree to falsify the records and not record some of the items that were excavated." Sarah started crying again.

No one spoke. No one wanted to interrupt her story. Anne expected Sarah to reveal Adrian as the murderer any second now.

"You see," Sarah looked around the table with a pleading look, "Thomas was trying to rope Adrian in into his smuggling scheme." Sarah looked at Emma. "Thomas had promised Adrian your job, Emma, in return. I'm sorry."

"Go on, Sarah," Emma said, her voice not betraying any emotion.

Anne realized the conversation she had overheard the night of the party had been between Adrian and Sarah. She tried to catch Emma's eye, but Emma was staring straight at Sarah.

"I told him he couldn't accept Thomas' offer. I told him I couldn't let him hurt you. You have been so good to us." Sarah turned to look at Ruth, who nodded in agreement. "But he was desperate. He wanted to get out from under Sir Hubert's thumb. He said he wanted to be with me." Sarah sobbed again, but this time was able to regain control of herself. "And the worst part was that Thomas was threatening to tell Sir Hubert about our relationship if Adrian didn't agree to be part of his smuggling scheme. Stupid Adrian had told Thomas the reason why he wanted a different job, away from Sir Hubert. He had told Thomas about our relationship."

Sarah broke down.

"Sarah, *mia cara*," Emma spoke gently to her and reached across to take her hand. "Are you telling us that Adrian is the killer?"

Sarah shook her head. "I don't know. I don't want to think so. But he was so mad that evening. What am I going to do?"

7 Longswords and other forms of exercise

"How was your coffee with Emma?" Marco asked as Anne walked back into the store.

"Well, actually, Ruth, Thomas' secretary, and Sarah, Emma's assistant, were also there," Anne said.

Anne's brow creased as she hesitated about how to proceed. "I thought we were going to talk about the smuggling, but the conversation took a different turn when Sarah confessed she was in a relationship with Adrian. And what's more, I think she thinks he's the killer."

Marco raised an eyebrow in response. Anne told him all that Sarah had said.

"So what do you think?" Anne asked Marco.

"Yes, it seems to explain everything neatly."

"You know, I was thinking, when I was driving back just now, Emma had mentioned that items in the storage room seemed disturbed and out of place. I guess the trafficking of stolen artifacts explains that mystery."

"Do you want some tea?" Marco asked and led

Anne towards his office.

Sitting across Marco's desk, Anne looked down at the cup of tea he'd offered her. "Did you know Ruth speaks English quite well?" she said.

Marco shrugged. "Lots of people speak English around here."

Maggie jumped in Anne's lap and Anne lifted the cup of tea above the cat so she wouldn't spill it.

"Yes, I know. But I mean, she speaks it without the usual Italian intonation. I don't know, it just made an impression on me. She seems like such a sad woman." Anne put her cup on the desk and stroked Maggie. "I think she must be about my age. She's the same age as Emma; they went to university together. And Emma is about the same age as me. But she seems so lonely. I can't get the image out of my head of her at the cocktail party. It was as if she was just hiding behind Thomas."

Maggie purred in Anne's lap. "Does it seem likely to you that Adrian is the killer?" Anne asked.

"Why do you say that?" Marco said.

"It's just that he's so young. What could have made him so angry with Thomas? He has his whole life ahead of him and his relationship with Sarah to consider."

"Young people could get very angry and sometimes they don't have the life experience to know how to control their anger," Marco said.

"But if it was Adrian, then the fact that Thomas was involved in smuggling becomes a moot point. Adrian killed him, if he actually had, because Thomas was putting pressure on him, threatening his career, and threatening to reveal his relationship with Sarah to Sir Hubert. But it wasn't about smuggling, per se." Anne sat thinking for a few moments, trying to collect her thoughts. "But what if it is about smuggling? Who would have a motive?" Anne leaned forward and nodded towards the newspapers on Marco's desk. "Did you find anything else interesting in the newspapers since this morning?"

"Nothing more than what we talked about. But Melinda Spencer has managed to be on a few radio shows since then," Marco said, patting the outdated radio set on his desk.

Anne picked up a different thread of thought. What if this Melinda is the killer? She knew about the smuggling, or at least strongly suspected it, but revealed it only after Thomas was killed. Why? Is she using it as a sort of alibi? Like, *'look how honest I am, I'm incapable of murder'*?

"But what would her motive be?" Marco said.

Anne felt the phone in her back pocket buzz, but she ignored it. She thought it would be rude to check her messages while talking to Marco. Plus, checking it would mean forcing Maggie out of her lap.

"I'm not sure. Maybe something to do with some priceless artifact that we are not aware of yet?...Something that surfaced on the black market that she wanted and couldn't get?...Some sort of argument she had with Thomas? She strikes me as so self-righteous, I wouldn't put it past her to dispense justice as she saw fit."

Marco didn't reply and Anne continued to pull at the mess of threads in her head that were her thoughts.

"Marco, is there something specific about this treasure that would make someone kill for it?" Anne said after a few moments.

"As far as I know, the treasure's worth lies more in its cultural value and is of value to the castles because of the light it can throw on their history. But I don't know if it has that much 'street value'. The newspapers are estimating several million. People have killed for less, I guess."

"Cultural and historical value," Anne said, almost to herself. "Don't you think it's strange how many people's careers have been disrupted since the treasure was discovered?"

"Hum," Marco said, nodding.

Anne continued, "The treasure should have been a career-making discovery for Emma and for her research assistant. But all of a sudden they find themselves pushed down the academic pecking order by the Board of Directors who invite Sir Hubert and his team to take the lead of the project. For Sir Hubert this is not a career-making project. He is already famous enough. But it's more of a high-profile, vanity project.

"What was the catalyst for this murder? What happened just before the murder?" For Anne, those were rhetorical questions, so she didn't wait for a reply from Marco. "The treasure was discovered and Sir Hubert arrived," she counted on her fingers. "One of those two was the catalyst," Anne said with finality in her voice.

"Oh, and Thomas was smuggling and selling artifacts from the storeroom. So, one of those three was the catalyst...Not a very smooth theory, is it?" Anne said, smiling.

"I guess we'll have to wait and see how the investigation develops," Marco said.

At that moment, the bells over the front door chimed. Anne got up to see who it was.

She was surprised to see Luigi standing at the front.

"Hi!" he said. Anne detected some shyness about him and wondered why that was.

"Hi Luigi. What's up? Do you need Marco?"

Anne turned to call Marco, but Luigi said, "No, I actually came to speak to you. Marco knows what I have to say."

Maggie jumped on top of the counter next to Anne and butted her head against Anne, as though pushing her towards Luigi. *What do you want Maggie,* Anne thought. *Are you matchmak-*

ing? I'm married!

At that moment, Maggie stopped and looked up at Anne. Anne stared back at the cat. *I'm sure you can't read thoughts,* Anne spoke in her head. *If you can, I command you to jump off the counter.*

Oblivious to Anne's thoughts, the cat laid on the counter and started purring.

Luigi cleared his throat. Anne had forgotten for a moment he was there.

"I'm sorry Luigi, what did you want to tell me?" Anne said, looking up at him. He was one of the few people around here who was taller than her.

Luigi cleared his throat again. "It's what I wanted to tell you this morning. I have a break and came to see you. It seemed so interesting and important when I told it to Marco, but now I'm not sure if it's even worth mentioning."

It surprised Anne that someone so good looking, who took so much care with his personal appearance, could be shy around women.

"What is it Luigi, you're freaking me out," Anne said.

He laughed, "There, now I've made it into a bigger deal than it is...It's just that when I read how that person at the castle was killed...and when I talked to Marco...the weapon caught my attention."

Anne nodded and encouraged him to continue.

"I have some buddies that belong to a European Martial Arts club in Milan. Do you know what that is?" Luigi said.

Anne shook her head.

"It's a club where they use medieval weapons to train. It's a form of exercise. Well, for some people it is; my buddies use it as a form of exercise. They throw axes at targets and such things, and use longswords to cut down things. It's great for upper body strength. Others join the club because they are weapons freaks." He paused and waved his hand as if to dismiss all he had just said. "Well, I just thought...We don't have a club like that around here. People who are into European Martial Arts have to go to Italy. Milan is the closest city with a club. There was even a local man who was club head at one point."

"Do you know his name?" Anne said.

"No, but I can find out. It's just such an odd weapon of choice, the *zweihander*. The thought just popped into my head that it could be a local person. Someone who was interested in medieval weapons. And since I know you're good at solving puzzles, I thought you might find the information interesting."

"Thanks Luigi," Anne said. "Let me know once you have the name of the local man who used to be head of the club. It could be a useful clue."

"I will," Luigi said, and turned to leave. At the top of the stairs he turned around and said,

"Why don't you give me your phone number, so I can text you when I have more information?" He walked back down and towards Anne.

Anne noticed Maggie was now staring up at her, half-closing her eyes with every purr.

Luigi handed Anne his phone so she could type her phone number. As Anne typed her thoughts raced: *Does he not know I'm married,* she wondered.

"You know, you should talk to my husband about getting some new roasts in your coffee shop," Anne said, hoping she sounded offhand and casual.

"Oh, yeah, I know your husband. Cool guy. A coffee expert," Luigi said with a smile as he took his phone back from Anne. "I'll text you soon," he said and left.

Anne looked down at Maggie and noticed that the whole time the cat had been laying on top of a newspaper, and while purring, had been clawing at a photograph in it. Anne took a closer look and saw that the shredded photograph was of Sir Hubert. A chill passed over Anne.

But before she could follow that train of thought, Anne's phone pinged. She took it out of her back pocket and saw a message from Luigi: *Stop by one day and we can discuss the merits of different roasts together.*

Anne smiled. But then she remembered that another message had come through while she was talking to Marco. She opened a message from Emma: *Adrian has been arrested.*

8 Man is not mightier than the sword

So that was that. Case closed, Anne thought, sitting at the kitchen table, dipping a chocolate cantuccini–the proper name for what Americans called biscotti, as she had recently learned–into her breakfast cappuccino the next morning.

Everything was nicely explained and tied up with a bow: Adrian and Sarah were in a relationship that they had to keep secret from Sir Hubert. Sir Hubert would fire Adrian if he found out Adrian was dating someone from the archaeology community. Why? Why was Sir Hubert so paranoid about rivals stealing his research ideas? And how would one even go about stealing an idea, anyway?

But Anne knew from experience that people in research and academia tended to be guarded about their research until they were ready to present it. So maybe Sir Hubert's behavior was a bit extreme, but not irrational.

She took a bite out of her now coffee soaked cantuccini, and savored the delicious mix of flavors.

Anne's focus returned to the murder and, between dips and bites, she continued listing the facts she knew: Adrian had approached Thomas for a job, attempting to get out from under Sir Hubert's influence. *Dip*. Thomas offered him a position on the condition that Adrian would join his antique smuggling scheme. *Bite*. Thomas needed someone to falsify records as he siphoned off Roman treasure to unscrupulous antiques dealers in Italy. *Dip*. Thomas even threatened Ardian with exposing his relationship with Sarah to Sir Hubert if Adrian didn't play along. *Bite*.

Yes, everything fits nicely, Anne thought.

And yet...her conversation with Luigi had planted a tiny doubt in Anne's mind. Why was no one talking about the choice of weapon?

Using a two-handed sword was such a brash way to kill someone. Why not just hit Thomas over the head with something?

Luigi seemed fixated on the weapon for some reason. Did it indicate to him something about the killer's mindset that she was not seeing? Anne made a mental note to ask him.

Anne took another cantuccini out of the package.

Is the killer a medieval weapons fanatic, she wondered. Adrian would have no problem swinging a sword. But was there even a hint in his past that he had any interest in swords and would know how to use one? Anne wondered if she would know how to use one. *Is there a trick to it, or do you just swing?* Emma had mentioned that according to the police anyone could have wielded the sword, but Anne made another mental note for a question for Luigi.

Anne looked at her phone. She had tried calling Emma after getting her text message yesterday, but there had been no answer. Anne assumed that things at the castle must be quite complicated at the moment. She would wait for Emma to call her instead.

With Sir Hubert now king of the castle, so to speak, who knew how things would turn out for Emma and Sarah. Or would Adrian's guilt tarnish Sir Hubert's reputation by association and he would return to England?

Poor Sarah, Anne thought. *She must be so distraught.* Her mind traveled back to the coffee they'd had together. Did Sarah know something more at the time? She'd seemed so sure of Adrian's guilt. Why?

Anne checked the time. It was close to nine o'clock; time to head to the bookstore. All this thinking about motives and weapons was getting her nowhere. She was just going in circles. She felt sorry for Sarah, but there was nothing she could do for her. Everything was in the hands of the police now.

Anne shut the heavy front door behind her as

her phone rang. She looked at the caller–it was Emma. Anne picked up immediately.

"Hi Emma," Anne said, anxious. "How are things?"

"Oh, Anne!" Emma cried out on the other end. "It's Sir Hubert. He's been beheaded too!"

Anne went numb all over. *What is going on at the castle?*

"Emma, I'm so sorry. Are the police there? Please get out of the castle if they are not!" Anne said, worried about the safety of her friend.

"Yes, they are here. I probably shouldn't be talking to anyone right now. I'll call you later once I know more. Just wanted you to know."

"Okay, stay safe, Emma," Anne said.

"I will," Emma said, and hung up.

Anne sat on the stone steps leading up to her front door. Her head was swimming. She needed a second to regroup before going to the bookstore.

Immediately her mind jumped to Maggie laying across the newspaper yesterday, clawing at Sir Hubert's picture. A chill crawled down Anne's spine, and, despite the warm morning, goosebumps broke out all over her arms.

She got up and headed to the store. Suddenly, she longed for the safety of Marco's company.

❖ ❖ ❖

"So we can assume Adrian is not the killer," Marco said.

"I guess that's what it means. But Emma didn't say when Sir Hubert's body was discovered, nor when he was killed. With so many tunnels and passages around the castle, it's possible that Adrian could have killed Sir Hubert yesterday, before he was arrested, and the body not discovered until this morning."

"Yes, we can't construct any meaningful theories before we have more details," Marco said, pensive.

"But what do you think connects Thomas and Sir Hubert? What could be the link between the two murders?"

Marco shook his head. "I didn't know them well enough to even make a guess why both of them would be murdered."

"Don't you think it has to be something that they have in common?" Anne said, unwilling to give up the discussion. "Like, the Roman treasure, or archaeology in general?...But you're right we don't know enough about Sir Hubert's death to make any guesses."

Anne and Marco sat together in Marco's office for a while, each seemingly lost in thought.

"I'm so worried about those women in the castle," Anne said. "Who knows what the killer's motives could be? They could be in danger. One of them could be an unwitting witness. Or one of them could be the killer," Anne said, and immediately froze, shocked that she would even think that. She couldn't picture a woman killing like that.

"The police are now there. I'm sure they will place a guard at the castle until they catch the killer," Marco said.

Anne was growing restless. She wanted desperately to talk to Emma, to find out more about Sir Hubert's murder. When did it happen? Who found him? In what part of the castle? Was Adrian still a suspect? And if he wasn't, then who was?

To take her mind off the murder, and to calm her wild thoughts, Anne went to do some work. Since the tragic cocktail party, she had done little at the bookstore.

She still needed to organize the digital copies of the maps Marco had given to Emma–the maps that had led to the discovery of the Roman treasure. Before handing the maps over, Marco had made sure Anne created digital files of them.

Unlike digitizing books, which was pretty straight forward, digitizing maps was a more intricate process. Because maps were large in size, larger than the scanner surface, they had to be scanned in sections. Then Anne used a specialized map software to correct for any distortion during scanning, splice all the sections together, and remove any overlap between scanned sections to recreate the original map. She also needed to adjust the contrast and play around with exposure to bring out faint details on the maps. Digitizing the original maps was a slow process.

Anne was fascinated by how details appeared and disappeared depending on the brightness and contrast settings. The maps showed sections of the castles long gone. Since their creation, the three castles had undergone a lot of changes, destruction, and renovation. The maps were not only valuable because they had led to treasure, but also because they showed the medieval footprint of the three castles. Connecting the digital files was like building a jigsaw puzzle, and Anne tried to visualize how the various pieces of the medieval maps fit in the modern-day ruins.

But Anne's head was not in her work. Her mind kept drifting to the new murder. She abandoned the files and went to talk to Luigi. Emma had clearly said that Sir Hubert was decapitated. So Luigi was right to think the weapon of choice was significant. The killer had used something similar again. Anne needed to find out more about European Martial Arts.

◆ ◆ ◆

"I heard back from my buddies, but they didn't know the last name of the local man. His first name is Luca, if that's any help."

Anne shook her head.

"I didn't think so," Luigi said.

With the morning rush for coffee over, Luigi had taken a break when Anne had approached him with questions about European Martial Arts.

They were now sitting in a small yard at the back of his cafe, closed off on all sides by tall stone walls. The walls blocked off the noise from the street, and a tall tree threw a dappled shade on their little table. Anne had no idea such a garden existed at the back of Luigi's shop. *It's too small for customers*, Anne thought. *How lucky for Luigi to have such a private place to escape to.*

"I'm sure they'll get back to me soon with his last name. One of them just has to go to the club to find out. But they all work full time and go there usually only on weekends."

"It's okay. I appreciate your friends trying to help," Anne said. "Yesterday, you seemed to think that the weapon was significant. Why?"

"Well, it just struck me that the killer knew which weapon to choose. Out of all the knives, swords and such things, the *zweihander* is the only one that can do the job, you know, to take off a head, without much effort. That sword does the job for you. You just have to swing. Oh, and it needs to be sharp enough." Luigi looked up at Anne, as if embarrassed by the information he was sharing with her.

Anne nodded, but said nothing. She was considering whether she would be able to swing a sword. *What mindset would someone need to be in to do that*, she wondered.

Her phone vibrated in her back pocket. It was a missed call from Emma. Anne hadn't heard it ring.

"It's one of the women from the castle. I'll need to call her back," Anne said. "Thank you for the coffee and the information."

"Of course. Any time. It was great sharing a coffee with you," Luigi said.

9 Lady Justice

Lost in thoughts of swords, suspects, and motives, Anne didn't notice how she got to Bellinzona.

Anne disliked driving so much back and forth, but Emma had sounded very distraught and Anne didn't think talking over the phone was the best way to help her.

She parked once again in the bowels of the parking lot under the castle. Instead of waiting for the elevator, she decided to climb the two levels up to street level. On the next level up, she saw a woman waiting for the elevator. *Why would anyone wait for the elevator for one level up,* Anne wondered, mentally passing judgement on the woman.

The woman, probably hearing Anne coming up the stairs, turned. It was Melinda. Anne, not sure if Melinda would recognize her, planned to pass by her without saying hello. But Melinda stared hard into Anne's face and Anne noticed the moment of recognition.

"You're that American woman," Melinda said. "The one that works for the bookseller in the wheelchair."

Anne flinched internally. She just nodded and moved to proceed climbing the stairs. She heard the elevator ping behind her.

"Are you here to see Emma?" yelled Melinda up the stairwell. "They won't let you in to see her."

Anne stopped and turned around. *What did Melinda mean?*

Instead of getting on the elevator, Melinda was climbing the stairs behind Anne. "The place is crawling with police officers. They won't let you in–"

"I'm not planning to go inside the castle," Anne said. *I'd rather not,* she added in her mind.

"–they've closed the place for tourists as well, not just the office space," Melinda continued.

Anne wondered why Melinda was telling her all these things and why she hadn't taken the elevator, but was instead following Anne up the stairs.

They reached street level.

Panting slightly, Melinda placed one hand on the wall to steady herself, and indicated with the other hand for Anne to wait.

Waiting for Melinda to catch her breath–*how could someone get winded by a single flight of stairs*, she wondered–Anne looked more closely at the woman in front of her.

Melinda was about the same age as her, maybe a few years older, but she gave off a completely different vibe. While Anne could pass for someone almost ten years younger, partly because of the graduate-student uniform of jeans and Converse high tops she wore, and partly because of good genes, Anne doubted Melinda had ever looked young. The image Melinda projected was of a President of a branch of the Women's Institute. Anne wouldn't have been surprised if she actually was one.

"Nasty business this," Melinda said, between breaths. "I can't believe the police allowed another murder to happen. Especially when they had a suspect in custody." Melinda took a pause.

Anne wondered what Melinda's point was.

"Oh, what a fate to befall Sir Huber!" Melinda said, a note of outrage in her voice. Anne wasn't sure if Melinda would be as appalled if the victim had not been noble.

Melinda leaned in closer to Anne. "Mind you," she continued in a confidential tone, "there was some dark blot on his past." Here Melinda paused to let the significance of her disclosure sink in.

"What do you mean?" Anne said. Even though she hated to admit to Melinda, she was curious.

"In his youth, while he was a graduate student, some scandal was hushed up."

"Do you know what it was?"

"I don't know the particulars, but one could

guess what wealthy young men get up to. Sir Hubert always had an eye for pretty women," Melinda said, and smiled demurely, lowering her eyes, as if to suggest she had once been one of his love interests. "I can only assume it was an unwanted pregnancy of an undesirable girlfriend." Her eyes returned to Anne, and her tone grew cold. "I only know that family connections were used to suppress the rumors. The old boys' network closed ranks and so on. His father, being a peer of the realm, couldn't allow a scandal to fester."

Anne didn't want to ask how Melinda knew all that.

As though reading her mind, Melinda continued, "We moved in the same social circles. Word gets around. Ladies talk over tea," she circled her hand up in the air, as if to illustrate the refined social circles she moved in.

Anne looked at her watch. She was running late, and she was desperate to talk to Emma. "Thank you for all of this information. It's very interesting. But I have to go. Have a good day."

And Anne walked away from Melinda before she could stop her.

Walking towards the cafe where she was meeting Emma, at the square with the seal fountain, Anne went over what Melinda had said. Could that dark stain on Sir Huber's past be the reason for his death? If so, how was that connected to Thomas' murder? Were the two murders connected at all? Or was someone just out to settle scores?

Anne got the impression that Melinda seemed to think that the unwanted pregnancy was terminated. But what if it hadn't? What if the mother was paid off to keep quiet, and the child provided for?

Anne stopped abruptly. *The kid would be in their twenties now.* She needed to think this through before meeting up with Emma.

That's Adrian's age, Anne thought. Was Adrian Sir Hubert's son? Did Adrian kill his own father? Did he know Sir Hubert was his father? *But why wait until now to kill him,* Anne wondered. *What was the cause?*

Anne continued walking. *His mother!* The theory suddenly popped into her head. What if he was given up for adoption and just met his real mother recently? *That's just too wild,* Anne told herself. *And who would the mother be?*

She brushed off the idea for a moment, but then reconsidered. *The mother would be in her forties now*, Anne did a rough mental calculation. Her thoughts jumped to the women connected to the case. Emma was about the right age. And so were Ruth and Melinda. *Could Melinda have been talking about herself just now?* Somehow, Anne didn't think so.

But let's say either Emma or Ruth were the

mother, Anne continued her train of thought. *They were at university together. When would either of them have met Sir Hubert? Did he visit Switzerland at some point?*

Anne would ask Emma a bit more about her university years.

When she arrived at the cafe, Emma was already sitting at their now usual table under a big chestnut tree.

As Anne sat down, she felt, for the first time, uneasy around her friend. Anne hadn't decided if she would tell Emma about her conversation with Melinda and the revelation about Sir Hubert.

"How are you, Emma?"

"Oh, not so good." Emma tucked some flyaway strands nervously, and Anne noticed that Emma's hair was more disheveled than usual, with wayward curls forming a frizzy halo around her head.

Emma shook her head from side to side. "I don't want to go to work until they catch the killer," she said. "I'm afraid, Anne," she said, and looked into Anne's eyes. "What is going on?"

"Do you know what happened? I thought Adrian was arrested for the murder? Do you know if Sir Hubert was killed before or after Adrian was arrested? How was Sir Hubert killed? And who found him?...I'm sorry for all the questions. We don't have to talk about it if you don't want to."

"Oh, it was awful. Ruth found him. She came running to me right after she did. She was shaking. It was a gruesome sight. Another of these longswords, a *zweihander*, like the first one, lay next to him. Where are these swords coming from?...Probably from our storage room. There are so many of them to keep track of. Piles of them. But how are the swords taken out?...The police had the room sealed off after the first murder and they said no one has used their card to unlock it since. So where are the swords coming from? You can't just bring something like that off the street?"

"Where was he found?" Anne asked. She thought maybe that would explain where the sword was taken from.

"That's another strange thing. The castle is full of these dead end passages. There are like three or four ways to get from the storage room to the offices and from the offices to the museum. But there are a few other dead end corridors, remnants from earlier times. He was found in one of them. What was he doing there?"

Anne creased her brow, thinking. "What was Ruth doing there?"

"She was on her way to the museum ticket office. The corridor goes by that dead end passage, and she saw a dark line. She assumed it was water leaking from somewhere and went to look, in case the stone ceiling needed to be patched up-...and she found him…" Emma trailed off.

"So, has Adrian been cleared of the murders, since he was in police custody at the time?"

"Not exactly. The police have been asking a lot of questions about whereabouts and times. He hasn't been released yet. They are still trying to establish a timeline for this second murder and whether Adrian could have committed it. It happened some time yesterday. They haven't told us exactly when."

"What about fingerprints on the swords? I can't believe that they haven't found any evidence like that. Or blood stains on clothes."

"Apparently there aren't any fingerprints. We all have these cotton gloves we use when handling artifacts. We all carry them in our pockets at all times. It's a habit. So we're all still under suspicion. But you're right about stains. I hadn't considered that."

"What about all the support staff? The staff at the museum, the ticket office? Did they not see anything? "

Emma shook her head. "Nothing."

Both women sat in silence for a few moments.

Anne wanted to discuss what Melinda had told her, but didn't know how to bring it up. "Have the police suggested any motive for Sir Hubert's murder? Do they suspect that the two murders are connected?" She paused. "Could it be something out of Sir Hubert's past catching up with him?" she said in a casual voice.

"They've said nothing to us. I guess plenty of people had motives. Sir Hubert apparently was a despot. He had already threatened to fire Adrian when he learned about his relationship with Sarah after Thomas' murder. Adrian was maybe trying to stop Sir Hubert from ruining his career." Emma sighed. After a few moments she said, slowly, "I guess I also have a motive to have killed Sir Hubert."

Anne shifted in her seat, but didn't dare interrupt. She worried about what would come next.

"He took control of the most significant discovery of my career. I'm still so mad about the Board of Directors' decision to invite him to take over the lead from me...But I guess now I don't have to worry about it...someone eliminated that problem for me," Emma said, with a thin smile. Anne could sense the conflicting emotions in Emma.

"So what happens now?" Anne asked, relieved that her friend didn't make a confession.

"Well, we continue as usual. The police will put a guard outside the storage room. We'll have to find a different place to store the Roman artifacts for now. We still have a lot of cataloging to do. Sarah has been such a sweet thing. Despite Adrian being arrested, she still comes to work to help clean and catalog the treasure. Says it helps get her mind off her problems."

This surprised Anne. She had expected Sarah to have taken a few days off. *So Sarah was also there at the time of the murder*, she thought.

"I don't feel well." Emma put her head in her hands. "I need to go home and lie down."

Anne looked at her. Emma had gone pale.

"Sorry for making you come all the way out here," Emma said, her voice strained.

"No problem. Do you want me to walk you home?"

"No, thank you. I'll speak to you soon." Emma said and walked slowly away.

Anne stayed behind to finish her coffee and collect her thoughts. Her gaze traveled towards the fountain in the middle of the square. She watched the water cascading–it jumped out of the seal's mouth and rolled down its back.

As Anne's thoughts began flowing with the rhythm of the water, she looked across the fountain to the building directly behind it.

The building was bathed in strong sunlight. Anne wondered why she had never noticed it before. Its neoclassical architecture gave it the unmistakable look of an administrative building. Anne didn't know what government department it housed, but a statue in the triangle above the building's entrance, the pediment, caught her attention.

Anne left money for her coffee on the table and went across the square to inspect the statue.

Yes, she had been right. The statue was leaning on a longsword. It was a statue of a woman–Lady Justice.

Ideas and connections began firing so rapidly in Anne's mind, she had a hard time keeping up with them. Of course, how could she have not seen it before. The killer was a woman. If Adrian was not the killer, the only other option left was a woman. There were no male suspects left. *Didn't Luigi say the longsword does the job for you? You just have to swing it.*

Running towards the underground parking, Anne texted Luigi: *Can a woman like me swing a longsword and behead someone?*

Anne kept looking at her phone as she ran. Almost instantly Luigi replied: *Yes!* Followed by: *Are you okay, Anne? Are you in danger?* The messages kept coming: *Where are you? Do you want me to come?*

She texted back: *On my way back. Don't worry.*

Anne needed to go back to the bookstore and make sense of all this.

10 The Executioner

So it's not about the treasure or the smuggling after all, Anne thought, while driving back to Ascona. *It's about justice. It has to be. The method, execution-style, fits.*

But justice about what, Anne wondered. She guessed it had to do with something that happened a long time ago. Probably something to do with the stain on Sir Hubert's past Melinda had referred to. *But what?* Anne wondered if she would be able to find something online.

And how was Thomas involved in all this? Was he murdered by mistake? Every man wore a dark suit the night of the cocktail party. Could the killer have mistaken Thomas for Sir Hubert?

When Anne got to the store, Marco looked like a parent waiting for a child to sneak back into the house after curfew. But what was Luigi doing here? Anne immediately assumed something bad had happened.

"What's wrong?" Anne said. "Why are you both looking at me this way? Luigi, why are you here?" Anne had no idea what was going on, but something strange was up. Luigi was usually at his coffee counter across the street.

"What happened, Anne?" Luigi said.

"What do you mean?" Anne said, confused.

"I got that crazy message from you asking if a woman can use a longsword to behead a person. I panicked. I was afraid you were about to get yourself into trouble," Luigi said.

"Oh, that," Anne said, and sighed with relief. "It's nothing. I just went to see Emma. Marco knew where I was," she said, a bit defensively.

"Yes, but when I showed him your messages, he got worried as well–"

"It wouldn't be the first time you've managed to get in a tight spot with a killer," Marco interjected. Anne felt herself get hot, but she saw Marco smile kindly.

"–yes, there's a maniac running around that castle slicing heads off. You should stay away," Luigi said.

"I wasn't in the castle. Just having coffee," Anne said, her voice rising. *What is this,* Anne thought, anger simmering in her head. *I'm not a child in need of reprimand.*

"So what did you learn from Emma?" Marco said.

Anne took a breath to calm down. She was thankful for the change of focus.

She told them about running into Melinda at the parking lot, her conversation with Emma, and seeing the statue of Lady Justice on the building across the square.

"–Seeing the statue, leaning like that on its sword, which thanks to these murders I can now identify as a *zweihander* longsword, was like an epiphany. It just hit me that the killer must be a woman. It has to be a woman. There is no one else left, if we exclude Adrian. I bet the key to the murders is some sort of long-overdue justice."

"Well, then you'll find this interesting," Luigi said. "The nickname of the local guy, Luca, who was head of the European Martial Arts club for a while, was 'The Executioner'."

Anne stared at Luigi. Even Marco turned to look at him.

"Sorry, they still don't have his last name," Luigi continued, unaware of the effect his statement had. "Seems the club's strength is not in its record-keeping. He hasn't been part of the club for a long time. Some sort of family trouble. Seems like everyone just called him 'The Executioner'."

"Why was he called that? 'The Executioner' is such a formidable nickname?"

"According to my friends, it's because his favorite weapon of choice when training was the longsword. He loved doing demonstrations at festivals with it. Chopping through stuff with it. Apparently he was a tall, big man, and looked a bit like one of those American wrestlers with the hair and the muscles." Luigi used hand gestures to illustrate the man's height and bulk.

"But one thing someone at the club remembered was that he had a daughter. No one has seen her; she never came to the club. But they know for sure he had a daughter," Luigi said, and looked earnestly at Anne. "It could be one of the women at the castle, you see?"

Anne felt her heart racing. She knew all of this was somehow connected. The murders at the castles, the longswords, the executioner's daughter, the family trouble. But there were still too many suspects. There were so many women connected to the case.

"We really need his last name, Luigi," Anne said.

"I know. I'll send it to you as soon as I have it." Luigi looked past Anne. "There is a crowd forming by the coffee stand. I need to go." Luigi leaped up the stone steps to the front door and was gone in a second.

"What do you think?" Anne turned to Marco. "Should we let the police know?"

"I'm not sure," he said, shaking his head. "It's all just guesses...All we know for now is that the killer is probably a woman. But by now the police have probably realized the same thing. As you say, there's no one really left–."

"Unless it's this 'executioner' guy, taking revenge for something that happened to his daughter."

"Melinda's information is interesting," Marco said. "But she's probably already reported it to the police. I doubt we have anything concrete to share with them."

Anne felt a bit let down. She had expected her epiphany about Lady Justice and her sword would get her somewhere. But it only brought up more questions.

She went to her office to continue her work. She had spent enough time on the case, driving back and forth to Bellinzona. While she was glad Marco was so understanding, it was time to finish the maps.

While putting map images together, Anne went over all she had learned today: Sir Hubert had a secret in his past. Was that why he was killed? Did he have a secret child? If so, was the mother one of the women working at the castle? Was it the child or the mother who had killed Sir Hubert? Was the mother the daughter of 'The Executioner'? Why wait so many years? And where does Thomas fit in? Were the two crimes even related?

"Ugh, it's all just suppositions and conjectures!" Anne yelled at her computer, voicing her frustration.

She leaned back in her chair and stared unseeing at the computer screen. Anne wasn't sure when the doubt had crept into her mind. Maybe it had been there all along, but she had been ignoring it. Once acknowledged, however, the idea started to grow.

"What if the murderer is Emma?" Anne spoke her hunch out loud.

The more Anne thought about it, the more clear everything became. Emma was angry with Thomas for being inept and for ruining her career in the process. She was angry that Sir Hubert had been invited to take over, and without being told. To add insult to injury, Sir Hubert was someone from Emma's past. Was Sir Hubert's relationship with Emma the dark stain Melinda had referred to? Was Emma the daughter of 'The Executioner'?

Anne had to admit she knew very little about Emma's private life. She knew very little about any part of Emma's life.

Abandoning the maps for a moment—*I'll get back to them in a second*—Anne opened the internet browser on her computer. She typed in Emma's name. A bunch of articles about the recent Roman treasure discovery appeared. Anne kept going back further and further into the search results: academic articles, links to the Bellinzona castles, links to the Ticino Ministry of Culture and its Archaeological Department. But nothing Anne could use.

What am I looking for, Anne asked herself. *Am I expecting to find a photo of Emma with a baby in her hands and a caption 'Sir Hubert's illegitimate child'?*

Both Adrian and Sarah were the right age to be Emma's child. But how could she find out if either of them was Emma's child?

Anne put in Emma's and Adrian's names in the search bar. Lots of articles about the recent murders, the Roman treasure, and castles came up. She switched to images. Again, just photos of the Roman artifacts, the castles, and the reception.

She put in Emma's name in combination with Sarah's and got similar search results. She switched to pictures; more of the same.

Anne searched for Adrian's name alone, but got overwhelmed with hits about his recent arrest and the murders.

Ready to give up her fruitless search, Anne switched to Sarah's name. She scanned quickly through more of the same–murders, treasure, castles. Except...a photo caught her attention. It was a photo of Sarah in a black fencing costume. Sarah was a local fencing champion.

Anne stared at the photo. *Is this photo even significant?* The photo triggered all sorts of questions in Anne's mind: Was Sarah related to 'The Executioner'? Was she his granddaughter? Was fencing Sarah's way of carrying forth his love for weapons? Was Emma Sarah's mother? Was Sarah Sir Hubert's child?

Anne thought back to the times she had seen Emma and Sarah together. Emma was always so protective of Sarah. Anne could almost say Emma's behavior towards Sarah was motherly.

Sarah, of course. Why had I never considered Sarah as a suspect, Anne wondered.

Suddenly Anne realized Sarah had exactly the same motives for killing Thomas and Sir Hubert as Adrian did. She could have killed both of them out of love for Adrian. To protect Adrian. Sir Hubert was blocking their relationship and Thomas was pressuring Adrian into illegal activities. Sarah could also have killed Sir Hubert to prove Adrian's innocence. Anne still didn't know if Sir Hubert was killed before or after Adrian was arrested, but what if Sarah killed Sir Hubert, after Adrian was arrested, to confuse the police?

Anne paused. *All of these arguments could be applied to Emma as well,* she thought with a sinking feeling. *What if Emma did all that to protect her child from these scheming, domineering men? Regardless of whether it's Adrian or Sarah. The motives work equally well for both.*

Anne sat for a few more moments arranging her thoughts. But the more she tried making sense of it all, the more muddles she got. Without any additional concrete information, she could go in circles for days, pinning the same motives on each of her suspects.

She told herself she needed to face the truth

sooner or later. Disheartened, she texted Emma: *Did you know Sir Hubert back in university?*

Anne's phone rang.

"What is this about, Anne?" Emma said as Anne answered, sounding irritated.

"Sorry, I didn't mean to..."

"No, I'm sorry," Emma sighed. "I can't get rid of this headache."

"I wanted to ask you about something I heard about Sir Hubert's past," Anne said, proceeding cautiously. She still didn't want to reveal what Melinda had said. She didn't want Melinda to be the next victim, in case what Melinda had told her was actually relevant to the killer. "Did you know Sir Hubert back at university?" Anne waited and didn't dare breathe. She wasn't sure how Emma would react, but she steeled herself, ready for the blow she knew was coming.

"I knew of him. He was a prick even back then, from what I had heard." Emma said. Anne was surprised how casual she sounded. "But I was at Cambridge for only one semester," Emma continued, "on an exchange. And he was at Oxford. And the two universities didn't really collaborate on archeological research."

Anne was confused. What was this about Cambridge and Oxford?

"I assumed you went to university here, in Switzerland," Anne said.

"Yes, I did. But I did a short stint during graduate school at Cambridge. Just a semester, as I said. But if it's something England-related, you could ask Ruth," Emma said.

"Why Ruth?" Anne was surprised for a second time.

"Ruth went to Cambridge," Emma said in a matter-of-fact tone.

"What?" Anne said. It was all she could muster. The revelation made her break out in goosebumps.

"Didn't you know? I told you we met at university."

"I assumed it was here…"

"No, no. Oh, I thought you knew," Emma said, her tone still casual and off-hand. "Ruth was doing a graduate degree in archaeology at Cambridge. I thought I had told you all that."

11 Of two maps

Anne knew Ruth attending Cambridge was significant. *But how?*

Well, for one, Anne had never really considered Ruth. She'd always been there, in the background, but Anne had never considered her as a suspect. But then again, Anne had never considered Sarah as a threat either. Could they be mother and daughter? Could they be in this together?

Or maybe Adrian was the killer, after all?

And what about Melinda? She seemed to know both men well. And she knew secrets about them, which she revealed only after they were dead. Was that a clever tactic to deflect attention from herself and her true motives?

Her thoughts spiraling, Anne told herself that she had to stop thinking about the murdered. She was driving herself crazy. She'd have nothing concrete to go on until Luigi found out the family name of Luca 'The Executioner'. *But even then*, Anne thought, *there is no guarantee that it will bring me any closer to the truth. The two things could be completely unrelated.*

Anne tried to go back to work, but her thoughts betrayed her. *If Ruth being at Cambridge is significant*, she thought, *then the key to the mystery must lie in England.*

The only sensible thing was to look up Sir Hubert online and see if she could get any information about the scandal his family had hushed up all those years ago.

Anne knew that the British press loved any sort of aristocratic scandal, and she wondered if there might be some tidbits that got leaked to the press. She hoped *Tatler*, the society gossip magazine, had archives going back twenty-odd years.

She knew it was a long shot, but gave it a try. But after a few minutes of searching, Anne had to admit defeat. Sir Hubert's reputation in the press was squeaky clean. If there had been any scandal, his family had dealt with it with an iron fist. The search pages were filled with reports about his death and achievements. The only thing Anne discovered was that the British press had decided Sir Hubert's death was connected to the Roman treasure and that he was the unfortunate casualty of Thomas Schmidt's antique smuggling ring.

Anne gave up on the internet. It wasn't getting her anywhere.

Looking at her work in front of her, Anne realized there was one puzzling aspect about the murders she hadn't considered fully yet.

Where were the swords coming from?

Anne leaned back in her chair and tried to remember all she knew about the weapons.

She heard the door to her office squeak. Someone was pushing it open, just slightly. She turned to see who it was, but the next moment Maggie jumped in her lap. Anne was always surprised by how Maggie could sense an empty lap.

Anne waited for Maggie to get comfortable in her lap and returned to her thoughts.

The two murders were done using the same type of sword, but not the *same* sword. Each time, the weapon was left by the body.

Why not use the same weapon? Why leave it by the body? Was it a message? Or was it logistics? Was it easier to get a new weapon than hide a bloody one?

Having two swords meant one of two things: either both murders were premeditated, and the killer had stashed two swords somewhere for later use; or the killer had a way of getting fresh swords.

But from where? Even if the killer had a collection of swords at home, it's not like one can just carry a sword into the castle. Someone was bound to notice.

So the swords were most likely coming from inside the castle itself. And most likely from the storage room. Emma herself had admitted that with such a large collection, it was hard to know if something was missing without doing an inventory check.

Prior to the first murder, everyone with a key card had accessed the storage room at some point, so anyone could have taken a sword out and hidden it in an abandoned passage. But how did the killer get the sword for the second murder? There was no record of anyone going into the storage room.

Was there another way in?

Yes, Anne suddenly realized. All needed lay in front of her. And she didn't even need the internet.

She started opening up the digitized map files on her computer. There were so many of them. Some she had already connected into bigger pieces, but some still needed to be placed in the correct configuration. She continued opening files until she found the puzzle pieces she needed.

Anne lined up the images on her screen. Judging by the position of the outside walls and main castle entrance, these pieces of the medieval map corresponded roughly to the present-day location of the castle offices, reception hall, museum, and storage room.

Then Anne took a piece of paper and drew a rough diagram of what she could recollect of the modern layout. She had visited the office area several times at the beginning of the excavation, bringing maps and documents from the bookstore to Emma after she had scanned them.

She drew Thomas' office, Emma's office, the museum, the reception hall with the bathroom, and the hallway beyond where Thomas' body was discovered. Then she took a red pen, compared her drawing to the medieval map on her screen, and began overlaying in red the medieval rooms, walls and passageways. Some of the outlines matched, but she was surprised to find big chunks of the castle missing. Anne played around with the contrast and brightness of the scanned files. Some of the lines were extremely faint.

At last, she was satisfied that she had the two layouts aligned. But as she looked down at her paper to see if anything jumped out at her, all she saw was a jumble of black (modern castle) and red (medieval castle) lines.

"Time to go home, Anne," Marco said, popping his head around the door. "It's after six. It's been a long day."

12 A secret passage

Anne spent part of the evening looking at the jumble of lines on her hand-drawn map.

Had she missed something?

The lines on the paper were just as tangled as her thoughts. She couldn't make sense of anything–neither her theories about the murders, nor the lines of the map in front of her. So many intertwining lines and threads.

She went to her empty bed, her head throbbing. Thoughts of failure swirled in her mind. She kept going back to her meeting with Wendy, to her old job, to her old life. Why was she even getting herself involved in these mysteries? It was up to the police to solve. And what was she doing at that bookstore? She had studied for so much more. It was time to look for a proper job.

Lying awake in bed, Anne felt the darkness closing in around her. She wished at least Ben was at home. But he was somewhere deep in a tropical forest, on the other side of the world, in a completely different time zone, without reception. Unable to call him and unable to sleep, Anne typed out a long email to him, telling him all about the events of the last few days–the murders, Wendy's visit, her doubts and regrets.

She tossed and turned for what felt like hours and was not sure when she finally fell asleep.

◆ ◆ ◆

The morning light stung Anne's eyes. *That's what happens when you don't get enough sleep*, she thought.

She walked to the living room and picked up her drawing of the castle off the kitchen table. The strain of trying to focus on the layout made her eyes water. She went to splash cold water on her face.

After she made herself a cup of coffee, Anne sat down with the piece of paper in front of her. While she drank her coffee, she studied the layout.

At first, the lines were just as meaningless as yesterday, but slowly, a picture formed in front of her eyes. She could see it. Yes, she definitely saw it. There was a passageway from the medieval map that ran in about the same area where the modern storage room was. Could this be a secret passage the killer was using to get access to the weapons unnoticed?

Anne needed to share this information with Emma. She grabbed her phone and took a photo of her sketch. She was about to send it to Emma when she stopped herself.

She couldn't send Emma the photo. It wasn't safe. What if the killer saw the message?

Anne dialed Emma. She was going to ask Emma to go for coffee with her, to get her out of the office. She'd tell her about the map then.

The call went to voicemail. Anne didn't leave a message. She didn't think it was safe.

What could she do? Was an email safe? Probably not.

And why hadn't Emma picked up? Wild thoughts raced through Anne's mind: What if Emma was in trouble? What if the killer (Sarah, Ruth or Melinda, or whoever it was) was picking off archaeologists for some reason?

What if Emma is next?

13 A dead end

Anne knew if she thought too hard about it, she would turn back and retreat to the safety of the bookstore.

But her friend was most likely in danger. Anne had to make sure everything was okay.

Plus, she had just figured out how the weapons were being taken out of the storage room. She needed to warn Emma. And the only way to do that was in person. Any other way of communication might tip off the killer that Anne was on to them.

Anne still had no clear idea who the killer exactly was, but she pushed that worry to the side. For now, getting to Emma was a priority.

She was driving towards Bellinzona. She had texted Marco that she'd be late for work this morning. She hadn't told him where she was going. Judging by his behavior yesterday, he'd try to stop her and tell her the police have figured it out already.

Anne now stood at the base of the castle. Her eyes traveled up the huge granite rock on which it stood. The rock had never looked so big and menacing. The castle seemed miles above her. She hesitated. To get to the castle she had to take the elevator that cut through the heart of the rock and brought her to the top.

Anne dialed Emma one more time. What could be the matter? Why was she not answering her phone? She sent Emma a text and got in the elevator.

At the top, Anne expected to be met by police. But she saw no one around. *How strange*, Anne thought.

She proceeded to the offices.

"Fermare!" Someone yelled at her. Anne jumped. A policeman was walking towards her. *So there are police officers around after all.*

He proceeded to say something in Italian, but Anne was not sure she understood completely. She could guess what he was saying, though.

Anne told him, in English, that she doesn't speak Italian, and that she had come to drop off some important research books for Emma. She had grabbed a few antique books from home, just in case she had to lie her way in, as she was doing now.

He hesitated, but took down her personal information and let her through. *It's obvious I'm not carrying a sword*, Anne thought. *It's not like I can't clobber someone to death with these withered volumes.*

Anne was half expecting to find Emma in her

office, but when she got there, Emma was not in it. Anne wondered what to do next.

She sat for a few minutes in Emma's office and then wandered down the hall to the other offices, but she didn't see anyone. Anne considered going back to the policeman and asking where everyone was, but decided against it. He might change his mind and ask her to leave.

She went back to the office. It was obvious that Emma was at work today. Her jacket and bag were here. Anne put her own bag on a chair. She considered leaving Emma a note and walked over to her desk.

Emma's desk was large and littered with books, printouts, and photocopies. A set of printouts on top caught Anne's attention. She went back to her bag and took out the hand-drawn diagram of the castle. The printouts on Emma's desk were the same sections of the medieval map Anne had been looking at last night.

Anne's heart started beating faster. She felt blood rushing to her head. Had Emma made the same discovery as Anne? Had she gone looking for the passage? Anne grabbed her hand-drawn map, felt to make sure that her phone was in her back pocket, and left Emma's office.

Once in the corridor, Anne stood for a few moments, trying to get her bearings. She was glad no one was around to ask what she was doing. She looked down on her diagram and closed her eyes to visualize where she stood in relation to the medieval map.

She turned left. She followed the corridor to the end. Here the corridor forked. The corridor in use continued to the right. Lightbulbs hanging from the curved stone ceiling illuminated the passageway all the way down to where it turned again.

But according to Anne's hand-drawn map, the passage she was looking for, the secret one that would lead her to the storage room, was to the left.

Anne turned left. Light from the corridor she'd just left illuminated the first few feet of this passageway, but without artificial light, Anne saw only darkness ahead of her. She took out her phone and switched on the flashlight. She did not know how quickly the flashlight would drain her phone, and hoped the battery would last long enough for her to reach the storage room.

She walked down the passageway, keeping the phone low and illuminating just a few steps ahead of herself. The light from her phone rippled over the flagstones on the ground. Her footsteps echoed, magnified by the stone walls surrounding her. As she got deeper into the passageway, the air was cool and still.

But after a few minutes the passage ended abruptly. She'd reached the end.

Anne turned around. She was confused. This

couldn't be right. Had she missed something? According to her map, following this passage would lead her to the storage room.

Stuffing the paper diagram in her pocket, she opened the photo of the map on her phone. It was easier to see, and she could zoom in. With a sinking feeling she saw that the original passage, the one on the medieval map, was much longer. This passage must have been blocked off at some point in the last few centuries.

Disappointment welled up in Anne. She had been so sure she had solved the mystery.

She stood in the darkness for a few moments, thinking. Then began retracing her steps back to where she had come from. But this time, instead of illuminating the ground, she moved her flashlight over the surface of the stones on each side of her. She had decided to check the walls.

Anne walked back slowly and switched her flashlight from one side of the passageway to the other, looking for any openings in the wall. As she moved her flashlight from the left wall to the right, a shadow caught her eye. She moved her flashlight back to the left-hand side.

Anne felt like the girl in the *Labyrinth* movie: she had found an opening in the wall.

While no wider than a slit, the opening was enough for Anne to squeeze through.

Anne inspected the space she now found herself in. It was another corridor.

Anne looked down at her map, but couldn't see any such passageway on her layout. She shone her flashlight as far as the beam could reach. The passageway went straight down and then either ended or turned.

She walked down to find out. The passage turned left, then right. By the next turn, Anne was completely disoriented. She had no idea where she was in relation to her map. Her map was of no use now. She wondered if she should go back.

But curiosity pulled her forward. She couldn't believe that she had found a passageway that no one seemed to know about.

Anne came to another turn. As she rounded the corner, her flashlight caught something black on the floor just ahead of her.

She jerked the flashlight back instinctively and froze on her spot, immobilized by fear. Her legs were about to give out from under her. She reached out to the wall to steady herself as blood rushed to her head.

Unwilling to bring the flashlight back to the black shape just yet, Anne focused on her hearing. She strained to hear any movement. But all was silent.

In the darkness, surrounded by the rough stone walls of the narrow corridor, Anne could clearly hear the pounding of her heart in her ears, but nothing else. She took a few deep breaths to calm down and slow down her heart, which felt like it was about to break out of her ribcage.

Moving her flashlight slowly along the surface of the floor, she began inching the beam of light back to the black shape on the floor. In her mind, she was already running back to the policeman for help. But first, she needed to make sure exactly what it was she had seen.

As her flashlight hit what looked like the legs, Anne held her breath, preparing for what she'd see next.

But as she moved the light up the legs to the torso, she realized that something was not right. This was not a person. She breathed a sigh of relief. It was some sort of one piece suit.

Anne got closer to examine it. The clothing looked like a boiler suit, but black. There was no dust on it, so it must have been left here recently. As she moved her phone along the suit, she shuddered. She couldn't be positive, but she saw patches of darker areas on the fabric.

At the top of the suit, where the head would be, Anne saw a weird black basket. She leaned over for a better look and realized what it was–a black fencing mask.

An icy wave of confusion washed over Anne. Why was there a fencing mask and a boiler suit here, in this abandoned hallway? Then her brain jumped to the only logical conclusion–*Sarah!*

Was angelic Sarah, with her shining blond hair, the fencing champion, the killer?

Suddenly all Anne could think about was getting out of here. She turned to go back, but she heard a faint noise in the darkness. She strained to hear what it was.

Then she heard it clearly. The sounds came soft, guarded, but their measured rhythm identified them, unmistakably, as footsteps.

Anne knew from experience that the corridors in the castle were excellent at carrying sound. She couldn't be sure how far away the person was, but she was sure they were walking towards her.

Had someone followed her here? Had Sarah somehow seen her come this way?

Anne's heart pounded, sending blood rushing through her ears with such force that she had trouble hearing the footsteps. Her breathing got shallow. Cold sweat beaded on her face. She was immobilized with panic. The only way out she knew was the way she had come. But that now was blocked.

Her instinct for preservation kicked in. Where could she go? Was there somewhere she could hide? She moved her flashlight frantically about. But it was hopeless. She was besieged by an endless stone wall.

And then she saw it. How could she have missed it? On the wall opposite the black suit, was a wooden door. With her beam of light focused the entire time on the suit on the floor, she had failed to notice it.

Anne leaped towards the door. She jerked and tugged the rough iron latch on the door, unsure how to open it. She prayed it was not locked. To her great relief, the door swung forward.

The lights flickered on, activated by a motion sensor, and Anne found herself in what looked like the castle's storage room.

14 The Executioner's daughter

Safe! Anne exhaled and closed the door gently behind her. She wasn't out of danger yet, but this was a good start. She glanced around for a second to get her bearings.

Tall metal shelves stood towering before her, stacked with all manner of antiques. Anne didn't have time to look at them.

The shelves, arranged along either side of the room, formed an aisle down the middle of it. Anne ran down the aisle and hoped she would find the main entrance door at the other end of the room.

She saw it. Her thoughts lightened. She knew the door had a police officer standing guard in front of it. She was safe.

Anne thrust forward and lunged towards the door, grabbed the handle, and turned it. She expected the door to open. But nothing happened. The door was locked. For a second she panicked again, but then relaxed. *Of course it's locked,* Anne thought. *The room is out of bounds and a police officer is guarding it.*

She started pounding on the door to get the police officer to open it. But no one opened the door. *Why is he not opening it?* Anne thought frantically. *Why is he not at his post? Where is he?* Had the police officer stepped away to go to the bathroom?

Anne leaned against the door. She'd try pounding on the door again in a second. She breathed in deeply to slow down her heart rate. Her mouth was dry and sticky. She needed a drink of water.

A creak in the back of the storage room caught her attention. Anne held her breath. The person in the passageway had caught up with her.

Anne's phone pinged in her back pocket, but she didn't dare take it out. Her eyes were glued on the aisle between the stacks. Yet, her mind wandered, unbidden, to how weird phone reception was at the castle. How could the signal get through these thick walls?

A figure came out of the shadows and into the aisle. The figure made a gesture Anne recognized–it wrapped a cardigan tight around itself. It was Ruth.

For a moment, Anne was puzzled. She had expected to see Sarah. *Wasn't the fencing mask Sarah's?* But then her mind started making connections–Cambridge, archaeology, Sir Hubert, a scandal. It was Ruth after all, but why?

"Hi Ruth," said Anne, trying to make her voice

calm and casual. She planned to pretend that she was clueless and had just wandered into the passageway and the storage room by mistake.

Ruth didn't answer, but just kept walking slowly towards Anne.

"What are you doing here?" Anne continued her routine.

"Don't play dumb with me, *Anne*," Ruth said in a cold voice.

Okay, thought Anne. *Let's go to the other extreme. Time for truths.*

Anne's new plan, the one she hatched just at that moment, was to keep Ruth talking and if Ruth got too close to start pounding on the door again. Someone must hear her.

"Okay, I won't play dumb," Anne said, emboldened by the thought that the police officer will be back any moment now. "What have you done with Emma? Where is she? Have you hurt her?"

"What?" Ruth stopped, and a mix of disgust and confusion came over her face. "Emma? No. Why would I hurt Emma?" Ruth resumed walking, stepping with each word down the aisle. "She's just in a meeting." She waved her hand in the direction of the offices. "I like Emma. She's really nice. She hasn't done anything...to me. There is no reason for me to kill *her*. She is not guilty. I only slay the guilty ones."

Anne shivered involuntarily.

Ruth now stopped next to a shelf. She disappeared out of view and Anne heard the scrape of metal on metal. Ruth was retrieving something metal off a shelf. Anne froze. She was sure she knew what Ruth was getting.

Ruth reappeared in the aisle, now with a longsword in her right hand, its tip dragging, grinding menacingly on the stone floor as she walked.

"And you, Anne," Ruth resumed her monologue, "are guilty of being a nosy parker. Curiosity killed the cat, you know?" Ruth let out a hollow chuckle at her own joke.

Anne's thoughts inexplicably jumped to Maggie. Anne worried that she would never see the black cat again. Maggie might have nine lives, but Anne didn't.

"How did you know I was here?" Anne asked, trying to avoid the topic of the murders.

"I came out of the meeting to go get something and saw you turn the wrong way. I waited for you to come back, but when you didn't, I figured out you had discovered what no one else had," Ruth said. "I'm really good at archeology, you know? I was at Cambridge. On a scholarship. Found this passageway and a few others."

Anne nodded. "Why did you kill Thomas?"

"I know what you are doing," Ruth said. She stopped walking, and a thin smile stretched across her face. Anne felt Ruth's cold eyes boring into her chest.

"It won't save you, you know?" her cold eyes

moved to Anne's. Anne felt a chill wash over her. "But okay, I'll play this game."

Ruth leaned on the handle of the longsword as an exhausted crusader might have done centuries ago. "Thomas?" she said, as though thinking. "Thomas was a feeble coward. He was also a thief and a cheat, but that's not why I killed him. It was because he was the reason Hubert was invited to come oversee the project."

She paused, staring in the distance. "I begged him to do something, to stop Hubert from coming. But he was powerless. The Board of Directors went over his head. He actually had the gall to ask me why I cared if Hubert came. Told me I was just a secretary. What did I care about who was in charge of the project? What did I know about archeology to question the decision of the Board? He actually laughed at me." Anne could see Ruth getting angrier, reliving her humiliation.

"But I couldn't tell him the truth. Made up some story about making Emma unhappy. But his fate was sealed then and there."

Ruth turned her gaze to Anne. Anne noticed the sword shift slightly. She stiffened. Anne willed herself not to think about what would come next. She hoped to buy herself time with more questions. Like in *A Thousand and One Night.*

"And what about Sir Hubert? Why didn't you want him to come?" Anne said, trying to keep the panic out of her voice.

"*Sir* Hubert," Ruth said with venom. "I met him while I was at Cambridge. At a conference. Can you imagine the sweetness that courses through your veins of being singled out by someone so dashing? A peer of the realm?" Ruth's voice became misty. "It was magical. Romantic. A fairytale. He seduced me. But it turned out he didn't want me, or my love, he wanted something far more precious."

"Sarah," Anne breathed out.

"What?" Ruth said sharply. "What does Sarah have to do with this?"

"Is she not your and Sir Hubert's daughter? Is she not the scandal his family tried to hush up all those years ago?"

"Sarah, my daughter?" Ruth laughed. "I thought you were smart, Anne."

Ruth paused. Her face resumed its faraway expression, and she gazed in the middle distance, as though unseeing. "His family hushed up a scandal, indeed, but it wasn't an illegitimate child. At the time, when he seduced me, I was working on a groundbreaking thesis about the Romans in England. It turned everything on its head. It was a once-in-a-generation kind of thesis. But Hubert stole it from me. It made him a world-famous expert on the Roman Empire."

A memory passed across Anne's mind: the day she'd had coffee with Ruth; Sarah had said that

Sir Hubert was afraid of lovers stealing ideas. Now Anne understood the source of his fear.

"Could you not fight back? What about your adviser? What about your university? Did they not stand by you?" Anne said, inflamed by the injustice. As much as she was afraid of Ruth, and what she would do next, at that moment all Anne felt was compassion towards the broken woman standing in front of her.

Ruth turned to look at Anne. "I fought," she said, resignation in her voice. "But it made no difference. Who was I to win against the old boys' club closing ranks and centuries of family connections among the upper class put in motion? In the end, they bullied my advisor into backing down and I had no way of proving that the thesis was actually mine. I had a mental breakdown and left without completing my degree."

"But why kill him now, after all those years?"

"Why not, when I had the opportunity?" Ruth said nonchalantly. "And now, story time is over."

"Don't get any closer to me," Anne warned. Anne knew she had no way of defending herself against the sword. But she hoped the police officer was back at his post. "I'll scream and the police officer will hear me."

Ruth, who hadn't moved from her position, laughed. "He's knocked out cold. I made sure of that before coming for you."

Anne looked around frantically. What could she use as a shield? There was just a cardboard box. As Ruth took a step towards her, Anne grabbed the box and threw it at her. But Ruth used her sword to deflect it. Anne screamed and started banging the sole of her foot on the door. Maybe the policeman on the other side of the door would revive.

Anne watched in slow motion Ruth wrap both hands–*zweihander* flashed through Anne's mind–around the hilt of the longsword, kick under the tip of the sword resting on the floor, giving the sword upward momentum, and lift the blade over the right shoulder.

She couldn't even scream. Anne pressed herself flush with the door. There was nowhere to go. She closed her eyes, preparing mentally to feel the impact of the cold steel blade on her skin.

It all happened so quickly. Anne felt herself being shoved sideways. She stumbled and fell to the ground. At the same time, she heard a man cry out an order in Italian and a steel sword cling against the stone floor.

Anne opened her eyes, surprised to be still alive. On the other side of the now open door was a policeman with his gun drawn and pointing at Ruth. Behind him was Emma.

15 Coffee and cake

"I was in a meeting all morning," Emma said. "The Board had scheduled an emergency meeting to discuss the leadership and PR crisis on our hands."

Anne was sitting in Luigi's garden, at the back of his coffee shop, with Emma, Marco, Alex and Luigi.

"That's why I didn't get your calls, Anne," Emma continued. "Plus, you know how patchy reception is at the castle because of those walls." She waved her hand towards the stone walls of Luigi's garden. "Ruth left to get something. When she didn't return, we decided to take a break. I don't think any of us suspected anything."

"What tipped you off to go looking for our Anne," Marco asked, and threw Anne a look that was between disbelief and admiration.

"I saw Anne's bag on a chair in my office. Then I saw the missed calls, but no message. I assumed Anne was in the castle, so I just poked around a bit, looking for her. I didn't suspect anything was wrong until I saw the policeman laying on the ground."

"Oh, Emma," Anne said, reliving all over again the elation she'd felt yesterday morning. "I was so happy when I saw you and the policeman enter."

"I tried reviving the policeman on the ground, but he was out cold. So I ran to get another police officer. I had no idea at the time that you and Ruth were inside the storage room. It wasn't until I came back with the second policeman that we heard the commotion inside and opened the door."

"And just in time, as Anne tells me," Alex said.

"Yes, I felt myself being pushed sideways, but had no idea what it was. But it was the policeman thrusting the door open." Anne shivered, speculating about what would have happened if Emma hadn't arrived on time. "Thank goodness police officers here have guns," Anne added.

"I could sense something was up," Marco said. "Maggie was acting up at the bookstore, going around as though looking for you."

Since coming back to the store yesterday, Maggie had shadowed Anne everywhere she went, not letting her out of her sight. *She's definitely one strange cat*, Anne thought.

"I knew you were coming in later, but I didn't expect you'd go snooping in the castle by yourself," Marco said with exasperation.

"I didn't really mean to," Anne began, "it just

happened. I got caught up in the moment, following my map." She hated having to explain herself, but knew Marco meant well.

"And of course you didn't get my message on time," Luigi said. "If only you had received it before going into the castle."

When Anne had been released from the police after questioning and statements, she at last got a chance to check her phone. Luigi's text message was the last name of Luca 'The Executioner'– *Weber*.

"So Ruth was the daughter of this man, 'The Executioner'?" Alex asked.

"Yes," Anne and Luigi answered at the same time.

"And do we know if the police were even on to Ruth?" Alex said.

"From what I learned while making my statements," Anne said, "they had surprisingly very little forensic evidence to go on. Ruth protected herself with that boiler suit and the fencing mask I saw. Plus, she knew all the secret and abandoned passageways around the castle, so she could appear and disappear unnoticed."

The group spent most of the next hour discussing the murders and the tragic circumstances that led to them, with Luigi fueling the conversation with coffee and Anne filling in with details on how she discovered each clue.

During a lull in the conversation, Anne saw

Emma give a nod to Luigi, as though communicating a silent message.

Luigi got up and disappeared inside the coffee shop. Anne wondered what was going on. When he reappeared, Luigi was carrying a cake.

"I have an announcement to make," Emma began. "I've been made Director of the Bellinzona castles!"

Everyone cheered and clapped. Anne was happy for her friend. She just wished it hadn't come at such a high cost.

❖ ❖ ❖

Anne received a text message from Ben. He had landed in Zurich and was taking the train. He'd be in Ascona in two hours.

'And I have a surprise for you.'

'What is it?' Anne texted back.

'I know I've been absent a lot. But I'm taking a few days off. I've booked us a getaway at a hilltop castle. I'm sure you'll love it.'

Anne sent Ben a heart emoji and put down her phone.

I hope this castle is not as deadly as the last one, Anne thought.

❖ ❖ ❖

Read Anne's next adventure in the Reckless Reprint (The Old Bookstore Two-Hour Cozy Mysteries Book 4) on Amazon.

If you enjoy this series, consider joining my Advanced Review Copy (ARC) Team to get advanced complimentary copies of my upcoming books. Check out **https://isabellabassett.com** for more details.

If you are curious to learn more about Southern Switzerland, head over to my website where you will find blog entries on the places mentioned in the *Old Bookstore Mysteries* series.

Plus, if you enjoy literary maps as much as I do, check out the map I created of Ascona, illustrating the fictional locations of the Out Of Print Bookstore and Anne's apartment, among other things.

See you at
https://isabellabassett.com

About The Author

Hi, I'm Isabella Bassett. Like Anne, of the *'Old Bookstore Mysteries'* series, I moved to Switzerland together with my husband for his job. But unlike Anne, I never had doubts about my decision.

I live in one of the picturesque towns of Southern Switzerland, about which I write, tucked in the folds of the Alps. I love exploring old places with forgotten histories.

The idea for this series came to me when walking through the winding cobbled alleys of Ascona. I wondered about all the secrets that may lie hidden behind the tall stone walls. So I invented a mystery series where I weave together bits of intriguing Swiss history into puzzling cozy murder mysteries.

Printed in Great Britain
by Amazon